Dog 281

Janet Vormittag

Dog 281

By Janet Vormittag

First Edition 2012
Second Edition 2019

Cover design by Pete Meade, a graphic designer from Ionia, Michigan. petemeade@mac.com

ISBN:
Softcover   978-0-9848542-1-9
eBook   978-0-9848542-5-7

www.JanetVormittag.com

Other Books by Janet Vormittag

More Than A Number (2nd book in the Save Five Series)

You Might Be a Crazy Cat Lady if ...

Acknowledgments

Although I started this book years before I met Tricia McDonald, I don't think I would have finished it without her encouragement. Thank you, Tricia!

I also want to thank members of two writers groups, the Monday Night Writers and the Sweet Potato Fries, who gave me support, feedback and encouragement.

Several friends and fellow writers read my manuscript and gave valuable feedback. They are: Lee Bradley, Rose Cole, Melissa Eefsting, Ellen Hosafros, Tricia McDonald, Sue Merrell, Pat Pritchard, Jeanne Urbanski and Wendy Wamser.

A huge thank-you to my friend Kate Lord for being my go-to photographer when I need photos of myself.

Cover photograph

Baxter was a purpose-bred dog born at a facility (a USDA Class A animal dealer) that breeds and sells beagles for use in animal research. He spent the first four and a half years of his life in a cage as the subject of numerous clinical trials. He didn't have a name. He was known only by a number. He didn't know love. He didn't know sunshine. He knew only pain and fear. Beagle Freedom Project, a rescue and advocacy group, negotiated with the lab for the release of Baxter and the nine other beagles at the facility. He was finally free!

Baxter now lives in West Hollywood with his human mom and his beagle sister Tashi (a death row dog from a high kill shelter). He is sweet, sensitive, inquisitive, and stubborn. In other words, all things beagle. He is making the most of his retirement years. He loves to hike and to go to the beach. He loves stealing snacks and snuggling on the couch with his mom. He loves playing with his fellow former lab dogs. Beagles LOVE other beagles. What he loves most, though, is finally being able to just be a dog.
~Caroline Christian, the guardian for Baxter.

Follow Baxter on Twitter @BFPBaxter

Dedicated to Fraser,
who never came home.

Chapter 1

Just as I summoned the courage to smash the window, distant headlights and the rumble of an engine interrupted me. I flattened myself belly down among waist-high dead weeds. A security light cast a pale glaze over the renovated red barn and surrounding area, me included. I prayed my form melted into the landscape. A chorus of spring peepers from a nearby swamp camouflaged the pounding of my heart, but I wished my hiding place wasn't ten feet from the kennel's door.

A car pulled into the circular driveway and parked behind a grove of blue spruce. *Did I trip a silent alarm?* The last thing I needed was to explain to my grandmother why her sweet, law-abiding granddaughter was in the county jail. Doors opened, and I heard rock music mingled with voices and laughter. Through the weeds, I could see teenagers. Four of them. They were sitting on the hood of the car and leaning against the fenders, sipping beer and eating pizza. The kennel was situated on an old homestead where trees and overgrown flower beds outlined where a house once stood. The seclusion made it a perfect party place for underage drinkers.

I worried the partiers would attract the police and panicked when a young man stumbled in my direction. He stopped so close I could hear his stream of urine drenching the weeds, and his feelgood sigh of emptying a bladder of spent beer. If there had been a breeze, I would have been sprinkled. I gagged at the pungent smell. It felt like the intruders stayed for hours, but, in fact, it was thirty-four minutes. Thirty-four minutes of my face pressed into

7

musty dry weed stubble, anxious about slithering snakes seeking my body heat and grateful that mosquitoes had not yet hatched. When they drove away, the teenagers left behind a grease-stained pizza box, empty Budweiser cans and me, a nervous, frustrated wreck.

Brushing dirt and dead grass from my sweatshirt and jeans, I got back to work. My first tap on the double-pane window with the ball peen hammer was too timid. The second whack shattered the glass, and it echoed like carillon music as it fell to the concrete floor inside. The nearest neighbor was a half-mile away, so I didn't worry about the noise. Wearing leather gloves, I snapped the leftover shards of glass from the window frame. I stepped on a weathered crate, leaned inside and dropped my backpack and a dog carrier to the concrete floor. Hoisting myself onto the windowsill, I paused to take several deep breaths to calm my nerves. I expected sirens, but all I heard were muffled barks and singing peepers.

Fumbling in my backpack, I retrieved my flashlight and put away the hammer. I switched on the light and its beam pierced the darkness and led me to the metal door that opened into the kennel. When I turned the doorknob and pushed it open, frantic barking assaulted my ears and a hot stuffy stench made me gag. The dogs were frenzied by my midnight visit, and they ricocheted around their wire-mesh cages. The flashlight's narrow shaft of light cast dancing shadows. Not much had changed from that morning. The hodgepodge of dogs were still trapped in filthy pens.

"Take me with you, take me with you," they begged in a doggie language I knew too well.

"Sorry guys," I said. "I'm looking for my dogs Cody and Blue."

At the end of the first row of pens was the closed door that hadn't been part of my earlier tour. Inside, six German shepherds were corralled in a pen. They jumped about, barking with excitement. None wore collars. They looked well fed and somewhat mannered. In the murky light they all looked alike, but one jumped a little higher and yipped a little louder.

"Sit," I commanded, trying to be heard above the ruckus.

The dog I had raised from a pup obediently sat on his

haunches. I opened the gate and Cody sprang forward, not waiting for an invitation. His tail wagged with such force he lost his
balance. It was a struggle to keep the other five shepherds from
dodging out as well.

"It's so good to see you," I said, ruffling his face between my
hands and kissing his cheeks. "Where's Blue?" It was a game we
played. Like a typical beagle, Blue would get on the hot scent of
who-knows-what and be gone. Cody and I would track him. We
searched the rest of the building. We found a room of caged cats
that hissed and squirmed when we disrupted their sleep.

Another door led to the interior of the original barn with its
wooden cathedral ceiling. It had a stuffy unused smell. I swung my
flashlight around the room and saw a Winnebago Motor Home, a
shiny red speedboat and two snowmobiles on a trailer. Whatever
Gary Jarsma is up to, it must pay well.

Near the door were bags of cat and dog food, cat litter and
stacks of dust-laden boxes. In one corner were bales of straw. I
wondered why the bedding wasn't in the dog cages. As I turned
to leave, I noticed a cardboard box of collars. I picked one up. It
was worn leather with two metal tags attached to it; one was a
dog license and the other a bone-shaped tag with a name and
telephone number stamped in the shiny metal. I stuffed it in my
pocket. I searched for Cody and Blue's collars but didn't find them.
Most of the collars had tags. I grabbed a handful of them, jammed
them inside my backpack and returned to the office. If Blue had
already been sold, maybe I could find a record of where he had
been shipped. There were three tall file cabinets. Piles of papers
were strewn across the desk. In the corner was a copy machine.
I flipped it on. As it hummed its warm-up tune, I grabbed what
looked to be the most current pile of paperwork and set it in the
automatic feed tray. Cody stuck to my side. He had no intention
of being left behind.

In one of the cabinets I found a file labeled "shipments." The
top paper had the previous day's date and listed eight dogs that
were sent to Southern Michigan University. I scanned the remaining papers and kept all the ones dated after my dogs went missing. *My dogs–already I thought of them as mine. Maybe Cody was
mine, but Blue belonged to my son. Always had. Always would.*

As the papers copied, the constant barking of the caged canines made me wonder what their fate would be. I didn't know any more than what the volunteer at the animal shelter had whispered to me that morning when I checked the shelter for my lost dogs.

"Look at Kappies Kennels," she had said. "He's a licensed animal dealer who sells dogs to research labs." Before I could ask any questions, the shelter director walked into the room and the volunteer scurried away. I introduced myself and asked about my missing dogs. He had me fill out a lost dog report and suggested I come back at least every other day to look for them.

"By law we only have to hold dogs for four days if they come in without a collar or microchip. Did your dogs have collars or were they microchipped?"

"They weren't microchipped. They had collars, but the information on the tags is wrong. I wrote it on the report."

"Collars can come off. We'll keep an eye out for them, but we get busy. You need to walk though the kennels and look for them on your own. You also need to put up some lost dog posters. An ad in the Lost and Found in the newspaper would be a good idea, too."

I thanked him for the suggestions and assured him I would check back at least every other day. He didn't mention dogs being transferred to an animal dealer.

"By the way, my name is Sam Grensward," he said. He read my report as he led me to the kennel area. "You must be Anna's granddaughter."

"I am."

"So how did you lose your dogs?"

"I didn't lose them. Someone took them from Grams' fenced-in yard."

"Why would anyone do that?"

"I don't know. All I know is the gate was closed, but the dogs were gone."

"Maybe you didn't close the gate and they pushed it open."

"I don't think so. The gate latches automatically when it swings closed. We checked. It works fine."

Sam didn't have an answer for the obvious theft of my dogs. He led me through the maze of kennels, and I didn't find Cody or

Blue. Since Cindi had already told me they didn't have any beagles or German shepherds, I wasn't surprised. He ushered me to the door.

"Remember to come back."

The comment didn't warrant an answer.

I recalled a green and white sign for Kappies Kennels tucked among towering blue spruce trees in the yard of an abandoned farm on Kirby Road. I drove there as soon as I left the shelter.

A middle-aged man greeted me before I could even get out of my car. He turned out to be the owner, Gary Jarsma, a balding, haggard looking bone-thin man with John Lennon wire-rim glasses.

"I'm Alison Cavera, and I'm looking for a couple lost dogs. A German shepherd and a beagle." His stare made me feel guilty. Guilty for looking for my own dogs. "They disappeared two days ago from my grandmother's house near Pearline."

"I don't think I have any shepherds or beagles, but you can look after you fill out a visitor's form. Wait here. I'll be right back." He turned and walked through an open garage door into a pole barn where I could see him talking with a young man. A couple minutes later he returned and handed me a clipboard and pen.

"If you don't mind, just fill this out."

The form asked for my name, address, telephone number and what type of animals I was looking for. He waited as I filled in the answers. When I finished, I handed it to him.

"They have collars, but the information on the tags is old. I just moved here." He wrote a note on the form, and then asked for my driver's license.

"Why?"

"Security. If you want in, I see your license."

I retrieved it from my purse. Jarsma compared the license data to what I had written. He scribbled my Chicago address next to Gram's address. He handed the license back to me.

"Follow me," he said, leading me into the pole barn and through a one-desk office. I scurried to keep up with him. As he swung open a heavy metal door, I was assaulted by a musty stench and the uproar of excited animals who sounded like they had been caged too long. He pointed to an aisle.

"Go ahead, take a look."

In the first pen a brownish-black terrier leaped and bounced off the front of its wire-mesh run. Next to it was a shepherd mix. Then a black lab-like dog with white paws who danced in circles. There were puddles of urine and piles of feces on the cement floor. In each pen there was a grimy food bowl and a coffee can partially filled with water.

I held my breath and hurried to the end of the aisle as Jarsma followed close behind. In the last pen five reddish-brown puppies tumbled over each other in play. Jarsma guided me around the corner and pointed to another walkway with pens on both sides. More dogs, some two and three to a pen. I didn't look too closely. All I wanted was to find Cody and Blue. I didn't.

"I didn't think we had your dogs, but if any shepherds or beagles come in I'll give you a call," Jarsma said as he walked me to my car.

"What do you do with these dogs?"

"They're used in medical schools, veterinarian schools, research labs. They'd be put to sleep at the shelter. Might as well use them to find a cure for cancer or something."

"But aren't they pets?"

"Not any more."

I got into my car and headed home. On the way I listened to the messages on my cell. One was from Cindi Owens, the volunteer at the shelter. She wanted me to call her at home. I pulled to the side of the road and called her.

"Hi Cindi? It's Alison. Did you find my dogs?"

"No, I just wanted to tell you that if you go to Kappies, don't tell him what kind of dogs you're looking for. I've heard that if he has your dog, he'll hide it in a back room so you can't find it."

"I just came from there."

"Did you find them?"

"No, but why would he lie?"

"He gets about $600 per dog. It's big money out of his pocket if he gives you your dog back."

"I don't believe it."

"I'm just telling you what I heard."

"Where does he sell them?"

"Wherever he can. There's a couple research labs near Kalamazoo, and several universities buy from him."

"For what?"

"Teaching. Research. Testing."

"Isn't that illegal?"

"Jarsma is licensed by the United States Department of Agriculture and has a Class B license. It means he can get animals from random sources and sell them wherever he wants."

"Random sources?"

"Shelters, pets people no longer want, other dealers. The county has a contract with him. Jarsma disposes of the bodies of euthanized animals in exchange for live dogs and cats. He's in here two or three times a week, checking out what we have."

"Do you think he steals dogs?"

"Nobody has proved it, but a lot of people suspect it. I've heard he doesn't ask questions when people bring him dogs. He pays $50 apiece. Some guys steal dogs for spending money. And in this bad economy, people who can't afford to keep pets are looking for new homes for them. Anybody who is a halfway decent liar can get as many free-to-good-home dogs as he wants."

She added that two people had been in the shelter in the last week looking for beagles. "I bet he has an order for beagles."

As I hung up, I recalled my visit to the kennel. I could see Jarsma talking to a teenage boy and then coming out and having me fill out the paperwork. I had already told him what kind of dogs I was looking for. Could that young kid have been hiding Cody and Blue as I filled out the search forms? I recalled seeing dirty empty kennels, which was odd when some kennels held several dogs. Damn him.

As I finished copying the files, I felt a twinge of guilt at rescuing Cody and leaving the other animals behind. Then it came to me, like an early-morning insight you get when showering, I couldn't take the other dogs with me, but I didn't have to leave them in this stink hole. I already planned on rescuing the adorable pups.

Back at their pen, two of them cuddled on a filthy orange blanket while the other three sniffed my ankles when I stepped inside their kennel.

"Come here you cute little babies. Where's your mama?" I said, as one by one I plopped them into the carrier. With the puppies safe and my backpack stuffed with papers, I looked around and took a moment to think of any clues to my identity I was leaving behind. I wore gloves so I didn't leave fingerprints. The tools were all accounted for. Maybe the pizza box and beer cans would help cover my activities. At the least, they would be misleading.

I propped open a side door. With Cody tagging along, I squeezed open the clips holding the cage doors shut. It took about 20 minutes to open all the kennels. With the fresh night air beckoning, the dogs ignored me and raced to freedom.

In the cat room, I opened a window before swinging the cage doors open. The cats hesitated. I caught a brown tabby and perched him on the windowsill. It didn't take him long to leap to freedom. Next I sat a calico in the window. The other cats watched as she disappeared outside. I helped two other cats onto the windowsill and left before they jumped. I could only hope the rest of the cats would escape after I left. I felt confident the fresh air and night sounds would entice them outside.

As I hiked to my car, parked on a two-track dirt road that ran alongside a nearby cornfield, I could see dogs sniffing around the yard and a couple cats dodging into a neighboring hay field. I had to hustle and get cruising before a vehicle came down Kirby Road and spotted the menagerie of animals.

One dog clung to Cody's side, and when I opened the car door he hopped in the back seat while Cody assumed his navigation post in the passenger seat. The newcomer's big brown eyes pleaded with me not to evict him from the car. I didn't have the heart to order him out. I put the carrier with its puppy cargo in the back seat, along with my backpack. As I drove away, dogs and cats were everywhere. *Run.* I thought. *Run as far and fast as you can.*

Chapter 2

I moved to Pearline in northern Michigan to keep my grandmother company after my grandfather passed. Grams and Gramps retired from farming years before but continued to live on the 60-acre farm where they had spent their entire married life. Grams appreciated my company, but she didn't think she needed anyone looking after her. Maybe I needed her more than she needed me. For six years I had taught fifth-graders, but after my son died, I couldn't handle being around young students and took a leave of absence. I doubted if I could ever go back to teaching. My future felt empty, like a journal waiting to be filled.

With Gramps gone, Grams stood her ground. At 69 she refused to rock on the front porch of Ludington Manor or anywhere else.

"I'm not moving to Chicago," she told my mother days after the funeral as they discussed her future.

I disliked hearing them argue, but I knew how to tune them out. You'd never know the two of them were mother and daughter. Everything about them seemed opposite. I learned to stay out of their disagreements years ago.

"You can't stay here alone," my mother said. She insisted Grams move to Chicago with her. I knew that would never happen.

"Oh yes, I can stay here. You can't make me leave."

"Mom, I'll be worried sick with you by yourself up here in the middle of nowhere."

"I'm not in the middle of nowhere. I've lived here most of my life. I have neighbors. I have friends. I'm not alone."

I was their compromise. I needed the distraction, and I knew Cody and Blue would love the space the farm provided. For Blue it would be a homecoming. Grams gave the blind beagle to my son. The pup's sky-blue eyes had fascinated Thomas and it was he who named the dog. Grams guessed the pup was born blind. Blue didn't know any difference and adjusted to new surroundings with ease. How right she was. When we got him home, he bumped into furniture until he remembered the layout of every room. We forgot he couldn't see until we took him out of his environment and saw him walking hesitantly and bumping into things. Cody soon became his eyes whenever we left the house. Blue usually could be found next to either Thomas or Cody, unless he smelled a rabbit.

A month after Mom and Gram's debate on where Grams should live, I found myself driving to Pearline. I chuckled as I drove through the farming community's business district. On one corner of the village's only four-way stop, stood a mill where farmers had their corn ground into feed, and shopped for seed, pesticides and fertilizer. The Pearline First Christian Reformed Church occupied another corner, as did Bob's Family Diner. A mini-mart with two gas pumps occupied the last corner. It saved locals a 15-mile drive to the Lake Michigan town of Ludington, a tourist mecca with a Wal-Mart, Meijer, Burger King and Holiday Inn Express.

Fifteen minutes after stopping at the downtown stop, I drove my 2004 Subaru into my grandparents' spruce-lined driveway. Moving to the farm had been a childhood fantasy. But in my dreams happiness surrounded the move, not the sadness that now held me hostage.

As I parked the car, a guy coming from the barn approached me. "You must be Alison," he said opening the car door. "I'm Cooper. Cooper Malecki."

He looked like a poster boy for Calvin Klein. Young, lean, with a head of sun-bleached blond hair. His blue jeans and green T-shirt were smudged with dirt. As I stared, he explained that Grams had hired him to take care of the horses and help around the farm.

Cody and Blue leaped out of the car and ran in circles around the yard before stopping to sniff Cooper's legs. He kneeled and held out a hand for them to sniff.

"Meet Cody and Blue," I said. "I hope you like dogs."

The screen door slammed as Grams came out. Racing in front of her were Elvis and Sinatra. Elvis, a cocker spaniel mix, had curly black hair. Sinatra, more than twice the size of Elvis, had slick black hair and four white feet. The four dogs sniffed their greetings to one another before tearing around the yard as if they had just been released from a week of confinement.

"I see you met Cooper," Grams said. She wore her standard fare, faded blue jeans with a button-down shirt tucked in. Her gray hair, wrapped in a bun with stray twirls dangling around her ears and cheeks, contrasted with her tan. She always had a tan, not from sunbathing but from hours devoted to gardening and other outside work. I gave her a hug and nodded yes.

"I didn't realize all the work Tom did around here, and I didn't want to burden you with it," she said.

Burden me? Feeding horses, mucking stalls, mowing grass and weeding flower beds would be less of a distraction than having a guy around. I needed to work.

"I planned on helping with the chores."

"He's staying in the upstairs apartment."

"I'll carry your bags in," Cooper said.

I popped open the trunk, and he started unloading suitcases and boxes. "What do you have in these?" he asked as he lifted out a cardboard carton.

"Books. And there's a laptop, too. Be careful."

When he got out of hearing distance, I turned to Grams and demanded to know why she had hired someone before talking to me.

She put her hands on her hips. "You're just like your mother, meddling."

"I'm sorry, but...."

"Don't be sorry. Just let me make my own decisions. If I want to hire somebody to help around the place, I will. And I did." She reached out and gave me another hug. End of discussion.

I didn't want to argue, so I let the matter drop.

I called Cody and Blue, grabbed a three-pound bag of carrots from the car, and headed to the barn. Built in the early 1900s, its red paint and green shingles always reminded me of Christmas. It just felt like a happy holiday whenever I visited my grandparents.

As a child I spent weeks on the farm during summer break while my parents stayed in the city. I hoed the garden, mucked stalls, and even learned to drive the John Deere tractor. Grams and I detested housework, but she made it fun. We'd play Frank Sinatra albums, sometimes Elvis Presley, and dance as we dusted, washed windows and swept the wooden floors. We did laundry in a wringer-wash machine in the basement and hung clothes outside to dry.

Every summer my grandparents planted a vegetable garden. Grams canned and lined the food cellar with quarts of tomatoes, dill pickles, peaches and pears. They leased land to neighboring farmers and boarded horses for a family who had a summer cottage on a nearby lake and only came up on weekends. Grams, a lover of anything with four legs, also baby-sat dogs for vacationing neighbors. She fenced in a portion of the backyard to give the boarders a place to run without the worry of them heading cross-country for home. The farm became a magnet for unwanted cats and dogs, drop-offs from irresponsible pet owners.

I stopped and inhaled the earthy smell of packed clay floor and the sweet scent of stored hay. Maggie meowed her greeting as she climbed down from the hayloft. The friendliest of the barn cats, she demanded head scratchings.

Opening the back door I stepped into the pasture and whistled. Dappy lifted his head. Gramps bought me the dapple-gray for my 12th birthday. Memories rushed in. Summer evenings, when the sun didn't set until ten. The three of us riding the backwoods trails of the Manistee National Forest. A day ride to the Big Sable Point lighthouse on Lake Michigan in Ludington State Park.

I whistled again. Like a stallion leading his harem of mares, the gelding galloped up the hill with the other three horses close behind. I loved watching them run. They slammed to a stop within feet of where I stood. Their muzzles tickled my palm as they gently plucked the treats from my hand. I scratched behind Dappy's dark gray ears and patted his neck.

"Did you miss me?" I whispered in his ear.

The barn door slammed closed, and I turned to see Cooper.

"Anna told me you'd be out here. She said the first thing you always do is go for a ride. Mind if I join you?"

I hesitated, not wanting to hurt his feelings. "If you don't mind, I'd rather go solo."

He didn't answer.

Cooper slipped the curb bit into Dappy's mouth and slid the headstall over his ears. After buckling the neck strap he handed me the reins and I led Dappy through the pasture gate. He offered to bring me a saddle, but I told him I preferred to ride bareback.

"Do you need a boost?" he asked as he interlocked his hands together and held them low for my foot. I accepted his offer.

I reined Dappy to the two-track road leading to the back-fields. Cody and Blue ran circles of excitement. Leaning forward and nudging his sides with my knees, I whispered, "Let's go." Dappy broke into a rhythmic canter. My body one with his, a sensation of flight. I slowed him to a walk by the irrigation pond and reined him to the trail leading to the river. The spring scent of apple blossoms drifted on the afternoon breeze. A cottontail rabbit, froze in a you-can't-see-me pose, broke rank and zigzagged in front of us. Blue picked up the scent, but he didn't have a chance of running the bunny down. Flute-like warbles of songbirds filtered from the budding maples and oaks.

At the river, I feasted on the quiet as Dappy munched grass. Three turtles sunned themselves on a log half-immersed in water, and a pair of mallard ducks floated by on the current.

The silence brought back memories of my last visit. A battle raged within me—live in the past with Thomas or get on with life. I seldom allowed myself the luxury of wallowing in the past. I closed my eyes as they brimmed with tears.

Last spring Thomas had been here with me, asking questions non-stop like a typical eight-year-old. What I would give to hear one of his silly questions now. I started keeping a journal the day I learned of my pregnancy. I never dreamed it would one day be all I had left of him, that and photographs. And Blue. Thomas and Blue had been inseparable with a stereotypical boy-dog friendship.

Rob and I split a few months after our son's death.

The sun hung low in the western sky when I remounted and started back. Dappy knew the way.

"Dinner's just about ready," Grams said when I went into the house.

"I'll clean up."

My suitcases and boxes sat on the floor of the second-floor bedroom that had been mine for as long as I could remember. The corner room had windows overlooking the front yard and the driveway. Braided throw rugs protected oak floors, and a flowery hand-sewn quilt covered the double bed. The walls were a little-girl pink, and Teddy bears snuggled among the bed's pillows. The desk, dresser and night stand felt sparse in the over-sized room.

I unpacked my laptop and sat it on the desk. Next I placed framed photos of Thomas on the bedside table; a family photo, one of Thomas with Blue and a close up of my son's sweet precious face. It had taken months before I could look at the photos without tears.

A red maple grew outside the front window and kept the room shaded in the summer. As a child, I would open the windows and pretend I lived in a tree house. Rustling leaves soothed me to sleep, and birds woke me when the sun beckoned them to song. I loved playing hide-and-seek with Grams in the old house. Under Gramps' desk, behind the couch, or scrunched between the bear-claw tub and the bathroom wall. Gramps' office occupied a corner of the family room, with its fieldstone fireplace, where on winter evenings the family soaked up the warmth of a hardwood fire.

Four bedrooms and a bathroom occupied the second floor along with a tiny apartment for hired help, which is where Cooper slept. The apartment could be accessed from the upstairs hallway and from its own staircase to the outside.

I heaved my suitcase onto the bed and rummaged through it until I found blue jeans and a sweatshirt. May nights were chilly. I took a quick shower and washed the big-city smell from my hair. Muffler exhaust, industrial fallout and whiffs of fast food dislodged to make way for fresh-cut grass, perennial fragrance and the sweet scent of natural fertilizer straight from the cow. Heavenly.

A spicy aroma drifted from the kitchen when I went back downstairs.

"Cooper likes to cook," Grams announced. "That's the real reason I hired him."

Cooper laughed. "Dad taught me the basics, and I've been experimenting ever since."

I joined Grams as he carried a tossed salad into the dining room. An off-white linen tablecloth covered the rectangle table. There were three settings of Grams' special-occasion china.

"I hope you like Italian food," he said as he returned with bowls of angel hair pasta and steaming marinara sauce. Next came garlic bread and a chilled bottle of red wine.

"I'm starved. It looks wonderful," I said.

Small talk and memories dominated the dinner conversation. Cooper, it turned out, was the grandson of one of Grams' childhood friends. He called San Francisco home, and instead of college, he decided to travel the country by motorcycle. When he reported home from Michigan, his mother suggested he stop and visit Grams. Needing cash to feed his cross-country adventure, he welcomed Grams' offer of work and the opportunity to spend time on a farm.

After dinner Cooper insisted on clearing the table and doing dishes by himself. Grams and I took our wine glasses to the front porch and sat on the hanging swing. Spring peepers, sounding like a sleigh-bell chorus, serenaded us from a distance.

Grams asked how my folks were doing. My parents, Catherine and William Chandler, never changed. My father, a criminal attorney, seldom worked less than twelve hours a day. My mother buried herself in her own work, a boutique that catered to wealthy women. As an only child, I felt more at home with my grandparents than I did with my parents. My mother hated her rural childhood and couldn't understand why I begged to visit Grams and Gramps. It took a long time to figure it out myself. It wasn't the country I longed for as much as the attention I got from my grandparents. My parents were too busy to be parents.

"They took me out to dinner as a going away party."

When our wine glasses were empty, Grams insisted I head up to bed. "You must be exhausted."

"I am, but it's a good tired. I can't believe I'm here to stay."

"At least as long as you want to be. I think you'll get bored before too long," she said, holding the door open for me.

"I don't think so. You know I've always wanted to live here."

We said our good nights, and I climbed the stairs to my room. Cody and Blue plopped down on their oversized pillow beds. They knew that's where they were supposed to sleep, just like I knew when I woke in the morning, they'd both be snuggled on the bed with me.

When I went downstairs the next morning, Cooper was already at the stove cooking pancakes. "Your grandmother shared her potato pancake recipe," he said.

I hadn't expected a personal chef. He poured me a cup of steaming coffee and told me Grams left for town an hour earlier. I let the dogs out the back door into the fenced yard. Soon Cooper set down two plates of pancakes, each with fresh strawberries and sausage.

"What are your plans for the day?" he asked as he pulled up a chair and sat down.

"I'm not sure," I said, as I took a bite of sausage. "What kind of sausage is this?"

"It's vegan."

"Vegan?"

"Meatless."

I spit it into my napkin. "Meatless? What's in it?"

"Soy protein. It's low fat. It's good for you."

"You can have it. Give me regular sausage."

"There isn't any."

"Don't tell me Grams eats this stuff."

"She's on a low-fat diet for her cholesterol. Besides she's a vegetarian."

"I didn't know."

After breakfast I drove into Ludington and bought groceries; bacon, sausage, hamburger and boneless, skinless chicken breasts. Cooper caught me stocking the refrigerator with the meat and informed me I'd have to cook it myself.

"I'm quite capable," I told him. So much for having a personal chef.

The next few days didn't go much smoother. Grams had indeed given up eating meat for her health. "It's good for both my hearts," she said. "I'm happier knowing I'm not the cause of an animal being slaughtered."

It looked like I made the wrong decision moving in with Grams, and I blamed it on Cooper.

Two weeks later, Cody and Blue disappeared.

Chapter 3

Shortly after I rescued the puppies from Kappies Kennel, they gorged themselves on beefy dog food until their tummies bulged. I put down straw in the corner of a stall and watched as they snuggled into it. One by one they quit wiggling, closed their eyes and slept. The babes had no idea how their lives had changed that night.

Cody and his newfound buddy reeked. "You guys are getting a bath," I told them. They followed me into the milk parlor where hot water and a tub, both leftovers from the farm's milk production days, provided an ideal grooming salon. Cody hated baths, but he quit trying to escape them years ago. On command, he jumped into the tub. I gave him a scrubbing with doggie shampoo while not inhaling through my nose. He didn't need coaxing to jump to the floor when done. He stood as close to me as possible when shaking off the excess water—a subtle way of getting even for the indignity of a bath.

The new guy cowered by the door. "It's going to be okay," I repeated over and over. He quit trembling at the sound of my voice. "What you need is a name. How about Stinky? Brownie? Shadow? You've glued yourself to Cody just like a shadow." Hearing his name, Cody jumped up, put his front paws on the edge of the tub and watched. His presence seemed to calm Shadow. I could hear Gramps in my head: "Give 'em a name, and they never leave."

We headed to the house when both dogs smelled fresh and clean. The outside security light lit the yard and eased my fear of the dark. Cody walked beside me with Shadow tagging behind him just like Blue used to. I looked the other way. How could another dog so easily take Blue's spot at Cody's side?

I had slipped out after Grams and Cooper went to their rooms so that darkness would conceal me. The night still blanketed the house. I eased the back door open and held it for Cody to go in first. I didn't turn on lights. I tiptoed up the stairs, but the quiet magnified the clickity-click of the dogs' toenails on the hardwood. I prayed Grams would be asleep. She wasn't. As her bedroom door opened, Cody, Shadow and I stopped in unison.

"You found Cody!" Grams said. She bent over and rubbed his head. His tail wagged in happiness to see her. "And who's this other guy?" Shadow weaseled his head under her hand to share in the welcome home.

"I've been calling him Shadow. He's Cody's new buddy."

The commotion woke Cooper, and he joined us in the hallway. "Where've you been? Where'd you find Cody?" he asked.

Like reporters, the two of them fired questions at me. They wouldn't let me slide with I'll-tell-you-in-the-morning answers. Instead they followed me into my bedroom and kept questioning. Cody jumped on the bed while Shadow sniffed his new surroundings. Grams pulled out the desk chair and Cooper plopped on the floor with Shadow.

"Start at the beginning," she said.

Exhaustion clouded my thoughts while I scrambled for a plausible tale. After an awkward silence, I opted for the truth. I began with my visit to the animal shelter and the whispered words of the volunteer. I told them about Kappies Kennel, the telephone call from Cindi, and my subsequent late-night return to the kennel. I held nothing back.

"That kennel owner is scum. As soon as I heard Cindi's story, I knew he had lied to me. I had to go back," I said.

"You didn't find Blue?" Grams asked.

"No, but I found some records of where he may have been shipped."

"What are you going to do?"

"I don't know." Before Grams could ask another question I told them about opening the cages and letting all the dogs and cats loose. Then I broke the news about the puppies.

"You stole puppies?"

"They're so cute, I couldn't leave them. I'll call Sara. She'll find homes for them."

Sara was an old friend who attracted dogs like a magnet attracted nails, and she thrived on the challenge of finding families for homeless pets.

Grams didn't seem surprised when I described the condition of the kennel. I asked her what she knew about the place.

"Not much. Over the years I've heard stories about Jarsma, but Tom always told me to mind my own business."

While Grams and I discussed the situation, Cooper sat cross-legged on the floor with his attention on Shadow. The dog's head rested in Cooper's lap. His eyes were closed and his body was limp as Cooper massaged his back.

"You did the right thing," Cooper said.

From then on I listened as Grams and Cooper plotted out the next day. They agreed I should take the puppies to Sara, and Shadow could stay at the farm. If anyone asked, he was just another stray who showed up at the door begging for a meal. I would call the shelter and tell them Cody came home and ask them to keep looking for Blue.

With a plan we all agreed to, Grams and Cooper finally left my room. I showered to rid myself of the kennel stench that enveloped my clothes and hair. But while the stink swirled down the drain and the soft scent of rose petals replaced it, the vision of the dogs I had seen that night bubbled to the surface of my thoughts. I fluffed the pillow and nestled between the sheets. I felt like I had drunk a pot of coffee for an evening snack. I tried to calm my mind by counting backwards from a hundred. Somewhere on my second countdown I nodded off, but it wasn't a comforting sleep. A jumble of beagles barked at me from behind bars, but none of them had blue eyes.

Sara and I became forever friends in first grade. Our friendship never faltered, not in high school, not when we went to different universities and not when she married her high school sweetheart, Ryan Hartwick. Sara and Ryan moved to Grand Haven, a small city in western Michigan, when Sara landed her dream job as an emergency room nurse in the town's only hospital. Ryan, a computer geek, made a decent living as a technology consultant, but his job forced him to be away from home for days at a time.

I debated if I should call Sara or surprise her. I didn't want to find myself standing on her porch listening to the doorbell echo through her house with no footsteps rushing to the door. I decided to call.

"I planned to go shopping in Grand Rapids, but I'd rather have a girls' day," she said.

I told her I'd be there in an hour, but didn't tell her why.

Cooper and I played with the puppies to tire them out before loading them into the carrier. He was gentle and playful--rolling them over one by one onto their backs and rubbing their bellies as they wiggled and licked his hand. They loved the attention.

"Do you want some company on the drive?" He asked as he lifted the carrier into the back seat and buckled the seat belt around it.

"I'd rather you were here for Grams," I told him. He gently closed the back door and opened the driver's door for me. I got in and rolled the window down. "I should be back by early afternoon."

Cody jumped up and stuck his head in the window. He loved to ride in cars. "You have to stay here with Grams and Cooper," I told him and patted his nose. I started the engine as Cooper called the dogs away from the car.

I loved the drive from Ludington to Grand Haven on U.S. 31. Stands of white pine, apple orchards, forests of oaks and maples and rolling farmland stretched for miles on either side of the expressway.

On Friday nights the freeway buzzed with city people heading to northern cottages. It came alive again on Sunday night as they drove back home for another five days of work. During the week, minutes could pass before another vehicle came into view. Compared to Chicago the roads were desolate.

Like Ludington, Grand Haven attracted tourists with its Lake Michigan beaches. For all the summers my father drove us to Pearline, we never explored the towns or beaches along the way. Sometimes we'd stop for a quick burger at one of the fast-food joints or for an ice cream cone. Most times Dad ignored the at-tractions along the highway, distractions, as he called them, and kept right on driving.

Sara and I explored the town in the months after she moved there. We hiked the dunes, walked the pier to the lighthouse and shopped the quaint stores. Every night during the summer, the dunes across the Grand River from downtown came alive with dancing water. It sprayed and twirled to the beat of well-know tunes and, like a rock concert, the water glowed under beams of colored lights that kept pace to the music. Tourists flocked to the bleachers and grassy knolls along the waterfront to watch the mu-sical fountain, one of the town's most popular attractions. The an-nual Coast Guard Festival, held in late July, also attracted tourists. Maybe this summer I could honor Sara's invitation to visit during the festival.

Sara and Ryan lived in a ranch-style house a few blocks from the beach, but close enough to the hospital that Sara walked to work. When I pulled my Subaru into Sara's driveway, she was sit-ting cross-legged, planting red, white and blue petunias along the edge of her perennial flower garden.

We hugged. "I have a little problem I'm hoping you can help me with," I said as I pulled the carrier from the back seat. The movement woke the puppies. Sara peered inside where a squirm-ing mass of reddish brown fur greeted her. I carried the load to the backyard before opening the carrier door. As the pups tumbled over each other and scooted around in the grass, I filled Sara in on their history and the last couple of days.

"Hot puppies. I love it," she said. I knew she would. Sara's game for anything.

"Hot, but I doubt if anybody's going to look too far for them. If anybody does, I'm sure you can come up with a good story."

"Like I found them in a box on my front porch after the door-bell rang mysteriously in the night?"

"Something like that."

Sara fostered puppies for the local humane society and al-ways had supplies for last-minute arrivals. I helped her carry a children's playpen from the garage into the house and ready it for the pups with water, food and a shallow cardboard box lined with a fleece blanket. We then plopped the tired youngsters in their new home.

Sara motioned for me to take a seat at the kitchen table. She poured us each a cup of fresh coffee and uncovered a cherry cobbler, bubbly hot from the oven. As she scooped us each a dish of the warm dessert, she told me Ryan left two days earlier for a conference in New York. She had a habit of somehow surprising him when he came home, and this time she painted the living room walls a cranberry red.

"He's not good at visualizing, but I know he'll love it," she said as she took a seat at the table.

I had no doubt he would. He worshipped her daredevil and independent style. He wouldn't even mind her taking the stolen puppies without discussing it with him.

"Are you all settled in?" she asked.

"I am, but Grams hired someone to help on the farm and I don't feel needed." She wanted to hear all about Cooper.

"Don't start getting ideas. I'm not ready for another relationship, besides he's a bit nosy and he's too chummy with Grams."

"What does he look like?"

"What does it matter? He's young."

"Ahh, you've been thinking about him," she said as she poured us more coffee.

"Drop it."

"What are you going to do about Blue?"

"I need to look for him. Thomas adored that dog, and I owe it to him to at least try to find him," I said. "Besides, it makes me angry that someone would come right up to the house and steal him from our fenced yard."

I reminisced about the day Grams gave him to Thomas. A story Sara had heard more than once, but she let me ramble on. For three years Thomas and Blue had been constant companions. With Thomas' diagnosis of leukemia, his friendship with Blue became even more important. Blue sensed a problem. Thomas cuddled with him like he would a stuffed bear and Blue didn't mind. When Thomas became too tired to get out of bed, Blue only left his room only to go outside to relieve himself. We even moved his food and water bowls into the bedroom.

Before I got too maudlin, Sara interrupted me. "Let's go for a walk and burn some calories," she said. We shared a love of walking.

We cut through town to the boardwalk that ran along the Grand River. The walkway ended at Lake Michigan where a pier, complete with lighthouse and keeper's catwalk, jutted into the water. The shops and eateries along the boardwalk were still closed for the season, so we had the wooden walkway to ourselves except for the brazen seagulls that swooped in low looking for handouts.

Sara asked about my parents.

"There's no news. They're still consumed with their careers."

The choppy water in the channel bounced around a flotilla of ducks as they searched for food. We walked in the center of the pier to avoid the occasional wave that crashed and swept across the concrete. The metal legs of a catwalk offered a place to latch onto if the waves got too aggressive.

"Have you heard from Rob?"

"No, other than when I called and told him of the move."

"What'd he say?"

"He wanted to get together before I left."

"Did you?"

"No. We had already said our good-byes. It's over. He doesn't want to face it. Getting together one more time isn't going to change anything."

"He's hurting as much as you are. You could at least talk to him."

I didn't answer. We reached the end of the pier and sat on the highest level of cement. We stared at the open waters. A nippy west wind blew in from across the lake.

"How do you think Blue is doing without Cody?" I asked.

"He'll manage. Hopefully he's with another dog he can follow."

"I wonder if he's still alive. What are the odds?"

"You'll go nuts thinking about it. I think you should let it go," Sara said.

I turned and stared at her. "You're the last person I expected to hear that from."

"He's gone. You already pushed your luck breaking into that kennel."

"I'm in the mood to push my luck. You know what they say. 'There's nobody more dangerous than someone who has nothing to lose.' That's me." I got up and started the walk back.

Instead of taking the boardwalk we followed the beach to the end of the state park and then trudged through the sand to the sidewalk. We didn't talk. Back at the house, I sat on the front step and poured sand from my shoes. "Thanks for taking the puppies," I said. "And thanks for the coffee and cobbler."

"No problem. You be careful and let me know what happens." We hugged good-bye.

I called the shelter when I got home to report Cody's homecoming. Sam Grensward said he'd keep an eye out for Blue. He didn't mention the break-in at Kappies or the flood of animals running loose in his jurisdiction, but he must have been suspicious. An hour later Sam, accompanied by Gary Jarsma, knocked on the back door. My thoughts sputtered as I tried to keep an innocent appearance. I stepped out on the porch leaving the dogs inside. Sam introduced Gary, and asked if I remembered him.

"Sure, I stopped at his place yesterday looking for Cody and Blue."

"Did you go back again last night?"

"Last night? No, I didn't go back. Why?"

"Someone broke in last night and let the dogs loose."

"I think maybe it could have been you," Gary said.

"Me?" I said trying to act confused. "Why would I go back?"

Sam held up his hand in front of Gary's face. "Let me take care of this."

"Since you were the only one at his place looking for a dog yesterday, he thinks maybe you had something to do with it."

"But he didn't have my dogs. He took me through the kennels himself."

Grams came out on the porch. She and Sam were old friends. He asked her where I had been the night before. With a poker face she told him I had been home all night. When he explained why he wanted to know, she asked if the break-in had anything to do with Cody coming home. Neither of the men answered.

Janet Vormittag

I waited a few seconds, hoping to give the illusion of analyzing what I had heard. "You mean you had Cody?"

Gary wasn't a poker player. "No, I didn't have your damn dog. I don't know what's going on, but it better stop," he said shaking his finger at me. His face turned an angry red, but his voice stayed a controlled monotone.

"You're saying it's just a coincidence that Cody came home after someone broke into your kennel?"

"I don't think it's a coincidence at all. I think you did it," Gary accused.

"Where's Blue?" I asked taking a step toward him. He backed up and Sam grabbed his arm.

"Cool it. Let's go," Sam said. He apologized as they stepped off the porch.

We watched as they drove away.

"That scared me," Grams said as we walked into the living room.

My legs shook so bad that I had to sit down. I dislike confrontations.

"We have to stick to our story. That's all there is to it," she said. "They can't prove anything. If they could, they would have."

32

Chapter 4

Cindi called an hour after Sam and Gary's visit. Sam had told her Cody came home, and she had questions. I hesitated telling her the truth, so I told her what I had told Sam; Cody returned on his own and Blue hadn't been with him. She wanted to talk and asked if I would come to her home. She gave me directions to her place, and I told her I'd be over shortly. I asked Grams how well she knew Cindi.

"She's been volunteering at the animal shelter for the last couple years. Sam lets her take dogs home when their time is up, so they aren't euthanized or don't end up at Kappies. She can only keep three dogs without a kennel license. Every once in awhile she calls to see if I can foster a dog until she finds it a home. I help her when I can."

"Can I trust her?"

"I would say yes, but the less people who know you're the one who broke into Kappies the safer you are."

Cindi lived ten miles away in an old mobile home on a desolate stretch of gravel road. Bright yellow daffodils and purple crocuses bloomed in a flower bed by the door. A chain link fence enclosed part of the front yard. It narrowed into a four-foot wide lane alongside the white and turquoise trailer.

When I drove into the driveway I spotted Cindi sitting on a weathered porch swing hanging from a massive oak tree. A gray cat curled in her lap and a black lab, which had been asleep next to her on the swing, jumped down as I got out of the car. Inside the fenced area two other dogs came racing from behind the trailer, barking. Cindi shouted at them to be quiet. They listened better than most kids.

A teapot sat on a chunk of wood next to the swing. I gratefully accepted when Cindi offered me a mug of the steaming brew. It smelled of apple pie spices and tasted the same. I savored its warmth.

"Did you hear about the break-in at Kappies?" she asked.

I shrugged. "Sam and Gary paid us a visit this afternoon and asked if I had anything to do with it." She didn't respond. I had the urge to fill the silence and struggled to keep quiet. I wanted to hear her version of the events. She finally spoke.

"The phone didn't quit ringing this morning. Everyone complained about dogs running loose," she said. "We brought four dogs to the shelter before we got the message from Jarsma and learned his kennel had been broken into. After that the rest of the dogs and cats we caught were taken directly to Kappies."

At the shelter Cindi had matched one of the dogs she had picked up to a poster for a lost dog tacked on the lobby bulletin board. She called the owners. Cindi's face glowed like a four-year-old on Christmas morning when she described the family reunion. The joy faded when Jarsma came to the shelter for the other three dogs. She tried to get Sam to stop him.

"Sam wouldn't listen," she continued. "I'm debating calling someone from the county."

"You should," I urged. "Cody must have been at Kappies. That's why he showed up at home last night."

She asked about the animals I had seen at Kappies and what rooms Jarsma let me go through. She listened intently as I recalled the details of the visit including the filth, the excited dogs, the stench and the way Jarsma made me fill out paperwork after I told him about my dogs.

"Was the place heated?"

"What's that got to do with anything?"

"The USDA cited Gary two years ago for not heating the kennel. He suspected I tattled and since then he won't let me in. By law, he doesn't have to. I used to take people there who were looking for lost dogs or cats. One time I knew he had this mixed breed mutt. I saw him pick it up at the shelter. Turns out the owners had been on vacation, and the dog-sitter didn't report the dog missing. I told them Gary had it. But when they went there, he claimed he didn't. Sam ended up going to Kappies with the couple. Like a miracle the dog appeared. He had a bullshit story about one of his workers putting the dog in quarantine and he didn't know about it. The guy is a liar."

Cindi told me she tried to get the county sheriff to investigate, but he relied on Sam to monitor Kappies, and Sam always gave Gary the benefit of the doubt.

"I'm beginning to wonder if Sam is involved in his scam to round up dogs."

"Could be. So, what do you think happened to Blue?"

She reasoned that if Gary had Cody, he probably had Blue, too. "Gary usually trucks dogs out twice a month. Beagles are the breed of choice for researchers. They're submissive and forgiving. He probably has a standing order for as many as he can get."

"Where does he send them?"

"I once followed his truck to a toxicology lab near Lansing. The next day Jethro here disappeared." She leaned over and gently ran her hand over the graying lab as he slept at her feet. "A couple hours later Gary brought Jethro home. He told me I'd better keep a closer eye on him or something could happen to him. I've been steering clear of the ass hole ever since."

"I see why. My gut knotted when I met him the first time," I said. "Then when he showed up on Grams' porch with Sam, he radiated nothing but deception and hate. He left me cold. It makes me sick to think he might have Blue. What should I do?"

"Odds are you won't see Blue again, but if you continue to look for him and ask questions, all I can say is 'be careful.' Keep your other dogs locked in the house when you're not home."

I asked her if she had any idea who broke into the kennel.

"You," she said without hesitation.

"You're crazy. Nobody else has a grudge against him?"

"Several people hate him and would like him to go away, but the timing points to you."

"I only wish I had the courage to do something like that," I said. To my surprise, dodging the truth came easy.

She asked about Grams and how I liked living with her.

"As long as I can remember I wanted to live with my grand-parents. It's too bad it took the death of my Gramps to make it come true."

"He was a kind old hoot," she said. "Not as soft as your gran-ny, but a good man. I only met him twice, but he treated me like an old friend."

I liked Cindi. I wanted to tell her about the collars I found at Kappies, but I held back. I thanked her for the tea, assured her I'd be careful and promised I would call if I found Blue. While driv-ing home, I told myself to keep in touch with her.

When I got home, Cooper had Gramps' horse saddled. When he spotted my car, he cantered in my direction. "Do you want to go for a ride?" He'd been bugging me to go riding with him ever since the day I arrived, and I always had a reason to say no. A ride sounded good, and not wanting to disappoint him again, I said yes.

Gramps' horse, Chester, took the lead on the narrow trail to the river. Dappy fell in behind. Riding single file made conversa-tion difficult, so we rode in silence. It gave me a chance to study Cooper from behind. He looked comfortable in the saddle and swayed in time with Chester's long stride. I swore he only owned blue jeans and T-shirts. I guess traveling on a motorcycle meant traveling light.

When the trail widened and we could ride side-by-side, Coo-per asked how the trip to Grand Haven had gone. I told him the puppies were in good hands and filled him in on the day's events, including the visit to Cindi's.

"You said you had papers from Kappies. Have you looked at them?"

"Not yet."

"Do you mind if I take a look at them?"

"No, maybe after dinner we can go through them." The thought of dinner reminded me of our clash at breakfast. I urged Dappy into a canter to rid me of the annoyance I felt at Cooper's existence in my life. Chester joined Dappy in the run. At the river, Cooper slid to the ground and tied Chester to a tree.

"Let's sit for a couple minutes," he said. The trunk of a fallen tree straddled the river. With arms out for balance, Cooper walked out onto the tree and slowly sat down.

"Come on, I won't bite," he said.

I gingerly slid my feet across the log and sat down next to him. Our feet dangled above the water. Usually I found solace in silence, but with Cooper the quiet felt uncomfortable. A rustling noise on the far bank made us both look. A white tail deer drank from the river, her ears perked for danger. She lifted her head and stared in our direction. After a few seconds of sniffing the air, she returned to her drink. When finished, the doe slipped back into the woods.

Seeing the deer started us talking again. I discovered Cooper had a talkative gene. I just needed to listen, that is, until he asked questions. I didn't like sharing my personal story. I bounced questions back to him and kept him talking. Everything in his life revolved around animals. His childhood home sounded like a zoo thanks to his mother's love of animals. He confessed that as a child he wanted to be a veterinarian. He even took pre-vet classes in college, but he dropped out. He wouldn't say why.

"Enough about me. Let's delve into your childhood," he said.

"Let's not."

"What skeletons do you have hiding in your closets?"

"Too many to discuss with you," I said. I stood up. I lost my balance, grabbed for Cooper's arm, and we both tumbled into the cold, waist-deep water. Cooper laughed as he made his way to shore. He looked like a little kid, hair plastered to his head with a T-shirt clinging to his chest.

"What's so funny?" I spit out river water and wiped the wet from my face. We crawled up the steep bank using trees to pull ourselves forward.

"Well, that was refreshing," Cooper said.

"Refreshing? It was damn cold. I'm sorry I pulled you in."

"No need to apologize. Give me a smile and all will be forgiven."

I gave a quick smile, then silence returned. Wet clothes made the ride home miserable.

The camaraderie Cooper and I shared by the river disappeared when we met again in the kitchen. I had just popped two chicken breasts and potatoes into the oven when he walked in.

"What's up?" he asked.

"I'm cooking dinner. I don't know how you can survive without eating meat."

"It's easy. You should try it some time."

"Why would I?"

"Tell me this. What's the difference between Cody, whom you love so passionately, and the chicken you're about to eat?"

"The chicken was raised for food. Cody's a pet."

"So raising an animal for food makes it okay to kill it to satisfy your need for meat?"

"Yeah, it does."

"In Korea Cody would be a main course."

"We're not in Korea."

"Right. Let me know when you're done with your carnivorous feeding," he said. He turned and left.

Moments later Grams came in. "What's the bickering about? I heard it all the way upstairs."

"We were just comparing dinner menus, and Cooper doesn't approve of mine."

Grams didn't approve either. When I invited her to join me, she informed me she planned on dining with Cooper.

"What's the big deal? It's chicken. Grams, you used to raise chickens. I remembered Gramps chopping off their heads and you plucking feathers."

"I always hated it. I didn't have a say back then. I do now. When the doctor told me I had high cholesterol and told me to cut back on eating red meat, it gave me the excuse to do what I had always wanted to do, not eat animals."

"But they're raised for food."

"So what?"

With that she left the kitchen. I read the newspaper until the potatoes were soft and the chicken, juicy and tender. I savored every bite.

After dinner, I left Cooper and Grams to their vegetarian cuisine and drove into Ludington to buy more dog food. Shadow ate non-stop, and I wondered what his life had been like before ending up with Jarsma. He must have been somebody's pet. He liked people and knew basic commands like sit and shake.

38

As I parked my car outside the supermarket, I noticed a white pickup parked on the far side of the lot. It struck me as odd. Why would someone park so far away from the door? The truck was still there when I finished shopping. I took my time loading the groceries into the backseat, all the time keeping an eye on the truck. When I pulled out of the parking lot, the truck's headlights blinked on and it pulled out behind me. I scolded myself for allowing my imagination to fill me with fear. I blamed it on watching too much television over the last year. I buried myself in make-believe lives rather than face my pain. I once read that people who watch a lot of television have a higher level of fear than those who don't watch TV.

Without using a turn signal, I switched lanes and swerved into a gas station. The truck slowed but stayed straight. I watched it disappear into traffic. I waited a few minutes and started home again. It didn't take long before I saw the truck parked along the side of the road, and sure enough, it pulled out behind me as I passed. When I slowed down, it slowed down. When I picked up speed, it picked up speed. Instead of going home, I drove into Scottville and pulled into a restaurant parking lot where a group of teenagers were hanging out. The truck followed. When it settled to a stop, I got out and walked towards it. A young man sat behind the wheel. When he saw me, he zoomed out of the parking lot so fast I couldn't read the license plate.

"Do any of you know the driver of the truck that just left?" I asked the teens. They didn't volunteer any information.

Back at home, I asked Cooper and Grams if they knew anyone who drove a white pickup. Neither one knew anybody. I told them what had happened.

"Do you think it could have something to do with Cody and Blue?" I asked. "Or are there young punks around here who like to scare women?"

"Are you sure he was following you?" Cooper asked.

"Positive. There's more going on here than we know."

"Like what?" Grams asked.

"I don't know, but I've got something to show you," I said. I went upstairs and retrieved my backpack. When I returned, I handed Grams the handful of collars I had taken from Kappies.

"What are these?"

"Collars I stole from Kappies." I stood, hands on my hips, waiting for a reaction.

She put on her reading glasses and inspected the tags on a red nylon collar. "I remember Winston. Jack and Martha searched for him for months," Grams said, as she read the information on a metal tag.

"When?"

"Last fall. If I remember right, he disappeared while they were on vacation and their neighbors were taking care of him."

"What kind of dog was he?" Cooper asked

"A chocolate lab who spent most of his time sleeping on the living room couch. Martha ran ads in the Lost and Found for three months and put up posters all around town," she said, adding that the couple finally gave up and hoped someone passing through the area picked up the friendly dog and kept him. "Jack and Martha were heartbroken."

The question of Winston's fate went unasked.

Grams didn't recognize the other collars or tags. One tag had a telephone number and Cooper called. He told the person who answered that he found a dog collar with their telephone number on its tag. From the one-sided conversation I could tell the person asked Cooper if he had the dog.

When Cooper finished he filled us in. The dog disappeared last summer on a hike in the national forest. He never came home even though he had been on familiar ground. The family hiked there often. They reported the cocker spaniel missing to the animal shelter and ran an ad in the newspaper. Like Jack and Martha, they never saw their dog again.

The other collars only had license tags. Without contacting the county, we couldn't get the names of the owners. I wondered if Cindi could get the names. If need be, I could ask her.

We went through the papers I had copied at Kappies. We divided them into thirds, and we each took a pile. We found two shipments of dogs shipped after Cody and Blue went missing. One went to Sweet's Research in Kalamazoo and the other to Doff Pharmaceuticals in Detroit. The paperwork didn't list the breeds, but it did show the payment. Jarsma got $425 for each dog.

I opened my laptop and did an Internet search of the companies. Both had websites. Sweet's was an independent toxicology lab that did contract work for a multitude of companies. The site listed clients, gave credentials of its department heads and showed pictures of the lab. The workers wore white lab coats, and counters were filled with vials and expensive-looking equipment. There wasn't an animal in sight.

Doff did research on new drugs. Like Sweet's site, Doff's website gave a lot of information about the company but didn't mention any testing of drugs on animals.

Neither one sounded like it held a promising future for a lost beagle.

Chapter 5

The muffled wail of sirens pierced my sleep, and I jolted awake wondering if the noise had been part of a dream. It took a minute to recognize the whine of fire engines, a sound not often heard on Oak Island Road. The green glow of the alarm clock displayed 3:18 as I reluctantly crawled from my cozy hibernation between flannel sheets. From the window, I could see red flashing lights as the trucks disappeared into the night. I stepped into the hallway where I bumped into sleepy-eyed Grams.

"Where do you think they're heading?" I asked.

"I don't know. Let's find out."

I slipped into yesterday's clothes and started down the hall.

Cooper peeked his head out from his bedroom door. "What's going on?" he asked.

"Fire trucks. We're going to see where they're headed," I said.

"Give me a second," he said, slipping back into his room to get dressed.

As we drove north, Grams fretted over whose home would be on fire. She knew just about everybody who lived in the county and prayed no one would be hurt. It didn't take long to see a red glow in the sky, and a few minutes later we spotted flickering flames above the treetops.

"Please tell me you didn't have anything to do with this," Grams said as Cooper parked in front of Kappies Kennel.

"Not a thing," I said. The wooden barn and its warehouse addition were engulfed in flames. The fire burned so bright I felt like my retinas were melting. I had to turn away. The century-old timber and bales of straw provided the perfect fodder. Even from the road we felt the heat. I closed my eyes as I thought of the dogs and cats frantically trying to escape their cages as the smoke and heat invaded their wire prisons.

"The dogs...it must have been hell for them," I said.

"Probably an easier death than what they had in store," Cooper said.

We asked a deputy standing guard at the end of the driveway what happened. He said he didn't know. A few minutes later Jarsma drove up. He got out of his car and just stared at the burning barn.

"I bet he's pissed," Cooper said. "With any luck he didn't have insurance."

I silently agreed with him. Gary Jarsma deserved to be put out of business, one way or another. His uppity air of righteousness was unbearable.

"With any luck they'll find it started by natural causes," Grams said.

"Natural causes?" I asked.

"You know, an electrical short, a coffee pot left on, something to do with an electric heater."

We saw Jarsma talking to the fire chief and decided to head home. Delicate pinks and lavenders glowed in the eastern sky as we drove away. Instead of going back to bed I took a shower to wash away the smoky remnants of the night. By the time I finished, Cooper had coffee brewing and pancakes sizzling on the griddle. We had just finished eating when a police car pulled into the driveway. Grams and I went to the door.

A middle-age man in a clean sheriff's uniform introduced himself as Sheriff Marc VanBergen. He reeked of Old Spice. I doubted he had been to the fire. Grams invited him in and offered coffee and a seat at the dining room table.

Sheriff VanBergen insisted we call him Marc as he sipped his coffee and asked how we were. After the token small talk, he reported he had been told we were seen at Kappies' fire and wanted to know why we were there. Grams told him the sirens had woken us, and we were curious about the fire and worried about neighbors. He asked if I had been home all night. This time Grams didn't have to lie.

"Do you know how the fire started?" she asked.

"We suspect arson, but we won't know for sure for a couple days," Marc said.

"Those poor dogs and cats."

"None of them died."

"You were able to get them out?" I asked.

"We didn't, but from what the first firefighters could tell, the cages were open and empty."

"Who got them out? The person who reported the fire?" Grams asked.

"No, a neighbor called it in but never went to the scene."

"What does that mean?"

"We suspect whoever started the fire let the animals out first," he said.

"Are they running loose again?" I asked.

"I don't think so. We haven't seen any dogs or cats."

"Where are they?"

"That's what we're wondering," Marc answered. With that he asked if I would mind coming down to the station to talk to a detective. The request caught me off guard.

"Why me?"

His eyes locked on mine. He took a step closer trying to intimidate me. "Mr. Jarsma thinks you had something to do with the break-in, and he's convinced you're somehow involved with the fire."

"That's crazy, all I did was go there looking for my dogs. He didn't have them, or at least he claimed he didn't. Ever since Cody came home after the break-in I've been wondering if he was at Kappies."

"We're looking into it. If you could answer some questions for us, it might speed things along. Can you come down and talk to a detective?"

I asked him when, and he offered to drive me. He promised to bring me home afterward. I looked at Grams. She said she'd be down to check on me if Marc didn't have me home by noon. He assured her I'd only be gone a couple hours.

On the drive to the station, Marc asked how I liked living with Grams. "Isn't it a culture shock after Chicago?"

One of the disadvantages of living in a small town is everyone knows everything about you. Or at least they think they do. Secrets are hard to hide.

"I'm much more suited for country living than living in Chicago. It's in my blood. It just skipped a generation." I explained how my parents detested almost everything about the country from the lack of fine dining to the farm-fresh air. He laughed.

Marc parked in front of a red brick, two-story building tucked on a side street near downtown Ludington. A blue spruce and two oak trees gave the police station a friendly appearance, but they didn't hide a small courtyard contained by chain link fence topped with taunt razor wire.

Once inside Marc took me to a small office and told me to make myself comfortable while he tracked down a detective. It didn't take long. A muscular guy with a graying mustache knocked on the door as he pushed it open. His caramel-colored suit clashed with a green shirt. A striped green and white tie only added additional woe. I made a bet with myself that he wasn't married. No wife would let her husband walk out the door dressed in a rainbow of greens. He introduced himself as Detective Bob Smith and took a seat behind the paper-cluttered desk.

"Tell me about the fire," he said.

I explained in detail how the sirens woke us up and aroused our curiosity. We drove in search of the fire and parked on the road to watch the firefighters work. He took notes on a yellow legal pad as I talked.

"Where were you yesterday afternoon and evening?"

As I outlined my day, I realized my life sounded pretty boring. In the excitement of the fire I had forgotten about the white pickup that followed me. When I remembered, I gave Detective Smith a detailed description.

"Do you think it's connected to the fire?" He ignored my question. It made me begin to doubt myself, and I wondered if the guy in the pickup had really been following me.

45

"What time did you go to bed?"

"I did some computer work, watched a little TV and went to bed after the eleven o'clock news."

He grilled me about Cody and Blue. He asked specific questions about their disappearance, where I looked for them and about Cody's homecoming. I stuck to my original story.

He wanted to know why I went to Kappies in the first place to look for them. I hoped I didn't get Cindi in trouble when I told him she had suggested it.

"Is it true none of the animals died in the fire?" I asked.

"Who told you that?"

"Sheriff VanBergen."

"It's an open investigation. We're not suppose to divulge information."

"So he lied?"

"No, he didn't lie."

When I got home I could hear Grams and Cooper arguing in the living room. It took me by surprise. They never disagreed on anything. In fact, their friendship aroused jealousy on my part. I listened but couldn't distinguish individual words. Grams was the louder of the two. When I opened the door they went silent. The only greeting was from the dogs who came running to me.

"Don't let me interrupt," I said, as I walked into the living room and sat down on the couch. I stared at them.

"It's private," Grams said.

"Nothing I do is off limits. Why do you get to keep secrets?"

Grams, who had been standing near the fireplace, shook her head and sat down next to me. "Tell her if you want," she said to Cooper.

Shadow jumped onto Cooper's lap as he took a seat in Gramps' over-sized stuffed chair. He started by making me promise not to tell anyone what he was about to say. "If you weren't Anna's granddaughter, I wouldn't tell you any of this."

"My lips are forever sealed," I said. I leaned back, making myself comfortable, and waited.

"I think I know who started the fire," he said.

"And they shouldn't have done it," Grams said under her breath. Her face was chiseled in anger.

46

It took Cooper a few moments to get past Grams' comment. "I called a friend who rescues animals and told him about the situation," Cooper said.

"A friend who rescues animals. What does that mean?"

Cooper ignored me and continued talking in a slow, deliberate voice telling me about an underground band of animal lovers who rescue animals in trouble. I couldn't believe it. He explained how he had given his friend details about Kappies. He didn't know if, or what, his friend would do with the information.

"But you knew they might use arson," Grams said. "And you knew they were adrenaline junkies."

"They do what they think is best."

"It's all going to cave, and you are going to be on the bottom of the heap. You promised you'd have no contact with those people," Grams said as she got up and stormed outside.

"What did she mean by that?"

Cooper turned and looked directly at me. "Have you ever heard of a group called ALL?"

"No."

"ALL stands for Animal Liberation League. What they do is illegal." He explained how the group existed in cyberspace and in the minds of a few hard-core animal extremists. Anyone could claim membership, but to be a member you had to rescue animals from abusive or cruel situations.

"It's called Save Five," he said. A website outlined the membership requirements and gave tips on how to bypass security systems, pick locks and generally not get caught. The rescues covered several areas of animal abuse.

"Abuse?" My comment stopped him, and I had to apologize for interrupting before he would continue.

"Wannabe members are asked to rescue animals from factory farms, fur ranches, hunting preserves, research laboratories and entertainment–something like a circus, zoo or rodeo. Wild animals, who can fend for themselves, are released back to the wild. Sanctuaries or good homes are found for the others."

"How are you involved?"

"I applaud anyone who recognizes abuse and does something about it."

"Are you a member?"

Cooper hesitated and turned to look out the window. I didn't think he was going to answer but he did.

"Yes."

He confessed that police wanted to question him regarding a fire at a horse slaughterhouse in California. A shipment of wild horses, which had been rounded up on public land and were being sent to the slaughter, had been hijacked. The truck was later found abandoned and the horses gone. The slaughterhouse burnt to the ground the same week, and the fire marshal deemed it arson. Cooper didn't admit responsibility for the theft or fire, but when he learned that authorities wanted to question him about the case, he took off on his motorcycle. His grandmother, Lucia Malecki, asked Grams if he could lay low on the farm for awhile. The two women had been friends since grade school and Grams couldn't say no.

I didn't know what to say. Cooper got up and announced he'd be in the kitchen making lunch. Although I only knew Cooper for a short time, I already realized cooking was his therapy. When things got tough, he disappeared into the kitchen.

I went to find Grams, who had retreated to the back porch. She sat on the swing, with her attention devoted to Maggie. The calico always appeared when she spotted a lap.

"At least Kappies is out of business for awhile," I said.

"But at what cost? We could all end up in jail."

"We just need to hang low and stick to our stories," I said.

"At this point, that's our only choice. And I hate it when I don't have choices."

A few minutes later Cooper invited us in for lunch. He had reheated minestrone soup, tossed together a spinach salad and toasted some garlic bread. Even I enjoyed the meat-free meal.

The rest of the day proved uneventful. I checked my e-mail and wrote to friends. When my fingers started to cramp, I unpacked my camera, called Cody and Shadow and went for a walk. I loved walking in the woods as much as I loved horseback riding. White trilliums, wild violets and spring anemones were in bloom. I focused on the beauty of spring, the land coming alive after the frigid air and blustery snow of winter. Of course, I couldn't resist more photographs of the dogs. When I returned Grams was sitting on the porch swing. She patted the seat beside her.

"There's still more to tell," she said as I settled in. She wanted me to know about her friendship with Cooper's grandmother Lucia. The two women had stayed in touch even though they lived on opposite ends of the country. They were pen pals who hadn't seen each other in years.

"We're like sisters," she said. They lived next to each other all through their school years. Grams' marriage and subsequent move to Michigan severed their day-to-day contact but didn't stop their friendship. When they were ten years old they each got a puppy for Christmas. The pups were from the same litter, and the identical gifts sealed their friendship in concrete.

Occasionally, Lucia would telephone and ask Grams if she had room on the farm for another stray. "I suspected she was involved in something not quite legal, but I didn't ask. I didn't want to know."

"Chester and Dappy would have been sold for meat if Lucia hadn't outbid the slaughterhouse buyer," she said. Lucia paid to have the horses trailered to Michigan.

"Blue came from her, too." Because of his obvious eye problems Grams had asked about his background. The pup had been stolen in a raid on a research facility that studied genetic eye disorders.

"You're kidding."

"No. From what I know they manipulated the genes of his mother to induce blindness in the offspring."

"Why would they do that?"

"Probably just to learn about genes."

"So why are his eyes blue?"

"Lucia didn't know. She guessed it was a side effect of the gene manipulation."

"Didn't you worry about giving him to me, knowing I would take him to a vet and for walks in the city where he would be seen? What if they were looking for him? He would have been easy to find. Everyone always noticed and commented on his eyes."

"As far as I knew, he was just another stray who showed up on my doorstep. Everyone knows I get cats and dogs dropped off all the time. I even have people coming here when they lose an animal or want to adopt a pet. They might know where he came from, but they'd never be able to figure out how he got here. And they couldn't blame it on me."

"Did my parents know anything about any of this?"

Grams laughed, and I realized the stupidity of the question. My folks were much too busy with their own lives to pay attention to mine, let alone hers. After that, we reassured each other everything would work out okay.

Cooper handed me a book as I headed to my room. "Read this. Maybe you'll learn something," he said. The title was "Diet for a New America." I flipped through the pages and saw black and white photographs of chickens packed in tiny cages, pigs confined in crates and calves packed in small stalls. Cooper's propaganda irritated me. I threw the paperback on my desk as I flicked on the television and put on my pajamas.

Chapter 6

I woke with an angry determination to find Blue. I couldn't sleep and when I did, dreams, no, nightmares filled my head. I woke with snippets. Blue restrained, men in white grabbing at him, doing things I couldn't see, and Blue howling in distress. It infuriated me that Blue, rescued as a pup, had disappeared into the unknown vat of animal research. But where to start? I needed to clear my head and think.

I had the kitchen to myself when I went down for breakfast. I let the dogs out the back door, made a pot of coffee and fixed a bowl of oatmeal with sliced banana and walnuts.

A few minutes later Grams came in from outside. "It's a perfect day for a ride to the lake," she announced.

Every spring for as long as I could remember we took a day to ride the horses to Lake Michigan. Our ultimate destination? Big Sable Lighthouse. It would be our first pilgrimage without Gramps. Grams read my silence and acknowledged my thoughts.

"Tom would have been out saddling the horses already."

"Getting away for the day sounds perfect to me."

"Should we invite Cooper?"

"Invite me where," Cooper asked, as he strolled into the kitchen invading our private conversation.

"On a ride to Lake Michigan," Grams said.

He didn't wait for an official invitation. "I'll get the horses ready," he said.

The intrusion dimmed the prospect of a good day. I helped Grams pack our traditional riding lunch of crunchy peanut butter and strawberry jam sandwiches, dill pickles, potato chips, red delicious apples and frozen bottles of water that kept the food cool and fresh. The water thawed enough to provide us with chilled drinks by noon. We packed everything in a saddlebag. I stuffed my camera into my jacket pocket. Cooper had Dappy, Chester and Lady Lu saddled and waiting for us by the time we were ready. We locked the dogs in the house, since the fenced yard was no longer a safe haven.

We rode down Oak Island Road for about a mile to a two-track trail that led into the Manistee National Forest. Grams gave Cooper an overview of the trip. If we stayed to the left whenever the trail split, it would lead us to Hamlin Lake. From there it was a short jaunt to Lake Michigan and the lighthouse. I let the two of them take the lead, happy not to be involved in their conversation. I had my camera to keep me company. I lagged behind as I snapped shots of pine stumps, spring flowers and the winding trail behind us.

We were only about a half-hour out when Grams felt Lady Lu favoring a back leg. Cooper investigated and found a stone lodged in the soft tissue of her hoof.

"She can't go on," he said. He offered to walk the mare home, but Grams insisted she would.

"You two go on. Lady and I'll have a leisurely walk home."

"I think we should all go back," I said.

Grams wouldn't hear of it. She untied her saddlebags and tossed them behind my saddle. Cooper tied them down.

"You know the way. Go, have fun and enjoy the day," she said as she loosened the cinch on Lady's saddle and started her walk back. I watched in disbelief as she deserted me. Cooper and I rode in silence until we reached the Big Sable River. We led the horses across a narrow wooden bridge. The trail followed the north side of the river until we reached Hamlin Lake, a 5,000-acre man-made lake created during the logging days as a holding pond for timber.

We stopped for lunch at a small sandy beach, the same place Gramps always had us take a break. We tied the horses to a sapling and retrieved the saddlebags. Cooper untied the blanket from behind his saddle, shook it out and spread it on the beach. Calm water, blue sky and a forest of white pines and oaks surrounded us.

"You didn't want me to come, did you?" he said as he sat down on the blanket.

"No, it's a family tradition. This is the first time without Gramps."

"I'm sorry I intruded."

I felt guilty for not wanting his company and offered a truce. "Let's just make the best of it and appreciate a gorgeous spring day." I sat down and handed him a sandwich and a bottle of half-frozen water. I spread the lunch on the blanket between us.

"Tell me about your grandfather," he said.

"He was a big guy, about six foot tall, on the heavy side from all of Grams' good cooking. He got up at five every morning, ate breakfast and then went out to milk the cows. I don't think Grams and he ever took a vacation, even after he sold the herd. He always said there was no better place to be than home."

"How often did you visit?"

"At least one weekend every month during the summer, and Thanksgiving and Christmas. Every summer I'd get to stay for two weeks without my parents. I constantly begged my mother to let me visit. I hated the city, and she hated the country."

I didn't want to talk about me, so I shifted the focus to him. "How'd you get involved in all this animal stuff?"

"My mother. She never pushed her opinions, but they rubbed off just the same. It all makes sense when you think about it."

"Like what?"

"Why do people think it's okay to eat cows and pigs but not okay to eat horses or dogs?"

"I don't see the problem."

"In some Asian countries dog meat is customary fare, and in France horse meat is as common as beef. It's preferred, since mad-cow disease has Europe in a state of panic."

The thought of eating either dogs or horses turned my stomach. "But cows, chickens and pigs are raised for food."

"Does that make it right? It just proves how anything becomes acceptable if it's done long enough and taught to children when they're young."

He started a sermon on dairy farming. "Small farms like your grandparents' might not be so bad. At least the cows are treated with respect. But small farms are a rarity these days. They've been replaced by factories where cows are nothing more than milk-producing machines. Calves are a by product and sold for veal. Cows are given hormones to produce more and more milk, their bags grow to abnormal sizes and almost drag on the ground."

"So you're saying it's wrong to drink milk?"

"A cow's milk is for its calf, not for humans. Only in the United States are people brainwashed to think they need cow's milk to be healthy."

He dared me to go visit a modern dairy farm and decide for myself.

"But they have to treat the animals well or they don't produce milk."

"Right, and if the cows don't produce, they're shipped off to the slaughterhouse. You know those tough cuts of meat? They're spent dairy cows."

He had an answer for every objection, but I'd had enough. I called a cease-fire and picked up my camera. I wandered along the shore framing pictures in my mind before taking aim and shooting. I even snapped candid shots of Cooper lounging on the blanket. I still thought he could be a Calvin Klein model. I tried to ignore my growing attraction and worked hard to keep him at arm's length. Damn Grams for setting me up. Had Lady Lu really picked up a stone? Or did she scheme to get us together in fun so we'd quit bickering?

After fifteen minutes of enjoying the serenity of the lake, we mounted the horses and pushed on. From Hamlin Lake the trail led into the dunes of Lake Michigan. It didn't take long before we could hear the faint roar of crashing waves. The top of the dunes revealed a picturesque view of the big lake, steel blue water with white foaming waves breaking on a sandy beach that stretched as far as we could see in either direction. To the south, the black and white Big Sable Lighthouse protruded from the dunes. We guided the horses to the beach and nudged them into a canter. Soon the red-shingled roof of the lighthouse keeper's home became visible.

The lighthouse, built in 1867, is the centerpiece of Ludington State Park. Years ago volunteers restored the landmark and opened it to tourists. The attached keeper's quarters provided a home to docents who served as guides and historians. Most of the time only hikers and mountain bikers had access to the area, but three times each summer buses traveled the service road to the lighthouse, carrying people, who couldn't hike or bike, the chance to experience it.

We tied the horses to a tree and went inside. A heavyset man with a plaid shirt and suspenders holding up denim pants welcomed us and pointed us into the gift shop. For a two-dollar donation we could climb the circular staircase to the top of the 112-foot brick tower. The prize for making the heart-pounding ascent was a spectacular view in every direction. The shop had an array of lighthouse collectibles including miniature replicas, T-shirts, magnets, books, calendars, key chains and everything else imaginable. I pulled cash from my pocket and handed it to the woman behind the counter. She asked for my zip code for their tourist statistics. When I gave her a local zip she looked up.

"Alison, I didn't recognize you. I'm so sorry about your grandfather. Is Anna here?"

The woman looked familiar, but her name eluded me.

"I'm Mary Tarman," she continued. "Anna takes care of our dogs when we go on vacation."

"I'm sorry. I couldn't remember your name. Lady Lu picked up a stone about a mile from home so Grams turned back." Sometimes it seemed everyone knew my grandparents.

"You're by yourself?"

"No, a friend is with me." I pointed to Cooper. "I didn't know you volunteered here."

"This is our first time. Bill is here too. We just got here this morning," she said as she took my money. "We're here for two weeks."

"Sounds like fun," I said.

"So far it has been. Enjoy your climb. Bill is on duty at the top," she said, closing the cash register drawer.

The open-grate metal stairs had a single railing along the outer wall. I clung to it. I hate heights. Cooper laughed at my slow secure pace and trotted up the stairs. He disappeared above me, the clanging of his shoes faded into the distance. When I finally made it to the top, Cooper and Bill were outside on the walkway that circled the glass-enclosed beacon. I preferred the inside. I could hear the history lesson Bill shared with Cooper, a lesson I almost knew by heart. Through the glass I took a picture of the two of them with the glistening blue water as a backdrop. I also snapped shots of Chester and Dappy waiting for us down below.

Bill insisted I step outside for the view. I tried to say no, but he wouldn't hear it. Finally, I gave in. For a few minutes the panoramic scene overshadowed my fear of heights. To the west, the steel blue water of Lake Michigan stretched to eternity. Its calmness consumed my essence. To the north and south, the water greeted the shore with a gentle hello. Seagulls scampered on the sand dodging the waves that washed ashore. After a few moments I relaxed enough to let go of the railing and take photographs. When a young couple with three kids came out onto the deck, Cooper and I took our leave.

Back in the gift store, Mary made me promise to say hello to Grams for her. I encouraged her to stop at the farm after her two-week stint at the lighthouse. "She'd love to see you."

By mid-afternoon we climbed in the saddles to head home. The lake shimmered in the sun as seagulls swooped over the shallow waters searching for dinner. I asked Cooper to stop so I could ride ahead and get a photo of him and Chester with the lighthouse in the background. I didn't need to encourage him to smile for the camera. His wind-blown hair gave him a boyish look, and he looked genuinely happy.

"How cool would it be to live here for two weeks?" Cooper asked. He couldn't quit talking about the lighthouse and the romance of keeping the light burning for ships passing Big Sable Point. He wished he had been born 50 years earlier so he could be a lighthouse keeper.

"Don't you think it'd get a little lonely being stuck out here in the middle of nowhere for months?" I asked.

"You'd have time to read books, a garden to tend. I could sit and listen to the waves forever."

"I bet within days you'd be lonely and talking to yourself."

"I do that now," he said with a laugh. "I don't need to be lonely to talk to myself."

I steered the conversation to Blue and asked Cooper if he thought the beagle might still be alive.

"There's always a chance, but research animals don't usually have a long shelf life."

"That's a heart-warming way to put it," I said. "What kind of research are dogs used for?"

"Do you really want to know?"

"It can't be that bad."

"What pile of sand do you have your head buried in? Research is nothing less than torture from the animal's perspective. At toxicology labs animals are used to find the toxicity of new products. They shave the hair off an animal and pour solutions directly on their skin. They force-feed it to them. They drip it into eyes or check the toxicity of fumes by pumping them into an enclosed area where the animal has no escape. The list is endless."

I couldn't answer. Blue. Sweet, trusting Blue, who wagged his tail and licked the hand of anyone who came near him.

"And if he's at the pharmaceutical company they're probably testing new drugs on him. Neither is a pretty thought." That tidbit sealed our silence for the rest of the ride.

By the time we got home, the temperature had started to drop. Grams sat in front of the television watching the local weather report. The meteorologist forecast freezing rain overnight. Cooper went back outside to put the horses inside for the night. Usually they were left outside with the freedom to go inside if they preferred, but with the upcoming storm, we thought it best they spent the night in the barn.

I woke in the middle of the night shivering. The glow of the alarm clock had disappeared along with the green power light of the smoke detector.

Downstairs I found Grams crunching newspapers to start a fire in the fireplace. Candles gave the room a deceivingly warm glow. The room was icy. We spent the rest of the night in sleeping bags on the living room floor. The dogs cuddled as close as they could, their body heat welcomed. The morning sun revealed a magical world of ice that sparkled like cut glass. Forsythia, with its yellow buds ready to burst open, drooped to the ground under the heavy load. Daffodils were encased and frozen in time.

Grams used a match to light the gas stove and put a teapot of water on for tea. She searched the hallway closet for the crank radio. Thirty seconds of cranking gave about a half hour of radio time. The news reporter said more than 30,000 homes had lost power. Crews from Indiana and Ohio were on the way to help fix downed lines, but it would take up to three days to restore everyone's electricity.

Sleepyhead Cooper seemed surprised to discover us camping in the living room. While Grams' worked on breakfast, Cooper and I went out to feed the horses and barn cats. The ice-encased branches creaked and tinkled like breaking glass as they swayed with a slight breeze. The driveway was transformed into a skating rink. We glided along the slippery surface like ten-year-olds learning to ice skate. I laughed as the California boy tried to stay upright, his arms flailing like tree limbs in a windstorm. On a slight hill leading down to the barn, I lost my balance, picked up speed and crashed into Cooper. For a moment he maintained his upright position and almost salvaged my fall. But not for long. We tumbled into a heap on the ground. The situation turned into a laugh fest when we tried to stand. We scooted along the frozen ground on our butts until we reached the barn.

The horses whinnied and stomped about, protesting the closed door that kept them prisoners. Grain and hay calmed their disposition. Willow and Maggie purred and weaved around our legs as we worked. We spent a few minutes sitting on bales of hay giving them some loving.

On the way back to the house, we walked on the lawn for traction. The frozen grass crackled under our weight as our footprints were cast in shards of green. Before we went inside, we stood still to admire the frozen landscape. The bushes and flowers were transformed into ice sculptures. Icicles hung from the wood fence like Christmas decor. I got my camera and recorded the beauty.

After breakfast we settled in for the day. With the fire crackling and papers spread across the floor, Cooper and Grams helped me plan my next steps.

Chapter 7

For close to an hour the three of us studied the papers I had copied at Kappies and the pages printed from the websites of Sweet's Research and Doff Pharmaceuticals.

"He has to be at Sweet's," Cooper said. The records revealed fifteen dogs had been delivered to Sweet's in Kalamazoo a week after Blue and Cody went missing. Seven dogs had been shipped to the pharmaceutical company in Detroit. The dogs taken to Doff's were large breeds; German shepherds, Labrador retrievers and over-sized offspring of mixed lineage, mostly identified as lab mixes. The animals sold to Sweet's were all smaller, mostly beagles.

"Look at this," said Cooper pointing to a line on one of the records from Kappies. "I bet this one is Blue."

I looked at where he pointed. It was a numbered list of dogs and the last one, dog 281, was a beagle with the notation "eye."

"It has to be him!" I said jumping from my chair. "It has to be." I grabbed Cooper and pulled him to his feet and gave him a hug. Then I did the same to Grams.

I recognized my good fortune at finding Cody when I did. He could have been in the shipment to Doff's. And if he had, odds were I would have never known the fate of either dog. I would be like the people whose dogs' collars we found in Kappies' barn. Always wondering, never knowing.

We focused on the pages from their website. They provided a wealth of information about the business, including backgrounds of key scientists, a list of customers and the services the company provided. They helped develop new products by performing safety evaluations and provided assessments and statistics on substances.

Sweet's Research, with its trusting, innocent-sounding name, specialized in both acute and chronic toxicology. The pages were sprinkled with words like dermatoxicity, inhalation, infusion, oncogenicity and neurotoxicology. I didn't know for sure what the words meant, but the root of some kindled my sense of urgency. They sparked the dark side of my imagination regarding research. I could only imagine what it all meant, or maybe I couldn't.

Their list of clients surprised me. The lab catered to well-known manufacturers of cleaning supplies, household goods, and personal hygiene and beauty products. They also did work for organizations that studied aging, diseases, alcohol and drug abuse, and genetics.

"Why do they do it?" I asked. The good news was dissolving as I learned about the research.

"To prove new drugs, products or chemical concoctions are safe. Because the government requires it. To protect their clients from lawsuits. Because it's the way it's been done for years."

"Can't they do it without using animals? Without stealing pets?"

"With today's technology they probably could if they wanted to, but it's human nature to resist change. And there's a good chance the scientists and researchers don't know the animals are stolen. It's legal to get animals from shelters if they're willing to release them."

Grams shrugged. "It's stuff we're better off not knowing about," she said. "What good does it do to make yourself crazy about something you can't do anything about?"

Her statement surprised me.

"I'd like to think we can do something about it," Cooper said.

I understood Grams' thinking, of not wanting to question the status quo. But I could also relate to Cooper's thinking—let's change the world! What did I think? I didn't know.

Cody, Shadow, Elvis and Sinatra sprawled on their sides soaking up the heat from the fire. I tried to imagine them as research subjects, locked in cages with scientists doing unspeakable things to them. The concept was too foreign for my imagination. They were pets. The thought of Blue being mistreated, like nothing more than a research subject in an experiment, made me mad. It gave me incentive to continue. No one had the right to steal my dog, my dead son's dog, and sell him to an animal hell.

The electricity came back on just after we finished a lunch of leftovers. Our cozy primitive morning came to a stop. The sun had already started to melt the magic of the ice. Television news showed pictures of downed trees and ice-glazed landscapes. A newscaster reported that main roads were clear, but some side roads were still blocked by fallen trees and limbs.

The morning session gave me an introduction to animal research and a possible location for Blue. But I wanted definite answers, not more questions, harder questions, gray questions. I liked things black and white with no confusing middle ground.

"So now what?" I asked.

Cooper didn't have any ideas.

Neither did Grams. "You're going to have to accept the fact that Blue is gone."

I couldn't. I wanted suggestions on how to proceed, not advice on quitting. I wasn't going to walk away. Yet, I didn't know what to do. I suggested a drive to Kalamazoo to knock on Sweet's door and ask if a blind beagle had been part of the latest shipment from Kappies.

Cooper doubted if they would even talk to me. "They wouldn't want the publicity of someone finding a missing pet at their facility."

"I'd promise not to tell."

"I bet they wouldn't even acknowledge they use dogs in the work they do. You'd be escorted out the front door as soon as they understood what you were asking."

"But you don't know for sure. I think that's what I'll do. Take a drive to Kalamazoo."

"And do what?" Grams asked.

"I don't know, but it'll beat sitting around here doing nothing." She tried to talk me out of going, but I had inherited her stubborn gene. The more she insisted I not go, the more determined I became.

"If you go, I go," Cooper said. He tried to console Grams by saying he would keep me out of trouble.

"But who will keep you out of trouble?" Grams asked. She threw the papers she had been reading onto the floor and waited for an answer.

"We'll be careful," was all I could muster. I could tell by her face she didn't like the answer. Neither Cooper nor I said anything more. I went upstairs, printed driving directions to Sweet's and packed an overnight bag. It looked like Cooper packed for a week. I kissed Grams goodbye and promised to be careful.

"Promise me you won't do anything illegal."

"I'm not going to make a promise I can't keep." I hated leaving Grams as angry as a wasp caught in a glass jar. But as much as I hated it, I did it anyway. After checking on the horses and opening the barn door so they could go outside, we left.

Sweet's was on the outskirts of the city. A mix of farmland and suburbia, with its subdivisions, strip malls and bike paths, surrounded it. The place looked deceivingly irrelevant with a plush green lawn bordered by flower beds. A large oak tree shaded the main entrance. An empty security booth fronted the driveway and about a half dozen vehicles rested in the parking lot. Ranch-style homes lined the street across from the entrance, and a farmhouse sat to the south of the facility. To the north, a hay field covered acres of land. It looked like an artist took a brush, dipped it in green and splashed it across a canvas.

We drove around to get a feel for the neighborhood. A half-mile away we found a grocery store with an attached strip mall. Cooper parked, and we hiked along the asphalt bike and walking trail that bordered Sweet's property. Their one-story building looked small from the front, but from an angle we could see it mushroomed in the back. It had a facade of red brick with a window on either side of a gray steel front door. A driveway alongside the building disappeared to the back of the acreage.

Cooper suggested we get a room for the night and come back after dark. "It doesn't look like they're worried about intruders," he said, noting the absence of surveillance cameras and fences. "We need to find out if they have a security system."

"How do we do that?"

"One of us, and I suggest it be you, needs to go inside and look for one."

"I wouldn't know what to look for."

We went back to the car where Cooper detailed telltale signs of a security system: stickers in the window announcing the presence of an alarm, cameras, magnetic door contacts, motion detectors, and a keypad near the door that provided a timed entrance. "If the right code isn't punched in within a programmed number of seconds after the door is opened, a silent signal will be sent to a monitoring company who will call the local police department."

I dropped Cooper off at a nearby park to wait for me. I hyped myself for action with thoughts of Blue. Blue as a playful pup bumping into furniture. Blue tagging along with Thomas and cuddling with him on his bed. Blue following Cody. It made me determined to bring the beagle home. It made going into Sweet's offices easier. I had nothing to lose and everything to gain.

I didn't even slow down as I drove past the deserted security booth. I parked in a visitor's slot and walked in the front door like I belonged. All the time I could feel my heart beating double time. A young woman sat at a desk talking on a telephone. It gave me time to look around. I didn't see any of the security items Cooper described. When she hung up the phone, she turned her attention to me.

"Can I help you?"

"Hi, I'm new to the area and looking for a job. Are you hiring? Could I fill out an application?" I asked.

"What kind of work are you looking for?"

"Office work, or anything you have."

"We're not hiring at the moment, but you can fill out an application. We'll keep it on file for six months." She handed me a two-page application, a clipboard and an ink pen. I took a seat in the lobby. As I filled in the blanks, I scanned the area. I still didn't see keypads, cameras or motion detectors. After a few minutes, I got up and told the woman I'd drop the application off the next day. She nodded. As I opened the door, I dropped my keys. Picking them up gave me time to check the door frame for anything that could have to do with an alarm. It looked clean to me.

"With no alarm, it'll be a breeze," Cooper said. We found a roadside motel about five miles away. Cooper asked if I'd register for the room. I finally realized he was taking a risk leaving the security of the isolation of Grams' farm. *Why? Blue didn't mean anything to him. Maybe he felt he owed it to Grams to keep an eye on me. He didn't owe me anything.*

I asked for two rooms, but the woman behind the counter said they were remodeling and only had one available. I reluctantly took it. One room? I didn't relish the thought of spending a night with Cooper in a motel room. I paid cash like Cooper instructed and scribbled my name making it illegible. Cooper didn't want a record of us having been in the area. The woman didn't ask questions. I guessed cash customers equaled tax-free income.

The door opened into a typical cheap motel room. The kind of place you forget as soon as you leave. To my dismay it had a king-size bed instead of two double beds. A flowery bedspread covered the bed. Curtains were made of the same florid print. A plastic framed landscape of pale browns and blues graced the wall above the headboard. High fashion—for the 1980s. Across from the bed a television rested on a low dresser, and on the far side of the room sat a round table with two wooden chairs. On the other side of the bed sat an overstuffed chair. Under the window a combination heater and air conditioning unit hummed and rattled when I pushed the vent button to get some fresh air from outside.

Cooper clicked on the television and cruised the channels until he found an old movie. "It'll drown out anything we talk about," he said in a low voice.

"Aren't you being a tad paranoid?" I tossed my bag on the bed and went in to checkout the bathroom.

"Probably, but you can never be too careful."

As soon as we were settled, which took about five minutes, Cooper suggested we go to a grocery store and get some food. I suggested he go. I needed some alone time. He returned less than hour later with two bags of groceries.

"How long do you plan on staying?" I asked.

"Sorry, but the way I see it we're stuck here with nothing to do but eat." He had veggie sandwiches from the deli, hummus, crackers, apples, celery, bananas, a can of mixed nuts, and a bottle of red wine.

"We might need it to unwind when we get back," he said as he sat the bottle on the table.

"Good idea. Maybe we could have a taste before we go?"

"I don't think so. We need to be sharp."

After eating the sandwiches, Cooper packed his backpack with tools he had in his duffel bag; flashlights, screwdrivers, wire cutters, duct tape, magnets, lock picks and a digital camera. It didn't take long to realize why he had looked like he packed for a week.

His preparedness put my expedition into Kappies to shame. "I get the feeling you've done this before," I said.

"A few times." He didn't offer any details, and I didn't ask.

We decided to take a walk to burn up our nervous energy. Just a jaunt around the neighborhood. When we returned, I got ice from a machine by the office to chill the wine. Cooper said we should wait until after midnight before leaving for Sweet's. We watched TV, then decided to try to sleep. Cooper insisted I use the bed--he intended to nap in the stuffed chair.

"It's a king-size bed. I think there's room for two of us," I said. I regretted saying it before the words were out of my mouth.

He didn't say anything, but got up and stretched out on the bed. We both clung to our sides of the mattress like a life raft. I hid between the sheets. Cooper stayed on top of the bedspread. There'd be no chance we would accidentally touch. No chance at all.

Sleep never came. Instead I replayed the last few days in my head. How had I ended up in a motel room with a guy I barely knew, waiting for the solitude of the early morning hours, so we could break into a research lab? It felt more like a movie plot than real life, especially my life, which until a year ago had been on a track of happiness and contentment. Death and divorce now defined me. I no longer cared about the future. I needed to get my life back on track but didn't know how. Finding Blue gave me a focus, something to think about other than the past.

The alarm buzzed at 1 a.m. Before we got into the car, Cooper muddied the license plate. We drove to the farm next to Sweet's.

With the headlights off, Cooper backed the car alongside the faded red barn that stood between the farmhouse and the lab. We waited to make sure no lights popped on in the house. A sliver of a moon eased from behind a bank of clouds and dimly lit the area. The silence swallowed me. No barking dogs, no traffic, no wind, not even mosquitoes. When it looked like no one had been disturbed, we tiptoed across a patch of lawn and ducked into a row of trees and underbrush that most likely marked the property line. The rustling of my clothes sounded gigantic. My heart thudded as I concentrated on deep, slow breaths. Cooper surveyed the area with binoculars. When he finished, he handed them to me. Floodlights lit patches of the lawn and the driveway that ran alongside the building. Silence enveloped the scene. Nothing moved. The place appeared deserted.

We worked our way through the trees toward the back of the building. I could see a loading dock with two overhead doors and an entrance door.

"Stay here until I call for you," Cooper whispered into my ear. He was so close I felt the warmth of his breath.

He took the lock picks out of his backpack and darted across the lawn and driveway. It didn't take him long to manipulate the lock and swing the door open. His flashlight swept the frame as he checked for an alarm switch. He disappeared inside for a minute before returning to wave me in.

Chapter 8

Sweet's didn't have any windows except in the lobby and in the offices at the front of the building. I expected darkness, but in the loading area a few florescent lights lit the room. There wasn't a pushcart, dolly, crate or kennel in sight. I anticipated something similar to Kappies; barking and an odor of confined animals. Instead, silence greeted us. Silence and a sterile, stuffy smell.

Cooper handed me a pair of tight-fitting latex gloves, having already donned a pair himself. "We don't want to leave any trace," he said.

A metal door with a small rectangular window led to a dimly-lit hallway with doors on both sides. It appeared to run all the way to the front lobby. One by one we checked out the rooms. I couldn't believe it. They were either empty or filled with cardboard boxes and file cabinets.

Near the office we discovered a large room with stainless-steel counters and tables. With no windows we dared turn on the overhead lights. The room lit up like a hospital. Finally, a room in use. Microscopes, scales, test tubes and a multitude of other equipment I didn't have names for filled shelves. Along one wall sat a large refrigerator. Through its clear glass doors I could see vials of liquids and Petri dishes. A stainless steel cabinet, built behind sliding glass doors, held glass fronted cubicles. I couldn't make out what inhabited each compartment, but something did.

Cooper slid open one of the heavy glass doors and a putrid smell drifted out.

"What are they?" I asked

"Rats," Cooper said. "Their backs have been shaved."

67

Cooper aimed his flashlight in the cubicles. One rat lay panting on its side with an oozing sore on its back. It didn't acknowledge the light or us. The rats didn't have food, water or bedding. Most of them looked dead. I couldn't tell. The nauseating odor must have been from decaying flesh. Their bodies rotting, yet their hearts kept pumping. I turned and gagged.

"They're doing some kind of chemical skin testing," Cooper whispered. While I held the flashlight, he took pictures of the pitiful creatures.

Another area in the room held dozens of mice. The tiny critters didn't have much space or any comforts. A few appeared lifeless, but several were wiggling about like Mexican jumping beans. Their backs were shaved and a dark ointment spread across the sensitive skin. Cooper snapped more photographs.

One little guy had his front paws on the rim of his compartment and stood stretched on his back legs. Cooper found a small plastic jar, punched an air hole in its lid with his jackknife, carefully picked the mouse up and deposited him inside the jar. I tucked the jar in my jacket pocket. Cooper searched through the papers on a nearby desk. "They're testing the toxicity of a new suntan lotion," he concluded.

"A suntan lotion? What could be in a suntan cream that would kill mice and rats?"

"It's a non-sun lotion. Whatever the chemical concoction is, it's probably supposed to give a golden tan without the danger of skin cancer caused by exposure to the sun."

"It's a skin dye," I said.

"It's insane."

I didn't see any kennels. "Where are the dogs?" I asked.

"I don't know."

We backtracked to a storage room where fireproof file cabinets were labeled by year, but they stopped at 2001. Cooper glanced though folders stuffed with papers. We went through the rooms one by one and concluded recent records were probably on computer discs and stored elsewhere. In the secretary's cubicle we found letterheads with a second address for the company.

"They have another building. That's why there's not much here," Cooper said.

"I knew it was too easy."

Realizing the information we needed wasn't there, Cooper wanted time to search the files.

"What are you looking for?"

"Nothing in particular, just curious to see what they're up to."

I thumbed through papers, not knowing what to look for. Each year had customers filed alphabetically. Records showed testing of the same product, using a variety of species from mice and rats to dogs and cats to primates.

Why are they testing the same thing on so many animals?" I asked.

"I'm not sure. I thought the FDA required results from one primate and one non-primate species." Papers of interest he slipped into his backpack, claiming if anybody missed a few, they'd figure they were misfiled. To prove his point he even mis-filed a few reports.

I wanted to leave. Cooper wanted more time.

"It's a once-in-a-lifetime chance to read this stuff," he said.

"Yeah, but Blue's not here."

Cooper didn't look up. "I know, but don't you care about what's going on here?"

"Sure, but what's being done is probably being done for a good reason." He didn't answer, but I swear I could hear his eyes roll.

"Just give me a few more minutes," he said, his eyes glued to the papers.

I timed him. After five minutes I tugged on his jacket. "Let's go." Just as we entered the hallway we heard noises from the lobby. We ducked back into the room and listened by the door.

"It's probably a janitor," I whispered.

Cooper put a finger to my lips to quiet me. I heard someone enter the room next to ours. Before we could sneak out we heard the door open again. Cooper grabbed my arm, and by the light of his flashlight, we tiptoed to the back corner of the room and squeezed between the wall and a stack of boxes. I couldn't control my breathing, and my heart raced. Cooper kept a tight grip on my arm. Then the door where we hid eased opened. I prayed. The overhead fluorescents flickered and flashed on. A file drawer opened. Papers shuffled. The sounds repeated seven times. Then the door opened and closed. I heard another door open and close. Cooper yanked me to my feet and pulled me toward the door. We ran as quietly as possible to the loading area. We were about to head outside when we heard a door opening again. Cooper peeked through the small window of the door that led to the hallway. A few seconds later I heard another door open and close.

"We're out of here," Cooper mouthed. With me on his heels he opened the back door and we slipped into the cool fresh air of the night. Cooper pointed, and I saw a black Jeep parked in the ramp of the loading dock. We flattened ourselves like chewed gum to the pavement. Everything remained quiet. Cooper got up to investigate.

"It's empty," he whispered. Ducking low we hurried to the safety of the trees.

"Why would he park in the back and go in the front door?"

"My guess is he doesn't want his Jeep to be seen, and he doesn't have a key to the back door."

We didn't dare use our flashlights. Instead we felt our way through the alley of trees and underbrush. We were almost back to the car when I tripped, lost my balance and tumbled to the ground making enough noise to wake the neighborhood. But it remained quiet. Instant pain shot to my brain. Cooper stopped and came back.

"What happened?"

"I fell. Give me a minute. I hurt my ankle." He held out a hand and pulled me up. Leaning on his shoulder I could stand, but I couldn't put weight on my foot. With his help, I hobbled along until we were out of the woods. Then, to my embarrassment, Cooper picked me up and carried me bride-style across the lawn.

I hoped the fall hadn't hurt the mouse. Once in the car I took the jar out of my pocket. By a muffled glow of the flashlight I could see the little critter moving. He sniffed my finger when I put it by the air hole. "Hang in there, little guy, we'll get you some food and water soon."

We decided to wait for the Jeep to leave. It took a few minutes for me to collect my wits, but Cooper didn't seem flustered at all.

"How do you stay so calm?"

"I'm not. I just hide it well. I love the adrenaline rush," he confessed. "I feel more alive when I push myself beyond my comfort zone."

I diverted my attention back to the mouse, dodging back into my comfort zone. I wanted to take the mouse out of the jar but didn't know how to handle him.

"He'll be okay till we get back to the hotel," Cooper said. "Why don't you name him?"

We bounced ideas back and forth and settled on Kal, a shortened version of the city we were in.

"Were they really testing suntan lotions on him?" I asked.

I could hear the anger in his voice as he spoke about the unnecessary and often duplicated research. "No matter what the results are, the first people to use a new product are the human guinea pigs," he said. "Is it really so important that we have another new suntan lotion?"

He challenged my naive view of the world, and I didn't like it. I stared out the window into the darkness and tried not to listen. Cooper spoke passionately about his belief that animals had their own lives to live and shouldn't be subject to the whims of man. I didn't agree with him but didn't dare say anything.

Fifteen minutes later we heard the Jeep start. We ducked our heads below the windows as it passed by with its headlights off. As soon as it pulled onto the street the headlights came alive. We followed, waiting until the Jeep turned a corner before turning our lights on to continue the pursuit. We weren't close enough to read the license plate numbers, so I retrieved the binoculars from the backpack and scribbled the numbers on the hotel receipt I had shoved in my pocket. I kept watching with the binoculars.

"It looks like an older man," I said.

"He must work there if he had a key."

After a few minutes, the Jeep pulled into Oak Estates, a newer subdivision with grandiose homes, manicured lawns, asphalt driveways and tended flower beds. It looked like a neighborhood where keeping up with the Joneses was mandatory.

We watched as the Jeep pulled into a garage. After the door rolled down, we drove by and collected the address off the mailbox. We knew where the mystery man lived, what he drove and that he had a secret. But who was he? And why had he visited Sweet's in the dark of night?

Back at the motel, the chilled wine took the edge off the throbbing pain in my ankle. Cooper put ice and cold water in a plastic laundry bag he found in the closet. He wrapped it in a towel and handed it to me to hold on my foot.

Cooper dried out the ice bucket, shredded some toilet paper into the bottom and put Kal in the cotton-fresh bedding. He washed the cap to the wine bottle and filled it with water for the little guy and gave him some raisin bread crumbs and a bite-sized chunk of apple. I found it odd to see such compassion in a man.

"I don't know what to do for his sore. I guess I'll just leave it," Cooper said.

"Now that he has room maybe he'll clean it himself."

"Whatever they put on him must be poisonous. Do you think it's safe to let him lick it?"

We decided to dab his back with a wet tissue to remove the remaining substance. Kal didn't appreciate the help. When Cooper finished, Kal drank a little water, nibbled on the fruit and crumbs and disappeared under the tissue. We took it as a good sign.

"How does it feel knowing you saved his life?" Cooper asked. He had poured himself a glass of wine and was on the bed with his back resting against the headboard.

I watched Kal explore his new home. I had never seen a live mouse up close. He stood on his back legs and stretched his front paws up the side of the ice bucket. Dark brown eyes, whiskers and a pointy little nose, which sniffed the air. He probably felt like he had died and gone to heaven. I put his new home on the table next to the bed and picked up my glass of wine. How did I feel about freeing him from a certain death? It felt good. But the feeling dissolved when I thought of the ones left behind.

"I can't take the credit. It took teamwork," I said.

"We wouldn't be here if not for your persistence." Cooper refilled my glass. "We have to finish it now that we don't have a top."

"I don't think that'll be a problem." The ice and wine dulled the pain and relaxed my soul after the harrowing evening. With a couple pillows behind my back I leaned against the bed's headboard. Cooper sat in the overstuffed chair next to the bed with his feet resting on the bed. We sipped the wine in a comfortable silence.

"In the morning we'll check out the other address," Cooper said.

"Do you think it'll be as easy to get into?"

"I doubt it. It's new, and with new comes high-tech security systems. They know there are people who don't approve of what they're doing. They need to make sure the truth stays behind locked doors."

"Great."

"It's just a minor complication. There's always a weak link. Somehow we'll get in."

"Is everything just a minor complication to you?"

"Pretty much."

"We also have to figure out who the guy is. I wonder what he was up to?"

"There are websites that'll give a name in exchange for an address. There's also one to get the name of car owners from license plate numbers. We can wait till we get home or try to find a library or Internet cafe to use."

"How's Kal doing?"

Cooper picked up the ice bucket and handed it to me. He moved to the edge of the bed and took over holding the ice on my ankle.

I could see Kal's tail sticking out from where he burrowed and the shredded paper above him rose and fell with his breathing. "I think he's sleeping."

"Good, we should be doing the same," Cooper said, taking the bucket and sitting it on the dresser.

I hobbled to the bathroom to brush my teeth and change into my sleepwear, an over-sized T-shirt. When I returned, Cooper had taken a blanket and pillow from the bed and rested in the armchair. It couldn't be comfortable.

"You won't get a good sleep there," I said.

"You're inviting me into your bed?"

The bluntness caught me off guard, and I didn't have a quick answer. Our eyes locked. He got up, the blanket falling to the floor. He stood inches from me wearing only a T-shirt and underwear. Without a touch he leaned in and kissed me full on the lips. His tenderness woke something that had been sleeping in me for months. I felt a desperate need for touch, a need for raw, bare flesh next to mine. I slipped my arms around his neck and returned the kiss.

"Do you have a condom?" I asked.

Cooper nodded yes. "I've wanted you since the day we met." He pulled the T-shirt over my head. His caress, tender but demanding, his body hard and lean. We explored each other with hands and kisses.

"Are you sure?" he whispered in my ear.

I pulled him down onto the bed. In the soft hue of streetlights sneaking between curtains that didn't close tightly, we made eye contact. I answered with a kiss. Our passion was relentless, built on adrenaline and fueled by wine.

Chapter 9

The sound of scratching filtered into my dream. Through the haziness of sleep, my brain recognized the clawing on plastic as something not ordinary. I'm not sure how long it took me to remember Kal...and to remember Cooper. I rolled over to find the bed empty. I heard the shower running and took a moment to enjoy the warmth of the bed and the memory of the night. Kal scratching at the plastic walls of his new home finally got me out of bed. He had tipped his water and made a mess. I was cleaning it, Cooper came out of the bathroom.

"Good morning," I said. The situation felt natural. He gave me a quick kiss and whispered in my ear.

"Not as good as last night."

I felt a blush spread through my face. "I'm taking a shower. We have less than an hour to be out of here."

Cooper was ready to leave when I returned. We did a last minute check for any left-behinds and turned in our room key.

"Do you want breakfast or lunch?" Cooper asked.

"It doesn't matter as long as there's coffee."

He drove downtown and found a mom and pop restaurant. It had a typical Midwestern menu of meat and potatoes with a few eggs tossed in for breakfast. I had a garden omelet and hot coffee. Cooper settled for hash browns, fresh fruit and dry toast with peanut butter and strawberry jelly. He saved some of his toast for Kal.

Using a GPS we found Sweet's other facility. To our surprise a group of people stood in front of the lab picketing. We parked

75

on the street across from the demonstration and watched. About twenty people held posters and banners for drivers and bicyclists to read as they sped by. The hand-written signs sported slogans like "Animal Concentration Camp," 'Animals Abused Here' and 'Buy Cruelty Free Products.' There were graphic posters of rows of white rabbits in head restraints, dogs with bloody wounds and monkeys behind bars.

Two police cars were parked near the security shack by the entrance driveway. Three officers, stern-faced with arms crossed across their chests, stood by the squad cars. They stared emotionless at the men and women who protested.

Behind them Sweet's white structure, with its six floors and a green metal roof, rose high into the sky. Evenly spaced narrow windows encircled each floor.

We parked the car in a nearby strip mall, rolled the windows down so Kal wouldn't get too hot, and went to talk to the demonstrators. We pretended to be just passing by and curious about the commotion. A young man handed me a fact sheet about Sweet's and directed us to a woman named Erica Armstrong, the group's spokesperson.

I guessed Erica to be in her mid-20s. She was short and plump with shoulder-length blond hair. Up close her startling blue eyes detracted from her other facial features. She looked like a stay-at-home mom, not someone who would demonstrate against animal abuse in a research laboratory.

Again, we pretended to be naive. Erica gave us an earful about toxicology testing and other research done at Sweet's. She hardly took a breath between sentences.

"How do you know so much?" Cooper asked.

"I worked there as an animal technician."

"How long ago?" I asked.

"Last year. I quit after two months. I couldn't take it any longer. I felt like I was losing my sanity."

"Did they use beagles?" I asked.

"They use a lot of dogs."

"But beagles. Did they use beagles?"

"A lot of them, why?"

"Mine is missing, and I think there's a chance he's there."

"What makes you think that?"

Before she could answer, Cooper interrupted. He looked around, uncomfortable. "Can we meet and continue this conversation somewhere else later today?"

"No, I'm busy the rest of the day. How about in the morning?" Erica suggested we meet at nine and gave us directions to a park. We thanked her and left.

Not wanting to use my cell phone, we searched for a pay phone to call Grams to give her an update. She sounded okay, but I felt a twinge of guilt for leaving her alone with all the farm chores to handle by herself. I promised her we'd be home tomorrow night.

With the day stretching empty before us, I suggested we drive to Grand Haven to visit Sara and the puppies. Plus, she had a computer we could use. Maybe we could figure out the identification of the mystery man.

I programmed the GPS for Grand Haven. Instead of taking U.S.131 to Grand Rapids and heading west on I96 I opted for scenic back roads. The GPS sounded like a backseat driver when I strayed from its chosen route, but it adjusted the course with a no-nonsense voice when I ignored instructions to turn around at my earliest convenience. We cruised past farmhouses, red barns, miles of green pastures with grazing cattle, freshly plowed fields with rows of corn peeking through the soil and rolling hills dotted with apple orchards.

After seeing a roadside sign for Fenn Valley Vineyards and Wine Cellar I made a last-minute detour to visit the winery.

"We have the time," I said.

"Michigan wine? I might be a bit biased. Remember, I'm a Californian."

"I didn't know you were a connoisseur," I teased.

"Now you do."

We parked in the shade so Kal would be okay in the car and went into the tasting room.

"Are you here for a tour?" asked a woman behind the counter. "Or just sampling?"

"What tour?" I asked.

"Of the wine cellar. It's eight dollars and includes wine tasting and a five dollar coupon toward the purchase of three bottles of wine."

"Sounds good to me," Cooper said, grinning.

We hadn't spoken of our romantic encounter the night before, but I could sense an intimate bond. We held hands while listening to the history of wine making in Michigan and learned the difference between red and white wines. We sampled several vintages. The shot-glass size samples went straight to my head, making me light-headed and carefree. I felt glorious, a feeling that had become foreign to me. How fast things changed. Not that long ago I had a son, a happy marriage, a teaching career and a future. Now I lived one day at a time, determined not to wallow in the past or plan a future.

I took photographs during the tour, including one of Cooper sipping from a glass of wine. A woman offered to take a picture of the two of us, and we happily posed. We both loved Lakeshore Sunset, a red semi-dry wine, and used our coupon to buy three bottles.

"What do you think of Michigan wines now?"

"I'm impressed," Cooper said.

I decided to call Sara to warn her we were coming, so we stopped in Saugatuck to look for a telephone. With the popularity of cell phones, the old-fashioned pay phones were becoming obsolete and hard to find. We didn't want to leave a trail of whereabouts that could be traced to cell phone records. We found one in a restaurant where we got coffee to counteract the wine. The call woke Sara. She had worked the night shift and just gone to bed.

"It's okay," she said. "Come. I want to meet Cooper. I can sleep later."

Back in the car, Cooper expressed concerns about Sara. "How much does she know about what's going on, and how are you going to explain our visit?" Cooper asked.

"I don't keep secrets from Sara. I'll probably tell her everything."

"It'd be safer for her and for us if you didn't tell her about some of the stuff that's going on, especially the break-ins."

"I hate secrets," I said.

An hour later we pulled into Sara's driveway. She greeted me with a big hug and Cooper, too, after I introduced him. I showed her Kal and she insisted on giving us a small aquarium that had a wire mesh lid so he'd have more room. She also gave him a larger water dish and some gerbil food.

While she arranged his new living quarters, I told her Kal had been rescued from a research lab and we didn't know what had been applied to his skin. She didn't ask questions and Cooper didn't say a word.

"His back doesn't look too bad," she said. "As long as he keeps his appetite, I think he'll be okay."

"How are the puppies?"

"Come with me," she said.

We followed her to a bedroom where she let the babies out of their kennel. All three of us sat on the floor while the pups scrambled about sniffing, licking and tugging on shoelaces.

"They've all been to the vet and had their first round of vaccines," Sara said. "And I think I have homes for two of them already."

"That's great," I said. When the puppies started to settle down, I asked Sara if Cooper could use her computer to check a couple of things on the Internet. After she got him online, we took the puppies into the backyard to romp. On the way out, I stopped by the car and got the camera.

"He's cute," she said.

I nodded in agreement as we sat down at a picnic table. "He's also nice, compassionate, funny and a good kisser."

"Tell me more."

"You don't need details, just take my word."

I filled her in on what had been happening, including why Cooper needed the computer.

"It sounds like you're getting in over your head," she warned.

"We're being careful."

"It doesn't matter how careful you are. Something could go wrong."

"You're such a pessimist. You should be glad I'm out and about and still not holed up in my room crying."

"I am, but you're breaking the law."

"It's the only way I can figure out how to get answers."

"Can't you just let it go?"

"No."

She asked about Grams and wanted to know if Grams knew what Cooper and I were up to.

I told her she knew everything except the relationship we had developed. "And I'm sure she'll figure that out real soon."

"You're probably right. You never could get much past her."

I asked about Ryan.

"Too busy. I'm tired of him being gone so much. He promised at the end of the summer he wouldn't be as busy."

"At least you have a job to keep you occupied."

"I love working nights," she said. "It's not so hectic. Once the tourists get tucked in for the night, this place is pretty quiet."

It felt good to chat about everyday stuff and get caught up. About a half hour later, Cooper came out. He sat cross-legged on the floor and played with the puppies. I took a picture of him with the pups crawling in his lap.

"Did you find anything?" I asked.

"His name is Daniel Madden. He's a scientist." Cooper had printed pages of Madden's credentials and papers he had published.

"I didn't take the time to read them yet, plus there's a lot more stuff about him online."

Cooper also did a search on Erica Armstrong and found a newspaper article about her blowing the whistle on animal abuse at Sweet's. The company was fined $20,000 for violating the Animal Welfare Act.

"I think she's going to be invaluable to us," Cooper said.

Not able to convince me of giving up on Blue, Sara turned to Cooper for help. Knowing he felt the same as she did, I was surprised when he stuck up for me. Sara laughed.

"I guess you wouldn't be here if you didn't agree with her," she said. Sara excused herself to make lemonade. Cooper and I busied ourselves with the puppies. They were healthy, fat and full of life. I knew I made the right decision when I stole them.

"Don't these little guys count as a rescue?" I said to Cooper as I lay on my back in the grass with the pups crawling over me. One struggled to untie my shoe and another wouldn't stop licking and tugging on my left hand. Cooper sat in the grass next to me and, using an old sock, played tug-of-war with one of the puppies. He let the little guy win.

"You're right, these little guys would be considered a rescue. I predict that before you're done with this, you'll be a bona fide activist. You're a natural."

"I don't think so. Dogs are my thing. I don't even remember what the Save Five are."

"Just think of the basic abuses: meat, fur, hunting, research, entertainment."

"It's really not for me. I'm only interested in finding Blue."

"Your heart's in the right place. You just need your eyes pried open."

"Have you done all five?"

"It's a goal."

"Tell the truth."

"I have, a couple times over. Not that I should be telling you. Talking is the biggest way of getting in trouble."

"If you can't trust me who can you trust?"

"That's it exactly. Trust no one."

"Have you ever been caught?"

"There have been a couple close calls and, like you know, there's always that little incident in California."

"With that hanging over your head, why are you taking such a risk helping me look for Blue?" The puppies continued to climb over me and tumble about with each other. Cooper held one in his lap, stroking its back. A couple minutes passed.

"At first it was for your grandmother. I could tell you weren't going to give up and she worried. But now I'm doing it for you."

Before I could answer, Sara came back with our drinks. We spent the rest of the afternoon lounging in the backyard. She quizzed Cooper on his childhood, his parents and how he came to be living with Grams. He didn't tell her about his activism.

Sara insisted on taking us out for dinner, so we walked downtown and checked out restaurant menus until we found one with vegetarian options. She tried to talk us into spending the night, but we wanted to get back to Kalamazoo so we wouldn't have to get up early for a long drive. We didn't want to be late for our appointment with Erica.

She offered to keep Kal, but I said no. I liked the little guy. "You're already doing plenty by taking such good care of the pups."

"But it's what I love to do. You know that." She hugged us both goodbye and made us promise to keep her informed on what we found out.

Cooper and I talked the whole way back to Kalamazoo, filling in the gaps of our lives and getting to know each other. I told him how much I appreciated his help. Before searching for a hotel room, we drove by Sweet's again. Even at that late hour, a guard sat in the security booth. Cooper noted the chain link fence topped with barbed wire that surrounded the complex. Security lights lit the place like downtown Las Vegas. And like Vegas money vaults, the place looked impenetrable.

"I think the weak link is going to be hard to find," I said. Gaining access looked impossible to me.

"But we have an ace in the hole: Erica."

"It'll be interesting to see what she has to say."

We drove by the park where we were to meet Erica so we'd know for sure where we were going in the morning. We didn't want to run the risk of being late or missing her. We found another small hotel. This time I asked for one room.

Cooper went to get some ice for the wine while I took a shower. I heard him come back and then heard a knock on the bathroom door. He stuck his head in the door and asked if he could join me. Such manners.

It didn't take him long to strip. I moved so he could get under the hot water, and he tilted his head back to wet his hair. I poured shampoo in my hand and massaged it into his scalp. He rinsed and I used my jasmine-scented bath soap to suds up his body.

The wine tasted delicious and, like that afternoon, it went straight to my head. We slid between the sheets. It didn't take long for our bodies to be hot with passion. We slept until the wake-up call jarred us awake. Time to meet Erica.

Chapter 10

We arrived fifteen minutes early for our rendezvous with Erica. The parking lot, built for dozens of cars, held two. Ours made three. Two women on a power walk sped by, and an older man walked a cocker spaniel on a leash. The park was designed for families. A 15-foot-tall wooden sailing ship dominated the landscape. Oh, to be a kid again. Or to have kids. Thomas would have loved to play on its decks, climb the ropes to the crow's nest, and turn the ship's wheel, pretending to stare out to sea. "Mom, look at me," he would have shouted.

"I hope she comes," Cooper said.

The sound of his voice bounced me back into reality. I left Thomas on the ship and continued to survey the park. There were weathered picnic tables, pedestal grills, swings, wood-chip covered walking trails and a lake with manicured grass mowed to its edge. The park felt lonely. A flock of mallards waddled toward us, looking for an early morning handout. Cooper opened his window and apologized for not having a snack for them. They answered with persistent quacks.

We watched Kal as we waited for Erica. The sores on his back looked like they were starting to heal, or maybe they were just less irritated. Either way he looked much improved. With a twitch of his nose, he would sniff my finger when I held it near him. He scampered about eating and drinking before curling up for an early morning nap. Activity and appetite were positive signs.

"He's so trusting. How can he be so trusting?" I asked.

Cooper didn't answer. He impatiently glanced at his watch every few seconds as he stared at the road and the park entrance.

"We should have asked for a telephone number," he said.

I didn't share his concern. Erica seemed as eager as we did to talk. We decided to walk down to the lake. Blue skies and bright sunlight made it look warm, but a morning chill had a grip on the air. The ducks followed us, and I regretted not having anything to feed the hungry crew. They were aggressive and acted as though we were holding out on them.

"Seriously guys, we don't have anything for you," Cooper said.

They finally believed him and waddled to the lake and swam away. We sat on a bench, but Cooper couldn't sit still. After a few seconds he stood, reached for my hand and led me to the playground. Morning dew covered the swings, but we didn't care. We sat and with a little knee action were soon sailing through the air with the abandonment of five-year-olds. The fun turned sour when Thomas invaded my thoughts again. He had loved to swing. I quit pumping and dragged my feet till the swing jerked to a stop.

"I'm heading back to the car," I shouted to Cooper. He followed and soon we were waiting again.

"I hope she shows," Cooper said.

Fifteen minutes after Erica was suppose to meet us, a rusted red pickup screeched into the parking lot. After getting out, Erica held the driver's door open and a collie jumped to the ground and came bounding over to us. Erica followed, carrying three coffee mugs and a thermos of coffee.

"You had me worried," Cooper said.

"I'm always late," she said with no apology. She poured us steaming coffee, introduced us to Webster, her five-year-old dog, and then sat down and asked about Blue.

Between sips of the hot brew, I told her how I had moved to northern Michigan to live with Grams and how Cody and Blue disappeared from the fenced-in yard. I pulled a small photo album out of my purse and showed her pictures of the two dogs. Photos of them playing together, of them snoozing on the couch and several with Thomas chasing after the pair at the farm. A photograph of Blue sleeping with Thomas shortly before his death was tucked into the album's cover.

Erica examined the pictures and asked about Thomas. I almost ignored the question, but realized she might be more sympathetic if she knew the whole story. I gave her the condensed version: a little boy dies and his faithful dog goes missing.

Erica listened and offered no platitudes, to which I was grateful. I was weary of responding to people's well-intentioned remarks about my loss. To me, my replies sounded as empty and pointless as the comments. I was beyond social niceties.

I explained about the animal shelter and the volunteer who told me to visit Kappies. I left out the part about my midnight social call to the so-called kennel. I told her a couple days later Cody showed up at home, and later I learned someone broke into Kappies and released the animals. I guessed Cody had been at Kappies, and if Cody had been there, Blue most likely had been there, too, because the two dogs were inseparable.

"Why do you think he's at Sweet's?"

I hated to lie, but I didn't know her well enough to be honest. "The same volunteer who tipped me off about Kappies told me Gary Jarsma had two primary customers and most of the smaller dogs went to Sweet's."

She confirmed Sweet's used small dogs. "They like beagles. They're friendly, submissive. They wag their tails no matter what they do to them. They also like dogs who are genetically random, not all from the same litter."

"Any ideas on how I can find out if Blue is there?"

"How long has he been gone?"

"Ten days. Cody came home a week ago––last Wednesday night."

She took a long slow sip of coffee.

"If he's been there over a week, is there a chance he's still alive?" Cooper asked.

"He could be. It depends on what they're using him for. The only way to find out is to get inside the lab and look for him. Are you up to that?"

I didn't know what to say.

"Maybe," Cooper said.

Erica finished her coffee and invited us to her apartment to talk more. "I have some stuff to show you," she said. She suggested we follow her, but Cooper asked for an address in case we got separated. He wasn't going to let her get away.

Cooper stuck close behind the red pickup. After ten minutes, it turned into the driveway of an old Victorian house that had seen better days. Its gray paint was peeling, the front steps sagged and a tangled mass of ivy was obsessed with the chimney. Crab grass choked the tulips that lined the driveway and branches littered the grass, which looked like it hadn't been mowed yet this year.

Part of the front yard had been converted into parking for tenants. It all seemed a slap in the face to the majestic house. Neighboring homes had the same affliction. I suspected the neglect offered inexpensive housing.

We left Kal in the car. How would we explain him to Erica? As soon as she saw the inflictions on his back she would know he was a lab mouse. There would be questions we weren't prepared to answer.

Erica lived on the third floor in what she described as the maid's quarters. The mansions were built for lumber barons who could afford the luxury of live-in help. Now the stately homes were divided into apartments. All of us, including Webster, were puffing by the time we climbed the two flights of stairs. Inside her tiny apartment, a window fan blew cool morning air into the living room.

The furnishings were as sparse as I imagined the maid's had been a hundred years before. But the styles were updated by at least a half dozen decades of style. In a tiny alcove a twin bed rested below a slanted ceiling. A four-drawer chest stood across from it with a tiny television perched on top. There was barely enough room to walk between the two pieces of furniture.

A kitchen occupied one corner of the living area. A plaid couch, a computer desk, filing cabinet and a Formica-topped dining table with two chairs consumed the remaining space. Through a doorway, I could see a small bathroom. The place was spotless, but there were stacks of books everywhere.

"I'm a bookaholic," Erica confessed.

She motioned for us to take a seat at the table. From behind the bathroom door, she pulled out a metal folding chair and joined us. She began her story with her employment at Sweet's.

"I worked there part time during my second year at Western," she explained. "They advertised for an animal technician, and since I was in a pre-vet program, I thought it would be good experience." She didn't stop talking even as she put on a fresh pot of coffee.

"At first I worked two hours a night and just cleaned cages," she said. "The previous technician quit two weeks earlier. I swear the cages hadn't been cleaned since he left. They were filthy. I could only clean with one hand because my other held a towel over my nose."

The majority of the animals Erica cared for were rats and mice, but there were also dogs, cats and white rabbits. She soon took over the task of feeding and watering the animals. Her boss laughed when he told her they didn't need much food. "Face it, they're on death row," she said, mimicking the man's voice and attitude.

She only worked every other night and realized no one else did her job on her days off. "Once I got the cages clean, the job wasn't bad," she said. She admitted she didn't follow directions on the amount of food to feed. "I always gave extra. It was the least I could do, especially when no one was feeding them when I wasn't there."

She skimmed over the conditions of the dogs as they progressed through whatever research they were being used for. They never got out alive. They either died during the experiments or were sacrificed at the end.

"I asked what the dogs were being used for, but they always dodged the question. They made it clear they didn't want me to ask questions," Erica said.

Erica befriended the truck driver who delivered dogs and cats. She checked the animals in and got them situated in the holding room. It didn't take long for Erica and the young man to become friends, and he didn't hesitate to say the animals came from a kennel up north owned by an animal dealer. He told her they were unwanted pets collected from animal shelters in the northern part of the state.

"When my classes changed for the winter semester, I had more free time so I asked for more hours. I didn't know what I was getting into." They gave her more hands-on work with animals. She still had to clean and feed, but she now helped with procedures and with documenting results. A lot of the animals she worked with were rats.

"I hated going into work. I don't know why I didn't quit."

At first, Erica thought Sweet's conducted medical research, but she discovered the majority of work they performed was product testing. They told her the government required safety testing on new consumer products. Diet pills, suntan lotions, lawn chemicals and new-and-improved cleaners were being examined for side effects and toxicity.

"I could rationalize in my mind if animals were sacrificed to find a cure for cancer or AIDS or some other fatal disease. But product testing? I was horrified to learn what they were really doing, but I needed the job, so I kept my mouth shut."

When a local animal rights group demonstrated in front of the facility, protesting the use of animals, it confirmed her heartfelt beliefs. She started to document everything. She kept a diary and took photographs and videos when she had the chance. In addition, she made copies of any paperwork she could get her hands on.

After about an hour Erica stopped talking, poured us more coffee and then retrieved a stack of photos from the file cabinet. "I'll warn you, they're not pretty to look at."

Cooper studied each photograph before handing it to me. All I needed was a glance to get the gist of the horrors the animals were going through. How could it be possible, I wondered.

In a monotone voice Erica explained each picture.

Several showed dogs with their backs shaved. Cone-collars around their necks prevented them from licking their backs. The hairless skin looked like a cross-stitched wall hanging of blisters and oozing sores.

"They were given a sedative, so records show they follow federal humane guidelines, but when it wore off, the dogs were in agony. I've seen dogs punched and kicked when they started to squirm from the pain. It didn't take long before they just whimpered and whined. I could see the pain and confusion in their eyes, but of course the bastards don't look into their eyes."

Some photos showed rats that were near lifeless from weeks of forced feedings. Erica explained the LD50 toxicity test. Over a period of time, a group of animals were given a high dose of a toxic substance until half of them died. LD50 stood for lethal dose, 50 percent. When half of them were dead the remaining animals were killed and all the bodies studied to see what affect the test substance had on their bodies.

There were rabbits in restraints whose eyes were used in what she called a Draize test for eye irritation. The test substance was placed in an eye and the changes in the eye were recorded. I looked at one photograph of a rabbit and that was enough for me. I turned away.

"How could you stand it?" I whispered. I could hardly stomach hearing about it.

"You learn to shelve your emotions when you walk through the door. I kept telling myself that what I was doing would help. I thought once I went public, they would be forced to stop."

Erica was detached as she talked, but she came back to life when she told us what happened when she turned over her documentation to the local media.

"It made the news for one day. A spokesman from Sweet's told reporters that testing was necessary to ensure the safety of new products. They even had the nerve to blame some of the horrific conditions on me. After all, I was hired to take care of the animals. And the photographs that revealed neglected incisions and dogs with gaping wounds were blamed on a worker they claimed they fired. But they couldn't reveal his name due to safeguarding his privacy."

In addition, they claimed the majority of the animals they used were rodents. "And it's true," Erica said. "People don't care about mice and rats, but the poor little things feel pain like we do. Just like dogs and cats. I should have given the documents to an animal rights group. They would have been able to bring more publicity to what was happening."

Next Erica pulled out pencil sketches of the layout of the lab, complete with security devices and a copy of the instruction manual for the alarm. She walked us through each hallway and told us what to expect in each room.

She even had a key to the back door but couldn't guarantee it would still work. "If they were smart, they changed the locks after I left." She suggested we wait a few days before making a move. "The protesters were there for just one day, but the big-wigs get nervous when they're picketed. If only they knew how harmless we are."

She told us the lab was empty on weekends except for whoever came to feed the animals in the mornings. Erica gave us a key to her apartment and told us to make ourselves at home when we returned. She had an inflatable bed we could use.

As we left she gave us a copy of the diary she kept while working at the lab and the videotapes she made. We thanked her, hugged good-bye and promised we'd be in touch.

Back in the car we were amazed to realize we had spent more than three hours with Erica. Kal was sleeping, his little body expanding and contracting with each breath. We decided to look for a place to eat and then head home.

We discussed the situation as we drove. We weren't sure if Erica was motivated by revenge or if she had a true desire to help animals. Either way we were grateful for her help. But halfway home Cooper became paranoid. "What if she's setting us up?"

The thought had never occurred to me, but then I'm trusting and usually take things at face value.

"Even if she is on our side, she's better off not knowing what our plans are," Cooper said. "When they discover someone broke into the lab, I bet Erica will be the first person they suspect."

We decided to come back Friday and not stay at her place.

Chapter 11

Cody ran in circles before jumping at the car door to greet us. Grams met us in the yard, too. "It's been too damn quiet around here," she said. Then she laughed a laugh that made me suspicious. She was up to something.

"I hope you don't have plans for tonight," she said.

"Why? What's up?"

"The County Board of Commissioners is meeting. They're going to discuss the county's contract with Kappies."

"Is it open to the public?" I asked.

"Sure is. They have a public comment time where everybody gets three minutes to talk. I've been rounding up people to go, and I need you both."

"As much as I'd love to go, I think it'd be a little too high-profile for me," Cooper said. "The last thing I need is my name in the paper."

While we carried our bags into the house, Grams asked an endless stream of questions about our trip. She sounded like a newspaper reporter.

"Let's sit on the porch. We'll tell you everything," I said. The blue sky begged us to be outside. The sweet scent of apple blossoms filled the air, as did the chirps and whistles of migrating songbirds. A perfect spring day, the kind I dreamed of when winter had its harsh grasp on the Midwest. Spring inspired me.

Grams sat on the porch swing, Cooper in a wicker chair.

"Wait just a minute," I said. I went back to the car and got Kal's fish tank.

I sat it next to Grams. She tilted back the lid, peeked in and moved the tissues to see what it contained.

"Isn't he cute," she cooed. She gently put a finger near Kal's nose for him to sniff. "Where'd he come from?"

We told her about the trip to Sweet's, how we didn't see any signs of dogs but did find mice. "He was the only one with any life left in him," I said. I pointed out the scab on his back where some unknown chemical had eaten into his flesh. "I don't think he received as big a dose as the other mice did."

"Poor baby." Grams picked Kal up and cuddled him in her hands before releasing him on her wrist. He scurried up her arm to her shoulder and perched there like a parrot.

I watched, amazed at how friendly and brazen he behaved. Did he know his name should be Lucky?

"His name is Kal, with a K," I said. "Short for Kalamazoo."

Grams laughed. "Cute."

Grams assumed we hit a dead end. I hated to tell her any different, but I did. "We were at the wrong place. When we started shuffling through papers, we discovered another address. The company has a new facility not too far from the first one."

"And you'll never believe this. Protesters were picketing it when we went there," Cooper said.

"For what?"

"Their use of animals. We met a woman who used to work there and she gave us a ton of information," Cooper said.

"Did you tell her about Blue?"

"She thinks there's a chance he could still be alive," I said.

"So, you're not giving up." It was a statement not a question.

"No, not when there's a chance of getting him back. We're going back tomorrow."

"I think that's all I want to know." She picked up Kal and put him back in his cage.

An uncomfortable silence settled over us. Cooper broke it with a question about the meeting. That got Grams talking again. The county had been giving Jarsma his pick of live cats and dogs in exchange for hauling away the bodies of euthanized animals, and the three-year contract with him was about to expire.

"The county doesn't make money on the contract, but the

commissioners figure they save a few thousand dollars each year on what they would have to pay to dispose of unwanted animals," Grams explained. She was upset by the fact that most pet owners weren't aware of Kappies, and once Jarsma got his hands on an animal, there was little chance of it being reunited with its owners. Plus, the animals Jarsma couldn't sell he killed. "He doesn't give them an injection. He puts them in a big barrel, several at a time, and pumps in carbon monoxide. It's a horrible way to die."

Grams had hand-delivered pamphlets from national animal welfare organizations to the commissioners. She handed me one. Besides discussing the ethical arguments against using animals in research, the pamphlets stated that tests done on animals were not reliable. They had examples of new methods of research that were cheaper, faster and more accurate.

She asked one of her friends to talk about alternative testing methods at the meeting. She had tried to get someone from one of the national animal rights groups to come, but no one could on such short notice.

"Did you talk to the commissioners?" Cooper asked.

Grams said she talked to them for as long as they would listen. She called each one at home last night to persuade them again to see things her way. "They listened, but they wouldn't commit to voting against the contract."

Cooper and I were appalled to learn the county had been selling pets to Jarsma for more than 20 years.

"Three years ago when the contract came up for renewal, a few of the volunteers at the shelter asked the county not to renew," Grams said. "It was a close vote. This time two of the commissioners are new, so there's a chance we can convince them to vote against it."

"Any idea how any of them are going to vote?" Cooper asked.

"No, but I think it'll be close."

Grams guessed about a half dozen people would be there to talk against renewing the contract. Jarsma's supporters would be there, including researchers who would try to convince commissioners that the use of shelter animals was necessary.

I hated to admit it, even to myself, but I wasn't convinced the use of animals wasn't needed. Thomas suffering with leukemia was never far from my heart. How many animals would I sacrifice for a cure? I didn't have an answer. But the one thing I did know, I didn't want my dog to be harmed. How hypocritical.

"What options are there besides using animals?" I asked.

Cooper rambled on for close to a half-hour about alternatives and how the results of animal testing couldn't be extrapolated to humans. "Cancer has been cured in mice, but guess what? The cure doesn't work in humans."

"I wish you could be there tonight," Grams said. But he couldn't, and Grams and I understood why. I spent the afternoon learning and jotting down notes about alternative testing and examples of bad medicine that came from testing on animals.

"You have to make them realize rats, mice, dogs and other species aren't furry little people. What works on different species doesn't always work on people and vice-versa.

"Odds are a new drug that could have cured cancer in people didn't have positive results in animals and was dismissed," Cooper said. He used aspirin as an example. The everyday headache and fever reliever caused renal failure and death in cats. Doctors advised people with high cholesterol to take a baby aspirin every day to help prevent strokes and heart attacks in humans, but aspirin caused birth defects in mice and rats. "If aspirin had to go through animal testing, it would never have made it to human clinical trials. Luckily aspirin was in use before they started testing new drugs on animals."

Another example was penicillin. The famed antibiotic was delayed for human use by animal testing. Although penicillin killed bacteria in a Petri dish, it didn't work on rabbits, so it was put aside for years.

Cooper had a point. Several points. The information overwhelmed me. "I need a break. I think I have more than enough to fill three minutes." I went for a walk to sift through all I had just heard and to try to condense it.

We arrived early to the commissioners' meeting, but there was no place to sit. People lined the side and back walls and some couldn't even get into the room. They stood in the hallway hoping to hear what happened. A television crew had a camera set up, and I overheard a newspaper reporter asking people why they had come to the meeting.

"I'm glad to see cameras here," I said.

Grams nodded in agreement. She informed me the Ludington Daily News ran a story about the contract coming up for renewal. "The timing couldn't be better with the fire and mystery surrounding Kappies," she said.

I agreed, but I wondered how the media attention would affect my search for Blue.

The meeting started promptly at seven. After approval of the agenda, and a few other cursory details, Chairman Donald Dykhouse asked for public comment. The first woman he called on asked if public comment would be taken when the commissioners discussed the contract with Kappies. He said normally they wouldn't allow it, but because of the high interest they would let people speak.

The contract was the first item on the agenda. Chairman Dykhouse told the packed room that there had been no changes to the agreement with Kappies. "It's just a renewal."

Someone asked for a copy of the contract, which brought the meeting to a halt while the secretary went to make copies. After she returned and distributed the copies, Dykhouse asked people to step up to the microphone in the front of the room if they wanted to make a statement.

"You'll each be allowed three minutes, and please don't repeat what others have said," he instructed. He held up a timer to show he would be timing each speaker.

Grams was the first in line. She described the bond between companion animals and their owners and how it shouldn't be betrayed by sending stray and unwanted pets to research laboratories. "The USDA licenses people to raise animals specifically for research. They should not be allowed to use pets," she said. When the timer rang after three minutes she concluded by asking the commissioners not to renew the contract with Kappies.

Cindi introduced herself as a shelter volunteer and said if the volunteers were given more time, they could find the owners of stray animals or find them new homes.

"Strays are only kept four days if they aren't wearing a collar or are micro-chipped. It is not always enough time to find their owners." She said there had been several occasions when someone came in after Jarsma had already taken his or her pet. "What am I supposed to tell them?"

The commissioners didn't respond.

Two more shelter volunteers argued the same point, saying they could find homes for the animals if they were given more time.

Dykhouse reminded people not to repeat what others had already said.

An owner of a missing Labrador retriever said his dog disappeared out of a fenced-in kennel. "He was stolen, and I've always wondered if he ended up in research." He added there seemed to be a high number of stolen dogs in the county, and he wondered if Kappies provided a market for them.

As we had planned, I questioned the validity of using animals in research. I wondered if emotional pleas from county residents about using pets in research would influence commissioners more than me trying to discredit the use of animals. After all, animal research was the status quo.

I talked about the drug thalidomide. It was given to pregnant women in the 1950s for morning sickness. Soon after it came on the market, babies were born with defected and missing limbs. It took a long time for doctors to connect the drug to birth defects and one of the reasons why was because it had been tested on animals. When it was finally pulled from the market, the birth defects stopped.

"It proves that animals aren't reliable test subjects for drugs that are destined for human use," I said. "Even after it was evident thalidomide was the culprit, they couldn't duplicate the birth defects in the majority of animals they retested it on. There was one species of rabbits where it caused birth defects in offspring, but it took extremely high doses," I said, adding that scientists could test it on several species and only report on the ones that produced the results they wanted.

My speech got a round of applause from a handful of people in the audience. Dykhouse interrupted the applause and said such outbursts would not be tolerated. He threatened to have anyone who clapped or spoke out of turn removed from the room.

Gram's friend talked about cell tests, clinical studies, autopsies and computer-assisted research. In addition, she talked about the time scientists wasted by experimenting on animals. An example she used was AIDS. Researchers focused their efforts on trying to cause AIDS in chimpanzees with dismal results.

"People are dying from AIDS, and the scientists are still playing with chimps," she said.

Grams was right to worry about who Jarsma would bring in to testify. After I talked, a researcher contradicted what I said and praised the inexpensive use of shelter animals.

"People are vulnerable to several of the same or similar diseases as animals, and there are parallels between human and animal physiology and pathology. Humans have at least 65 infectious diseases in common with dogs," he said

He added that vaccines, surgical advancements, cancer therapies and drug safety all were made possible by animal research. "They're going to die anyway. So why not let some good come from their lives?"

I was horrified when a man introduced himself as Daniel Madden from Sweet's Research in Kalamazoo. I recognized the name from Cooper's Internet search. He was dressed in a black suit with a white shirt and blue tie. He was balding and what hair he had was gray. His brown horn-rimmed glasses gave him an outdated look. I guessed his age at 60. His voice commanded respect. I realized he alone would probably convince the commissioners to renew the contract.

Madden touted the use of animals. "They're irreplaceable." He told a story from 1933 when more than a dozen women were blinded from using permanent mascara called Lash Lure that contained an untested chemical. He added that the Food and Drug Administration required all manufacturers of cosmetics to prove the safety of their products. "We're working at reducing the number of animals for cosmetic testing, but in some cases it's still necessary."

He added that sunscreens, antidandruff shampoos, fluoride-containing toothpaste and anti-acne creams must be proven safe on animals because they contain ingredients that cause a chemical change in the body that could be harmful.

Grams was fuming by the time he finished, and she took to the microphone again. "The only reason he likes strays is because they're cheap and they're trusting. Animals bred for research aren't socialized with humans and are hard to work with. A dog that was once a human companion will wag its tail while it's crucified."

When Grams finished, the public comment was closed. I wondered why Jarsma didn't stand and defend himself, but I guess he had rounded up enough heavyweights to do the persuading for him.

The commissioners didn't make any comments or ask any questions. Instead the chairman thanked everyone for their input. "You've given us a lot to think about. I think we should table the renewal of the contract to give us time to digest what we have heard," Dykhouse said.

The motion was seconded, voted on favorably and the commission continued with the agenda.

Back at home we stayed awake for the 11 o'clock news. While we waited, we filled Cooper in on the meeting. He wasn't surprised.

"Scientists impress people. Everyone thinks they're going to discover a cure for cancer, when in reality they haven't even been able to find a cure for the common cold," he said.

When the coverage came on, it showed Cindi pleading for more time to find the owners or new homes for shelter animals. Next a scientist said the cost of research would go up if the supply of shelter dogs stopped. The reporter tried to interview Dykhouse, but he only said he needed time to reflect on what was said.

After the news Grams went to bed. Cooper told me he had read Erica's diary. "She's a gutsy woman. I don't think I would have been able to work there as long as she did." He offered the diary to me to read, but I declined.

I didn't want to fill my mind with horrific details that I would never be able to erase. My focus was to bring Blue home for Thomas. I didn't want to get sucked into Cooper's activism. I was already learning more than I wanted to know about what went on behind closed laboratory doors.

Cooper and I planned on heading back to Kalamazoo the next afternoon, and I wanted a good night of sleep. But I didn't get it. Vivid dreams of dogs pleading to go home filled my head. I kept looking for Blue, but the aisles of cages went on forever. Every corner I turned produced penned up dogs as far as I could see. And they all stared at me as if I was their only hope.

Chapter 12

We gave Grams instructions on how to take care of Kal, which she probably didn't need. I hated to leave again but wouldn't allow myself to even think about backing out. The whole situation had me infuriated and focused. Operating on dream-plagued sleep added fuel to my determination.

We filled the drive to Kalamazoo with small talk, childhood memories and laughter. We avoided anything serious or sad. Of course my favorite childhood memories were visiting my grandparents and their menagerie of animals. Cooper didn't grow up in the country, but that didn't stop his family from collecting pets.

"We always had a house full of dogs and cats. Usually it's the kids who drag the homeless and injured animals home, but at my house my mother and grandmother were the culprits," he said. Their home attracted strays much like Grams' farm.

"It was natural for me to grow into an animal rights activist despite my dad's effort to steer me elsewhere," he said.

"Your dad wasn't on the same page?"

"I don't think my mother would have dated or married him if he wasn't. He's just not as committed as she is, but he supports her one hundred percent, which is cool."

"And what does he think of your radical lifestyle?"

"He's not pleased, but he understands. He would have preferred I followed a legal path like becoming a lawyer and working on behalf of animals through the legislation and courts."

"Why didn't you?"

"It's too slow, and there's too much compromise."

When we got to Kalamazoo, we drove by Sweet's to scope out parking for our after-dark visit. Two blocks away we found a 24-hour superstore where an extra car wouldn't be noticed.

Cooper decided we shouldn't stay at the same motel as last time, so we drove around till we found another cheap room. I put on my best happy smile when I checked in and chatted non-stop to the guy behind the counter. On the registration form I wrote sloppy, transposed two numbers on the license plate numbers and then paid cash, all the time keeping him talking about places to eat and things to do in the area. I told him we'd probably stay a second night, but I'd let him know in the morning.

The room looked clean but smelled stale. Cooper unpacked the cooler he had stocked at the farm. Nerves kept me from eating, but they didn't stop Cooper. He spread the food out on the table like a picnic: salad, sandwiches, grapes and wheat crackers. I watched cable news. When Cooper finished eating, he pulled out Erica's sketches of the floor plan at Sweet's. When we had the layout of the building engraved in our memories, Cooper took the papers and burnt them over the toilet and flushed their charcoal remains.

The square building had six floors, each with almost identical floor plans. The back of the first floor had an entrance door, loading dock and two garage doors so trucks could pull inside the building to unload. There was also a holding area for animals. Offices and a small lobby filled the rest of the first floor. The remaining floors had a system of corridors that created a square within the facility. The main hallways ran along the exterior windows, leaving the interior of each floor devoted to laboratories. Erica noted which species each lab was set up for. Most were for rodents. The top two floors had larger rooms where animals such as cats, dogs, monkeys and rabbits could be used.

When we did a drive-by of the facility, we noted a black wrought-iron fence topped with strands of razor wire surrounding the property. The grounds were landscaped like a city park with mowed grass, flower beds, evergreens and deciduous trees. Vehicles going in had to stop at a guard shack. A gate opened before they drove into the property. Cameras perched on the guard shack added to the security.

We waited until midnight before heading out, our coat pockets filled with tools. Cooper carried a backpack with other stuff we might need, including a collapsible shovel. We parked the car at the store and decided we should go in and buy some gum and candy in case anyone noticed us. When we left the store, we walked in the opposite direction of Sweet's and strolled around the block. We held hands and chatted like lovers.

We snuck across back lawns to the fence by the back of the building. Security lights lit the driveway and back parking lot like downtown Las Vegas. Erica had told us there weren't any cameras in the back, a money-saving cut that made things easier for us. Cooper dug under the fence until he had a trench he could crawl through. He told me to wait by the fence until he signaled. He crouched as he ran to the door; why I don't know. Anyone looking would have seen him if he were upright or if he crawled.

I watched as he put Erica's stolen key in the lock. A couple of seconds later I saw the door open and Cooper disappear inside. Erica had given us several codes for the alarm, but she didn't know if any of them would still work. Sooner than I expected, Cooper came outside and waved for me to join him.

"I can't believe they didn't change the locks or the codes after Erica quit," he whispered.

"Stupid on their part," I said, as I surveyed the dimly lit room. I felt hopeful and excited. It could end tonight, and I prayed it would end in a good way with Blue coming home.

Cooper pointed to a vehicle parked at the end of the garage area. "I wonder if someone is here," he said. "Or if it's stored here."

"I don't know."

Erica suggested we look first in the holding area. My excitement soon turned to disappointment. There were four dogs, each in separate pens, and none of them were beagles. Their tails wagged when they saw us. My stomach knotted, knowing we had to leave them. A dozen or so cats stared with distrust, maybe knowing their fate. A gray tabby hissed. A row of cages contained albino rabbits, and several plastic boxes contained mice and rats. I took several pictures.

Erica predicted Blue wouldn't be there. Dogs were ordered

and delivered as needed. It had been ten days since Blue disappeared, and assuming he had been at Kappies with Cody, it meant he had been shipped out eight or nine days ago.

Next to the freight elevator, we found stairs and climbed to the fourth floor. The door had a sign saying 'restricted area.' We ignored it and found the next room Erica suggested we check. We were about to go in when I heard a noise. "I think somebody is coming," Cooper whispered. He had the door open so we dodged inside the dark room.

"I bet it's a security guard. Hopefully making a routine check," Cooper said. We stood next to the door, so if it opened we'd be behind it. We strained our ears and listened. Sure enough, footsteps. I felt a flush of adrenaline. But nothing happened. The footsteps faded. We took a few seconds to calm down.

"It's an interior room. I think it's safe to turn on a light," Cooper whispered.

I heard him feel the wall for a switch and with a click the room filled with light. Totally empty. Not even a chair or file cabinet. But there was another door. As soon as Cooper opened it, I knew. An odor of rot and dog hit me hard. I held my breath to keep from retching.

Two overhead lights lit the room. A row of large cages lined the back wall. My heart leaped into overdrive. There were six beagles, each in its own cell. They cowered in their cages. Each had a plastic cone around its neck that prevented it from turning its head. I avoided looking at their backs. I didn't want to know what the dogs weren't suppose to be licking. They didn't bark or make eye contact.

"Blue. Come. Blue," I called. I expected a bark. One by one I looked at the eyes of each dog. They were all normal. Taking photographs distracted me from my disappointment.

Cooper began sifting through papers on the desk. "They must be keeping records on the computers," he said. A flat-screen computer sat on a desk. He started looking through drawers.

"Bingo," he said. Taped inside one of the drawers he found a list of what could be passwords. "They have to be for the computers." He turned on one of the computers and when prompted, entered the first string of letters and numbers. The screen flickered with life. Cooper plugged in his travel drive and started to copy files.

"This is going to be interesting to read," he said, as he put the travel drive in his pocket and turned off the computer.

"Let's find the next lab," I said.

"I don't like that there's a security guard wandering around," Cooper said. "I wonder why Erica didn't mention it."

"Maybe they didn't have them when she worked here. They could have added extra security after she left and when they started getting negative publicity."

"True, but you'd think they would have changed the locks and alarm codes."

We were about to leave when we heard footsteps in the hallway again. Cooper turned off the lights. He grabbed my arm and we ducked under the computer table and pulled a couple chairs in front of us. Not the best hiding place, but the only other choice was sitting on the chairs.

The door opened and the overhead lights flickered back on. Whoever it was didn't walk around the room. They must have just looked. It seemed like minutes, but I'm sure it was only seconds before the lights flickered out and the door closed. We heard the outer door open and close. Then silence.

We waited a few minutes. Then Cooper whispered, "He probably won't be back for awhile. Let's hustle." We tiptoed out of the room, down the hall and into the next lab. Every noise we made reminded me of opening a bag of candy in a quiet movie theater.

The next lab was set up identically to the first one. I braced myself for what we would find, but preparation was impossible. In the dimly lit room I saw a row of restrained rabbits, their necks held in stanchions. Most appeared lifeless, their faces distorted with swollen, oozing eyes.

"They're probably testing new ingredients for shampoos," Cooper whispered. One rabbit twitched and struggled to free itself. Cooper cursed, grabbed some paper towels and held them firmly over the rabbit's nose and mouth. After an eternity the animal quit struggling.

I turned away, tears filling my eyes. I took photos by pointing the camera without really looking.

"Let's get the hell out of here," Cooper said. I could hear the anger in his voice and didn't know how to react. I wanted to leave, but we weren't done.

"We can't until we check all the labs," I whispered. He took forever to answer.

"Okay," he finally said.

We listened for the security guard before going back into the hallway again. This time we heard voices.

"I bet the alarm panel indicated the back door had been opened and the security guard saw it when he got back from making rounds," Cooper said.

We listened as whoever it was systematically went into each room. When we were sure they were inside a room with the door closed, we slipped into the hallway and ran to the loading dock door. As we opened the door, the alarm started wailing.

"Damn. I forgot to enter the security code," Cooper cursed.

"Too late now."

We ran to the fence and crawled through. Looking back, I didn't see anyone in pursuit, but I knew they would be shortly. We backtracked across the backyards and then, walking fast as to not draw attention, we went straight to the car.

I wasn't sure if my heart pounded from fear or exertion. Probably both. Cooper started the car and drove us back to the motel. Disappointment enveloped me. My heart felt hollow. Neither of us said a word until we got back to the motel.

"We won't be going back there again," Cooper said once we were safely in the room. "Security will be so tight, nobody will ever get in."

I put on my pajamas, slipped into bed and pulled the blankets up around my neck. Cooper slipped in beside me. His chest was my pillow. He held me tight. The next thing I knew the sun glared in around the edges of the curtains. It was a comfort not to wake alone.

We debated about stopping to see Erica and decided we should keep her informed. We needed her knowledge and hoped she had another idea. We found a pay phone and called her. She asked that we bring donuts.

Erica had coffee brewing and eagerly poured us each a cup.

She liked her coffee strong. She didn't seem surprised when we told her we had already gone to Sweet's.

"I couldn't wait," I told her.

"What did you find?"

"There was a security guard inside so we couldn't stay long," Cooper said. "Then I forgot to enter the code when we left so the alarm went off."

"Not good. They really beefed up security," Erica said.

"There were beagles on the fifth floor, but not Blue. We didn't get to all the labs. And we never made it to the sixth floor," I said.

"I don't know what to say. Maybe you could apply for a job."

"That's not going to happen," Cooper said.

Speaking from experience Erica acknowledged it wasn't pleasant. "But you could do it," she said. "I want that place closed. Out of business. Not everything they do is illegal, but it is wrong. More people need to know what they are doing. Maybe a second whistle blower would add credibility to what I reported."

I knew Blue's chance of still being alive grew slimmer as time went by, but I couldn't stop. Like Erica, I wanted people to know pets were being stolen and sold into research. To their owners it must seem like they walked off the face of the earth. Little did they know that their beloved pets really walked straight into a living hell.

"I still have the application I picked up when I snooped for security details at the other building."

Erica offered me her neighbor's apartment, which she was watching for a month while they were out of state for work. I could use the address on my application. She also had a couple of friends she would call to ask if I could use them as references.

She said Sweet's liked to hire students. "Tell them you plan on enrolling at the university in the fall and will be studying biology and your goal is to be a veterinarian."

Cooper again voiced his disapproval. "I doubt if you could even get hired. After their experience with Erica going to the media, I'm sure they screen applicants closely. Your background of teaching elementary school wouldn't qualify you for a job."

I thrived on a challenge. Tell me I can't do something and I'll do my best to prove you wrong. Cooper had just motivated me.

Chapter 13

It was a long, soul-searching drive back to Pearline. *Should I give up? If not, what should I do next? Did I really want a job at Sweet's? Could I handle it?* Thoughts ping-ponged around in my head. I was tired and knew better than to make a decision when not feeling par. But that didn't stop my brain from working overtime.

I sat in the passenger seat and paid slim attention to the scenery as Cooper sped along U.S. 131. The blue sky didn't even lift my spirits. It was Saturday morning, 12 days since Blue went missing. Kid Rock's "All Summer Long" played on the radio.

"What are you thinking?" Cooper asked.

"About what I should do next."

"It would be okay to walk away from it. You already did more than most people would have done."

"But it doesn't feel finished. I'd really like to know what happened to Blue."

"Maybe the files we downloaded will have an answer. You don't need to make a decision right now."

"True."

I appreciated Cooper letting me know the decision was mine. I knew he would support me no matter which road I took. It felt good to have someone on my side, a confidant.

We arrived back at the farm shortly before noon. Cody and Shadow barked and ran in high-speed circles in the fenced back-yard when they spotted us. We went to the fence to say hi. A lunch of salad and vegetable soup awaited us, compliments of Grams. She had the dining room table set for three with her best china.

"Why the good stuff?" I asked, picking up one of the bone white plates with its intricate design of laced roses.

"You're home," she said.

I reached out and gave her a hug. "Home. It's good to call this place home."

She ladled the steaming vegetable soup into a tureen and Cooper carried it to the table. I carried the salad while Grams got a pitcher of ice water from the fridge.

"It looks delicious," I said. The salad of fresh greens, sliced apples, mandarin oranges and walnuts was lightly dressed with a homemade mix of olive oil, vinegar and the juice from the canned oranges. The soup was homemade with vegetables Grams grew herself.

"I heard Jarsma hauled in a trailer to use as a temporary office and is building kennels in the old chicken coop behind his barn," Grams said.

"Damn. Why can't he just go out of business?" I asked.

"He's already cleared away the remains of the barn and is supposed to start construction on a pole barn next week."

"He moves fast," Cooper commented.

"The chicken coop isn't heated, so he has to have a new barn ready by winter."

After lunch Cooper helped Grams with dishes, and I decided to go for a ride. Dappy came trotting when I whistled. It only took minutes to get him bridled. Cody and Shadow tagged along. I guided Dappy down the trail to the river. The same place I rode on my first day. Hard to believe only three weeks had passed.

My brain started buzzing with dates. One year, three months, twelve days since Thomas died. Eight months, two weeks since the divorce. I tried to bring Thomas' face into focus. It was getting harder every time. I didn't want the memories to fade. But I realized the images in my mind were becoming replicas of photographs. Moments not captured on film were being stolen by the continuous march of time.

Live in the moment. I inhaled. Held it for 30 seconds and slowly exhaled. Inhale. Exhale. Breathe. I focused on Dappy's rhythmic stride. The delicate green of newly emerged leaves. The earthy aroma of the river.

Cody and Shadow zigzagged along the trail, stopping to sniff whatever interested them. They never strayed out of sight. The serenity of my surroundings took a backseat to my thoughts. This time my present predicament took center stage. I reviewed the last three weeks, and asked myself what I wanted in my future. If I quit on Blue, what would I do tomorrow? What would I feel when I drove by Kappies' new kennel?

I couldn't quit. The only path that felt right was to continue looking for Blue. I needed an answer. With that I called the boys, turned Dappy around and headed home.

"Anyone here?" I yelled as I went into the house. The dogs plopped on the floor, tired from their long run. Grams had left a note on the table saying she went to visit Clare, and Cooper wasn't around. I checked voice mail. The only message was from Cindi, asking that I call her at home.

"I've got a problem," she announced when she heard my voice.

"What?"

"Thursday morning a woman brought a stray beagle into the shelter. When I came in Friday it was gone. Sam said the owners claimed it. But later in the day a guy came in looking for a beagle. His description of the dog fit the beagle that came in Thursday. His dog had a healed broken tail. The dog at the shelter had the same injury. What are the odds? When I looked for the paperwork on the dog, I couldn't find it. I'm so tired of this crap."

"What did you do?"

"I told the guy the truth. If someone claimed the dog, there should have been paperwork. There wasn't any. What that usually means is Jarsma took the dog."

"Did he know about Jarsma?"

"Yes, he said he had read in the paper about the fire and the missing animals."

"What do you think he'll do?"

"Look for his dog at Kappies. I told him not to go alone, and to tell Jarsma he's looking for anything but a beagle. To take a photo of the dog and proof of ownership like vet records. I told him to take a cell phone to call for help."

"When's he going?"

"He probably went yesterday afternoon."

"Is he going to let you know what he finds?"

"I asked him to, and I asked him not to say I sent him."

"Is there anything I should be doing? Or *we* should be doing?" I asked.

"I don't know. Wait, I guess."

"Well, keep me posted."

"I will. Thanks."

I wandered around the house, restless. I decided to drive into Ludington and do some shopping. I needed new underwear. The thought made me laugh out loud. New underwear. I hadn't bought any new clothes, under or outer, in years. I owed the need for silky, sexy bras and panties to Cooper. He made me feel alive. Made me feel like a woman. I decided not to dwell on it. Just go with the flow. "Just go with the flow," I said out loud.

I bypassed the big box stores in favor of the downtown shops. Most catered to tourists who liked shopping while on vacation. I went to Mary's Boutique, an upscale women's store. I selected some fine under things and tried on two blouses and a skirt. Work clothes, I thought. No, but maybe interview clothes. I bought a couple things that made me blush and a burgundy blouse.

As I got into my car, I noticed the white truck parked on the street. I panicked and went back into the store.

"Do you have a bathroom?" I asked the clerk.

She pointed towards a back hallway.

Once inside I pulled out my cell phone and called the house. Cooper answered.

"Thank God you're there. I'm in Ludington and the white truck is parked across the street from where my car is."

"Let me think," he said. "How's this sound? Wait about ten minutes. Get in your car and drive down towards Scottville. I'll be on the bike on the corner of Stiles. Turn on Stiles and head for home. I'll pull out and follow the truck and see where it goes. I'm assuming they know where you live and won't follow you home."

"Sounds good."

I watched the time and browsed in the shop. After ten minutes I thanked the clerk and left the store. The white truck was still there. I could see someone slouched in the driver's seat. I got into my car, started it and pulled out onto Ludington Avenue. The truck followed. My heart started racing, but I maintained the speed limit. A few minutes later I approached Stiles, and I slowed down. When I spotted Cooper, I put on my turn signal. I turned and the truck kept going. Cooper pulled out behind it.

At home I watched the clock and waited. What did I get Cooper into? A half hour later I heard his bike pull into the driveway. I ran out to meet him.

"I was worried."

"You were? How sweet."

I swatted his arm. "What happened?"

"It stayed on U.S. 10 for a bit and then turned south on Scottville Road. I followed him until he turned into a driveway of an old farmhouse on Chauvez Road. Then I came home."

"Did you get an address?"

"No, but I know which house it is, and it's for sale. We can go back at dusk and look around a bit more."

When Grams came home, we asked her if she knew anyone who lived on Chauvez Road. Cooper described the location of the house. She thought the owner had died last year and didn't know what happened to the farm.

"I think we should go have a look around," Cooper said.

"Why? What are you thinking?" Grams asked.

"I don't know what to think. But twice the white truck followed Alison. It would be interesting just to look around."

In May in northern Michigan, the sun doesn't set until nearly 9:00. It meant we had a couple hours before heading to the farm. We had a leisurely supper of BLT sandwiches, with avocado substituted for the bacon. Grams talked about her visit with Clare, a woman she first met shortly after moving to Pearline.

At 8:00 we changed into dark clothes. I put my camera in my pocket, said goodbye to Grams and promised we'd be back shortly.

We parked the bike in a grove of trees about a half-mile from the farmhouse. Cooper brought his hand-held GPS unit and had it hanging around his neck.

"If anyone stops us, we'll say we're geocaching," he said.

"Geocaching?"

"It's a high-tech version of a hide-and-seek. People hide things and post the coordinates on a website. Anyone can retrieve the coordinates and hunt for the hidden treasure."

"Sounds like fun. But won't they know if something is hidden on their property."

"Well, you're not supposed to hide stuff on private property without the owners' permission. But we're lost...we wrote the coordinates down wrong."

"You always have a story."

"It's best to be prepared."

Cooper suggested we walk along the tree line of a plowed field and come up to the farm from behind. From our vantage point I didn't see the white truck, but just because we couldn't see it didn't mean it wasn't there.

The farm had several out buildings––a big wooden barn with fading red paint, an old chicken coop, a two-stall garage and an outhouse. We watched the place for 15 minutes from under an oak tree, its low branches providing cover. Nothing moved. We slowly made our way to the farm. My heart beat overtime, again. It didn't take much to pump my adrenalin.

The inside of the chicken coop smelled musty. Cobwebs filled the corners and draped from the ceiling like a patchwork of threads. Chickens hadn't called the place home in years. Dusty, dirty straw filled the nesting boxes and grime coated the windows.

In the garage, we found a gray and red Ford tractor parked in one of the stalls. The other stall was cluttered with an array of tools and equipment––a John Deere riding lawn mower, an assortment of hoes, rakes, shovels and a workbench with hand tools and soup cans of screws and nails. Nothing of interest to us.

The barn was a different story. We found a dozen empty dog kennels and a garbage can half-filled with dog food.

"He must to be connected to Jarsma," Cooper whispered.

"How?"

"He could be a buncher––someone who picks up dogs and sells them to Jarsma."

"Could he be the one who stole Cody and Blue?"

"It's possible."

We snooped around for whatever we could find. Like at Kappies, I found a box of dog collars. Some with tags attached.

"Looks like he's definitely involved," Cooper whispered.

I didn't answer. I was staring at two collars on top of the heap. One a sky-blue nylon, the color of Blue's eyes. The other one purple. I bought both for Christmas presents. I picked them up and held them out to Cooper. He read the names on the tags.

"Damn," he said.

"We've got to find out who this guy is," I said, no longer whispering. My fear turned to anger. I wanted to march up to the house and demand answers. Cooper grabbed my arm and hushed me.

"Listen."

It sounded like a truck. A few seconds later a car door slammed. We stuffed as many collars as we could fit into our pockets and headed toward the back door. The sun hung low in the western sky.

"We can't risk being seen," Cooper whispered once we were outside. He pointed to the outhouse. "I bet that's not in use any more. Let's hide there until it's dark."

We spent 20 minutes huddled in the windowless forerunner of the portable toilet. Not romantic. Luckily the door didn't fit tight, and we could see the outside world. When the sun sank below the tree line, we made our way across the yard. We were back at the bike in 10 minutes.

Grams waited for us on the porch swing, an almost empty glass of red wine in her hand.

I dropped Cody and Blue's collars in her lap.

She picked them up and looked at the tags. "Where'd you find them?"

"In the barn. There were dog kennels--all empty. Some dog food. And a box of collars." We handed her the rest of the collars we had taken. Tears rolled down her cheeks after she read the tag on one of the collars.

"This is Papa Bear's collar. He's the Clinton's dog. A black lab. He disappeared last fall. I used to watch him when they went away. He was a gentle soul who was crazy about people."

"So whatever is going on has been happening for awhile," I said.

She nodded.

Cooper got up and returned with the bottle of wine and two more glasses. Stars dotted the night sky. Spring peepers made a ruckus in the marsh across the street. Forget sipping, I downed my first glass of merlot in seconds.

"We need to find out who lives on that farm," Cooper said.

His statement jarred me back to reality. I had been drifting. "Easy enough. All we need to do is call the real estate agent who is handling the sale."

"I'll call in the morning," he said.

"I'm going to bed," I announced. I wanted to be alone.

After bringing in the dogs, we said good night and each made our way to our rooms. I sat on the side of the bed. Finally I pulled out the job application and stared at it. Something told me to look at Sweet's web site. A heading for "Careers" popped out at me. I clicked on it and found an online application and a list of job openings. I read about their recruiting and hiring practices. I knew I would never pass a background check using false references. They sounded too thorough. There was an opening for a temporary office clerk. The job description included typing, filing and a need for computer skills. That fit me perfectly.

I used my real name and the address Erica gave me for her neighbor's apartment. After filling out the application, I attached my resume and pressed submit.

Chapter 14

Mom and Dad surprised us with a phone call early Sunday morning, announcing they were driving up for a short visit. They would be pulling into the drive in less than two hours and insisted on taking us to lunch at Scotty's. No surprise there. The Ludington restaurant was their favorite place to dine with its menu of homemade soups, prime rib, charbroiled burgers, steak and seafood. And cocktails.

Cooper stocked his room with food and drinks. He planned on staying out of sight with only Kal for company during the duration of the visit. Mom and Dad didn't know Grams hired anyone, and she decided she didn't want them to know. Her decision. We played along.

The folks were checking to see how we were doing and seemed pleased with what they saw––I had color in my cheeks and a new outlook on life.

Grams invited them to spend the night. "Tomorrow is Memorial Day. Don't you have the day off work?"

They indeed had the day off work but were planning on going sailing on Lake Michigan. Their sailboat had been put into the water two weeks earlier. Dad wanted to leave. "Why have a boat if we don't make the time to use it?"

"If we leave early tomorrow, we'll still have time for a sail," Mom answered. She convinced him to stay.

My thoughts drifted to Cooper, stuck in his room for the rest of the day. Instead of sitting around the house, I suggested a trip to the Little River Casino in Manistee. It was a half-hour drive north, and I knew my folks loved The Willows restaurant at the resort. Not to mention their love affair with slot machines.

"Great idea," Mom said.

Within an hour we were on our way. I kept the conversation light. I didn't want to answer a thousand and one questions about my life. Once at Little River the need for talk dissipated. The gaming floor echoed with excitement, and I felt a tingle of anticipation in the smoke-filled air. Slot machines whirled while people sat on stools fixated on the spinning wheels. Others tried their luck with video poker. There were games I knew nothing about. Gray-haired women were fixated on animated screens with the only sign of life an arm lifting and a finger pushing buttons. Men wandered around listless in search of the winning machine, slipping in their playing cards and leaving a trail of mismatched cherries and bars.

Dad pressed fifty dollars into my hand. "Have fun. Be lucky."

"I will," I said, thanking him.

We sat side-by-side playing video poker while Mom and Grams wandered off to find quarter slots. Grams once won $800 on what she called her lucky machine, and she had been determined to repeat the good fortune ever since. She always played it first. If she didn't, the outing would be a bust. But she usually lost. The fun was in the playing, in the chance of taking home big money.

"So how is it really going?" Dad asked.

"Great. No problem. I'm enjoying the peace and quiet. Getting a lot of riding in."

"Have you thought about getting a job?"

I didn't have to lie. "Actually, I put in an application last week for some office work." It felt good to make him happy. I prayed he didn't ask where. Just when I thought he would, three aces popped up.

"Look," I said, pointing to the screen. "And I'm playing the max, five quarters."

I saved the aces and pressed the deal button for two new cards. The fourth ace appeared. The light on top of the machine started flashing, summoning an attendant. I jumped off my stool in surprise.

"I don't believe it."

"Wow. Way to go," Dad said, giving me a pat on the back.

A guy in a casino uniform appeared. "Congratulations," he said.

"What did I win?"

"$1,000." He paid me with $100 dollar bills.

"Must be your lucky day," said a stranger who shook my hand.

"Lets go find Mom and Grams," Dad said.

They were surprised too. I'm not usually a lucky person. I always leave casinos with less money than I start with. The reversal of fortune felt good.

"We're not having any luck. Why don't we go eat?" Grams suggested.

"My treat." That felt good, too.

The talk on the trip home focused on the casino, and once there we had wine on the porch and talked about past summers on the farm. I found myself enjoying my parents' company. For once they weren't dictating how I should run my life. Maybe they realized I had grown up, that I was an adult.

Unfortunately, Mom and Dad's bedroom stood between mine and Cooper's. I considered sneaking him a snack but didn't want to risk getting caught. Dad was a light sleeper. I figured Cooper could survive on the stockpile of food he had stashed in his room. Plus, he had probably made himself a fine meal while we were at the casino.

Grams made French toast for breakfast. With that and hugs and kisses, Mom and Dad were gone. Soon after, Grams left with friends for the Memorial Day parade in Ludington.

When both cars pulled out of the driveway, I rescued Cooper. I showed him the hundred dollar bills and told him of my lucky afternoon at the casino. He showed me what he found on the computer files we had copied at Sweet's. "There's a ton of information, but I don't understand most of it. I did find records of all the animals they bought in the last three years." He scrolled through lists of documents, stopping on acquisitions. There were sub-files for species. Under dogs, it listed the breeds, date of arrival, the price paid and someone's name.

Two days after Blue went missing the record showed six beagles bought for $200 each from Kappies for a Dr. Daniel Madden.

"Daniel Madden? Isn't he the guy we followed from the lab? The one who testified at the Board of Commissioners' meeting?"

"One and the same. I looked at Sweet's website and found this on him," Cooper said, handing me a sheet of paper. I had seen the information before when surfing the site but hadn't paid much attention to it. Knowing he had a connection to Blue put it in a new light. A spotlight. The printout had a headshot and a biography. In the photograph Madden looked young and had a full head of brown hair.

"This must be an old photo. He looks so young."

"It was probably taken when he started at Sweet's 15 years ago."

Brown-framed glasses with tinted lenses perched on his nose, and a smirk dominated his face. He looked like a weasel. The picture didn't do him justice. In real life he came across as intelligent, in-control, convincing and trusting.

Madden was the Executive Vice President of Sweet's and the Director of Research. He earned his PhD at Iowa State University and had more than 26 years experience as a toxicologist. The bio also listed the places he worked before coming to Sweet's.

"What do you think?" I asked Cooper.

"I bet one of the beagles shipped to Sweet's was Blue."

"I don't believe it. He was shipped the day I went to Kappies. I must have just missed him."

"So the question is––is he still alive two weeks later?"

"My gut says yes. Why couldn't we make it though all the rooms? Just think. If we had, we probably would have found him."

"I'm sorry."

"It wasn't your fault. It just happened."

It was then that I told Cooper I sent an application along with my resume for an office job at Sweets. It took him several seconds to answer.

"I really don't think it's a good idea. Besides, what are you going to learn from working in the office?"

"I don't know. What other options are there?"

He couldn't come up with any. Not one.

While cooped up in his room, Cooper also had researched the house on Chauvez Road. It belonged to a Mary Bradford who died a year earlier. Her obituary listed a son and one grandson.

"Maybe her grandson is living in the house and driving the white pickup," Cooper suggested. "We need to call the real estate agent and make an appointment to see the place. We got lucky having the place up for sale."

"That's me, Miss Lucky."

With that, I got the phone and dialed the number Cooper had written down. With the bad economy, the housing market at a standstill and real estate prices tumbling, the agent sounded like she was smiling when I asked about the farm. She offered to meet us there at 5:00. She didn't care about it being a holiday.

We had a few hours before the appointment and decided to go for a ride.

"I just need to change my clothes," I said.

"Do you need any help?"

It didn't take long to say yes. Before I knew it, we were in my room tearing at each other's clothes.

We packed a picnic lunch and rode to the river. The freshness of spring was fading with green growing into the new normal. Spring flowers shriveled in the shade brought forth by the leafy canopy. Cody and Shadow tagged along, sniffing and investigating as they kept up with the horses. Shadow was becoming a new normal, too. It's funny how life changes can be so instant and devastating. How you feel life will never be the same. And it isn't. You just get used to the new.

Cooper pointed to Cody and Shadow. They were about twenty feet off the path and frozen in place, staring intently at something on the ground. I couldn't see what they were looking at, so I dismounted and walked slowly toward them. Cooper did the same. We were almost next to them when I saw what they were looking at.

"It's a fawn." The baby was curled in a tight ball ignoring the activity. Its soft brown coat with white splotches blended into the forest floor of decaying leaves and branches.

"Mama must be close. Let's go before she spots us."

I tugged at the collars of the boys, convincing them to turn and walk beside us as we made our way to the trail. "How cool was that? My luck continues. Not everyday do you get to see a newborn fawn."

We stopped at the same place we had on our first ride, where we both had taken a tumble into the icy water. We laughed at the memory.

"You weren't happy, that's for sure," Cooper teased.

"Watch it or you'll get a repeat performance."

We grabbed the sandwiches and apples from the saddlebags and balanced our way out onto the downed tree. With our feet dangling within inches of the water, we savored the peacefulness of the river and enjoyed lunch.

"It doesn't get any better than this," Cooper said.

I had to agree. It was a perfect moment. "No, it doesn't," I said, rubbing his thigh with my hand. He leaned over and we kissed.

"I think I'll order this for lunch every day," he said.

"You're getting spoiled."

"And I like it."

After about an hour of hanging out by the river, we headed for home. It felt absolutely wonderful to be riding Dappy. I could tell he enjoyed the outing too. He needed no urging to follow the trail along the river. His ears perked forward listening to every sound. Instead of turning around, we took an old logging trail that led to the road near the house. I seldom took the trail because I worried about the dogs being loose for the last bit along the road. But with the holiday, there wouldn't be much traffic.

We invited Grams to go see the house with us. She declined, worried she might know the agent. "I'm sure you two can come up with a more convincing story without me."

We pulled into the driveway of the farm promptly at 5:00. We took Cooper's motorcycle in case the owner of the white truck was home. No doubt he would recognize my car. But the only vehicle in the yard was a blue Taurus. A woman got out of it and walked toward us.

"Hi, I'm Barbara Sanford from Century 21. You must be Alison," she said, as she shook my hand.

"I am. So pleased to meet you. This is my friend Cooper."

She asked a few personal questions. I lied and told her we were engaged and looking for a hobby farm.

Barbara delved into the history of the house; its square footage and the improvements that had been made over the years. "It has a new furnace. The shingles were replaced last year, and the electrical is up to code," she said, as she led us through the front door.

"Is it rental property or is the owner living here?" Cooper asked.

"The owner, Mary Bradford, passed away and left the place to her son who lives in town. He's renting it to a young man, Blair. He's gone for the weekend."

Cooper had been right.

We watched for anything that might connect the guy to Kappies as we wandered through the house. "Does Blair work around here?" Cooper asked to keep the conversation alive.

"He works at a kennel. Sometimes when they're super busy he brings dogs here. But he doesn't bring them into the house. He keeps them in the barn."

After going through the whole house, basement included, Cooper asked if we could see the barn. Mary said sure. She led the way out back, opened the barn door and stepped aside for us to enter. Nothing had changed since our earlier visit. Cooper asked how old the shingles on the barn were. Mary had no idea. They looked for signs of water damage on the inside roof boards, but didn't find any signs of wetness or rot.

"It looks in great shape for a barn that was probably built over a hundred years ago," Cooper said. "Plenty of room for horses and maybe a couple goats or cows."

After a quick glance at the chicken coop and outhouse, we thanked Mary for her time and said we'd be in contact if we were interested. She reminded us the farm was priced to sell and the Ludington State Bank would be able to finance the sale for qualified buyers.

Back home, Grams and Cindi were sitting on the porch swing sipping wine. Cindi wanted to update us on the latest happenings at the shelter. She bubbled with excitement, like a 10-year-old walking through the gates of Disney World for the first time. The alcohol probably added to her animation. I introduced Cooper as an old friend visiting from California.

It seems the owner of the beagle, a guy named Patrick, did as she suggested and went to Kappies looking for a Jack Russell terrier. Jarsma insisted he didn't have any Jacks but let the guy go through the kennel anyway.

"And guess what he found?"

"Did he really?"

"He did!"

"What did he do?"

"He pulled out his wallet and showed Jarsma a photo of his beagle with its injured tail. He had adoption papers and vet papers. He said Jarsma was fuming."

"Did he let him take the dog?"

"Not at first, but when Patrick pulled out his cell phone and threatened to call the police, Jarsma changed his mind."

"So that's the end of it?"

"Hell no. Patrick called the police from his car in the driveway. They came and he made them take a police report. Seems he's a lawyer. Isn't that the best?"

"He's a lawyer?"

"Yup. He's demanding a full investigation into how his dog ended up at Kappies after it had been at the shelter for less than the seven days required by law."

"Do you have proof the dog was at the shelter?"

"Sure do. Three volunteers, me included, saw it. And thanks to its distinct tail, there's no denying it's the same dog."

"Wow."

"I think Sam is in big trouble."

"How big?"

"Well, Patrick took his police report to the newspaper, and they're doing a story on it. They called me with questions, and I told them everything I knew. No holding back."

"Are you going to go back to the shelter?"

"Hell yes, but not alone. I'm not that crazy. The volunteers talked it over and decided there should never be just one person alone at the shelter with all that's going on."

Grams asked if she truly feared for her safety.

Cindi didn't hesitate to say yes. "Not so much from Sam, but Jarsma is a different story. His livelihood is on the line. He's feeling threatened."

"Are you okay at home? Don't you live alone?" Grams questioned.

"I do, but I have my dogs. No one is coming in my house uninvited. Plus, I keep a baseball bat under my bed and my cell phone close."

"You're welcome to stay here until things get settled," Grams offered. "We have an extra bedroom and plenty of space for your dogs."

Unfortunately, Cindi turned her down.

Chapter 15

I woke up exhausted. The stress of the last few days gnawed at my sense of well-being and continued to invade my dreams. When Grams announced she was planting her garden and could use some help, it sounded like the perfect project. Cooper had plowed the small plot a few days earlier to prepare the earth for new life. Grams bought plants, fertilizer and seeds at Miller's Farm Market on Saturday.

"Here, wear Tom's old hat," Grams said, handing Cooper a wide-brimmed straw hat. "He always wore it at planting time."

"Are you sure?"

"It'll be like part of him is with us if you're wearing his hat."

In all the commotion since Blue went missing, I realized I hadn't given enough thought to the fact that Grams had lost her life partner. We avoided the subject of death by keeping busy. Focusing on Blue distracted me from the everyday pain of loss.

Cooper plopped the hat on his head and jiggled it in place. He looked like a farmer.

"Cute," I said.

"As handsome as Tom," Grams noted.

We carried the trays of plants and packets of seeds to the garden. We left the dogs in the fenced-in yard. They loved helping to dig holes, but it wasn't the kind of help we appreciated.

We planted rows of big-boy tomatoes, cherry tomatoes, zucchini, green peppers, watermelon, muskmelon, butternut squash and sweet corn. She had seeds for carrots, radishes, green beans, lettuce and collard greens.

"What will you do with all this? You can't possibly need this much food," Cooper asked.

"She takes most of it to the food pantry at church," I said.

"Plus I plant extra so when the deer, raccoons and rabbits are full, there's something left for us," Grams said laughing.

With all the plants tucked into the dirt, Grams pulled Henry out of storage. The scarecrow had stood guard over the vegetables as long as I could remember, his clothes faded from the sun and rain. The scrawny make-believe man wore Gramps' discarded clothes and was stuffed with old hay. Every spring he got a new outfit from whatever clothes Gramps had that were beyond mending.

"We have a whole closet to choose from this year," Grams said. She hadn't gotten rid of any of Gramps' things yet. "You go pick something out."

"I don't think I can. Not without you." It took some persuading, but she gave in and joined me.

Every garment had a memory. It took us an hour to decide on a red and blue plaid flannel shirt and a pair of dark blue work trousers.

"It'll look like Tom himself watching over us," Grams said. She burst into tears. "He is watching over us."

While we had picked out clothes for Henry, Cooper had whipped together lunch. I was starting to get used to his no-meat meals. They were convenient, since I hated cooking for one. After lunch, Cooper and I went out to dress Henry while Grams cleaned the kitchen. I think it was her way of avoiding handling the clothes. We took Henry to the picnic table and laid him out like a cadaver in a university medical classroom. I unbuttoned his shirt and started to take it off, but the shirt held the stuffing to form and without it the musty hay fell everywhere.

"I have an idea. Just put the new shirt over the old one. It can't hurt, can it?" Cooper suggested.

"Good idea." I followed his lead and within minutes we had Henry dressed and were poking the old clothes out of sight behind the new.

"It just makes him a little chubby. More to scare the birds away," Cooper said.

We attached Henry to the metal stake in the center of the garden. Grams came out as we finished.

"He looks good," she said, handing me the *Ludington Daily News*. "This just came. Look at the front page."

Above the fold was a picture of a man with a beagle. The headline read, "Ludington Man Demands Investigation."

We sat down at the picnic table, and I read the article out loud. The story was almost identical to the one Cindi had told us. She was even quoted, saying unflattering things about how the shelter was run.

Cindi told the reporter that the beagle had been at the shelter and disappeared before the seven-day hold period expired. Its paperwork disappeared too. And it wasn't the first time it had happened, but it was the first time someone had come looking for a dog she knew had definitely been at the shelter. She knew because the dog's tail had a distinct kink from being broken.

"I think her days as a volunteer might be over," Cooper said. "Even though she's right, the newspaper isn't the place to say it."

"She tried doing it the right way and she's been ignored. This is perfect. Let the people know what's going on, and if they don't like it they'll demand change."

Donald Dykhouse, the Chairman of the County Board of Commissioners, told the reporter he wasn't aware of the incident but would look into it.

At the end of the article it said Sam Grensward and Gary Jarsma were unavailable for comment.

"Figures they wouldn't have the guts to talk," Cooper said.

"It looks like they have something to hide," I said.

When we went back into the house there was a message from Cindi asking that I call. When I did, she sounded frantic and refused to discuss what was bothering her on the phone.

"Please come over. Can you?"

When I pulled into Cindi's driveway, the place looked deserted. Not like the first time I visited when she sat swinging under the oak tree in her front yard. There were no dogs barking from the fenced-in yard and no lights shining from within the house. The front door opened before I stepped out of my car. Cindi greeted me in the driveway.

"Thanks for coming," she said, giving me a hug.

"No problem. What's up?'

Once in the trailer, she offered me a glass of iced tea. I took a seat at the kitchen table and had a chance to look around while she played hostess. It was my first time in her trailer. It was clean and comfy, but smelled of pets, a musty wet-dog smell that's impossible to get out of shag carpet.

Cindi wasn't her bubbly talkative self. Even her dogs looked worried. They were lying on their beds, but their eyes watched every move Cindi made. Two cats sat on the back of the couch keeping an eye on her, too.

She sat the glass of tea in front of me. I heard the ice cubes clink. Cindi took a seat across from me at the kitchen table and stared out the window.

"Cindi, what is it?"

"Jarsma is missing. The sheriff came this morning and asked me questions. He wanted to know when I last saw Jarsma. I told him it was at the Board of Commissioners' meeting last week. He kept asking if I saw Jarsma at the shelter. I haven't seen him there in months. Jarsma knows what I think of him and knows which days I volunteer. He steers clear of me, which is fine by me."

"When did he go missing?"

"I don't know. The sheriff wouldn't tell me anything other than they couldn't locate him."

"Did you see today's paper? The article about the beagle?"

"I did. I think I said too much."

"But all true."

"Nothing I haven't said before, but this time they listened."

"So why are you so worried?'

"I don't have an alibi for last night. I was home alone. The sheriff kept asking if anyone could vouch for me. I said no. I live alone. Most nights I'm home alone, watching TV, reading, doing whatever. Then he asked about my relationship with Jarsma. I told him I couldn't stand being in the same room with him. He made my skin crawl."

"You shouldn't have anything to worry about. I'm sure Jarsma just ducked out of sight after the incident with Patrick. He'll show up acting all innocent."

"You're probably right."

"And if something did happen to him, you wouldn't be the only suspect. There are a lot of people who wish him a one way ticket to hell, including me."

I stayed for two hours trying to convince Cindi everything would be okay. She insisted the sheriff suspected her of something. I asked if she was guilty of anything. She said no, but immediately our conversation dwindled to good-byes.

"I don't think you have anything to worry about," I told her as I opened the door to leave. I turned, gave her a hug and left.

When I got home the sheriff's car was parked in the driveway. I took a deep breath before I got out of the car. Taking extra air into my lungs was like inhaling Cindi's paranoia. I understood why her fear clouded her innocence.

In the house, Grams sat at the kitchen table with Sheriff Marc VanBergen. I remembered his inquisition after the fire at Kappies and again related to how Cindi felt after he questioned her.

After hellos, Marc went straight to business, asking where I had been.

"Visiting Cindi Owens."

"So you know why I'm here?"

"She said you couldn't find Gary Jarsma." I almost said more, about how his relentless questions made even an innocent person feel guilty, but I kept my thoughts to myself.

"Where were you last night?"

"Here with Grams. Cindi stopped by in the evening and told us about the beagle being found at Kappies."

"Why do you think she did that?"

"Maybe because my beagle is still missing and she cares."

"And after Cindi left?"

"We talked awhile and then went to bed. I watched a little TV in my room before going to sleep."

"You swear you were here all night? Never slipped out the door after your grandmother was asleep?"

Grams slammed her open palm on the table. "She said she was here all night. How many times does she have to say it?"

"Just once more," he said turning, staring me straight in the eyes. "Were you here all night?"

"Yes, I was here all night," I replied, with an emphasis on all.

He thanked us and apologized for taking our time. "I'm just doing my job," he said with a smile. Then he asked if we could think of anyone who might want to hurt Jarsma.

"Just every animal lover in the county," I told him.

He handed me his business card and asked me to call if I remembered anything of importance.

After he left, I called Cindi and apologized for not being more sensitive to her worries. "Sheriff VanBergen just left. He was waiting for me. Luckily I was home all night and Grams said so."

After discussing the sheriff's questions, we wondered why he didn't ask about our whereabouts during the day. His was only concerned about the evening and overnight hours.

"I bet someone saw him during the day. Maybe he didn't show up for work this morning," Cindi said.

"I bet that's it."

I felt better after talking to Cindi. With any luck, Jarsma cleaned out his bank account, left for Mexico and would never come back.

Cooper came downstairs after the sheriff left. We told him Jarsma couldn't be located, and we guessed he had disappeared sometime in the evening or overnight.

After dinner, Cooper asked if I wanted to go for a ride. It sounded relaxing, so I said yes. I had hoped for a laid-back day, but thanks to the disappearing Jarsma it hadn't been as restful as I had hoped.

We saddled Dappy and Chester and took the usual trail down by the river. Cody and Shadow were as eager for a run as the horses. After a few minutes of letting the horses have their head, we pulled them to a stop. Cooper suggested we take a break. We let the horses munch on grass and we sat on the riverbank talking of the past and the future. There were too many variables to make definite plans. I was still taking it a day at a time, and Cooper was wanted for questioning in California. Where did that leave us? In the now.

Cooper offered a back massage. I laid on my stomach on the soft spring grass, my head resting on my hands. He kneaded my taut muscles, and I found the relaxation I had been searching for all day. Birds tweeted their mating calls. The air was filled with a kaleidoscope of spring smells. I slipped into a state of bliss, but the distant barking of the dogs ruined the tranquility.

I rolled over and sat up. Cooper called for Cody and Shadow, but they didn't respond. We tied the horses to a tree and followed the riverbank downstream. The barking grew louder. Finally we could see the dogs. They were standing on the bank barking at something in the river.

"Another fawn," Cooper suggested.

But it wasn't a fawn. It was a human body. Floating face up, lodged in the crook of a fallen tree.

"Oh no, it's Jarsma," I whispered.

We shushed the dogs and stared at the body as it bobbed in the current.

"What do we do?" I asked.

"Let's think for a minute. We got time, he's not going anywhere."

"The only option is to tell the truth. I couldn't handle answering any more questions if we lie."

"The only question is, do we report it or do you report it."

"I can do it. I'll say I went for a ride and the dogs took off and I followed their barking."

We convinced the dogs to leave their find and went back to the horses. At the barn, Cooper unsaddled Chester and left Dappy tied to the fence. We told Grams what we found. I picked up the business card Sheriff VanBergen had given me and dialed his cell number.

He answered, and I explained the situation.

He asked if an ambulance could get to the river. I told him it could get most of the way but the last hundred feet was wooded. He said they'd be over within a half hour. I went to the barn and put Dappy away while I waited.

Instead of going into the house, I sat on the picnic table. I noticed bits of hay on the ground, remnants of the morning fun. Planting the garden and dressing Henry was already a distant memory. I heard sirens and knew they'd be arriving soon. Besides the ambulance, a state police car and an SUV screeched into the driveway. I pointed out the trail we needed to take.

"It's at least a mile back," I told them.

They decided to leave the police car at the house. The state trooper and I rode in the back seat of the SUV. The sheriff and another deputy rode in the front. I showed them where to park and led them to the body. Jarsma, still snagged on a fallen tree, bobbed in the current. The deputy pulled out a camera and started taking photographs. The sheriff asked me to repeat my story of how I found the body.

"Listen closely," I said. I had no patience left. "I went for a ride after dinner. I took my dogs, like I always do, and they disappeared. When I stopped I could hear them barking. They wouldn't come when I called, so I went and looked for them. I found them on the riverbank barking towards the river. When I got close enough, I saw what they were barking at. A body, face up. I recognized it. I went back to the house and called you." VanBergen scribbled notes in a pocket-size notebook as I talked. When I finished he thanked me.

"Can I leave?"

"Where?"

"To the house. You don't need me here, do you?"

"If you wait, we can give you a ride."

"I don't mind the walk."

He thanked me for the help and said I could leave. The walk to the house was peaceful. The sun glowed low on the western horizon, and the trail, sheltered by giant oaks and maples, was shrouded in evening shadows. Back at the house, Grams and Cooper waited.

"They're taking photos like it's a crime scene," I told them.

"It's not. It's apparent he floated to the spot and got caught by the dead tree," Cooper said.

He offered me a glass of red wine and I gratefully accepted.

"I'm sorry you had to handle it alone."

"No problem. When it's truthful it's easy, or maybe I should say easier."

"It's been one heck of a long day," Grams said.

About an hour later we saw the trio of vehicles leave the driveway, their headlights lighting up the night. The three of us finished the bottle of wine before saying good night.

Up in my room, I decided to check my e-mail before showering. The one that caught my eye was from Sweet's--they had received my application and wanted to set up a time for an interview.

Chapter 16

I broke the news about Sweet's request for an interview to Grams and Cooper over breakfast.

"You're taking this too far. You can't get a job there and be sneaking around. You're going to get in trouble," Grams said.

"I agree with Grams. As much as I hate to say it, I think Blue is beyond help," Cooper said. "With Jarsma turning up dead, there's going to be a lot of questions and you leaving town won't look good."

They were both right, but my stubborn gene flared up. "I probably won't even get hired," I said. "And that'll be the end of it, but I've come this far. I'm determined to see it through."

After morning dishes, I called Erica. She was still okay with me using her neighbor's apartment. I then called Sweet's and set up an appointment for an interview at 9:00 the next morning. I called Erica again and informed her of the interview time and asked if I could come this afternoon. She said to come any time.

Cooper stomped off to the barn after hearing I was leaving in a few hours. Grams continued to try and convince me not to go as I packed a suitcase with clothes and toiletries. The more she talked, the deeper I ground my heels into the premise that Blue waited at Sweet's for me to rescue him.

"Nothing you can say will stop me from going," I told her. "I can be as stubborn as you, and this time I've made up my mind." She stared at me for a few moments and then left the room without another word.

After I packed, I didn't feel like having any more confrontations, so I called Cindi and invited myself over for a visit. Grams wasn't around when I went downstairs, so I left her a note saying I was heading to Cindi's and would be back before leaving for Kalamazoo.

Cindi had the iced tea already poured when she welcomed me into her trailer.

"I heard on the news this morning that they found Jarsma's body," she said.

"Did you hear where they found him?"

"In the river."

"Yeah, the river behind Grams' farm."

"You're kidding?"

"No, I found it." I relayed the entire story to her, leaving out Cooper's part.

"Could you tell how he died?"

"No, but I didn't look that close. He was floating on his back and that was all I saw."

We speculated on what might have happened. Suicide? Accident? We kept returning to murder.

"Everyone who knew what he did hated him," Cindi said.

"Hated enough to kill him? I hated him and wished him nothing but the worst, but I couldn't have killed him," I said.

"I hope Patrick had an alibi. He was furious."

"I bet everyone who read the newspaper was steaming mad."

Our conversation led us to wondering about the future of Kappies. Cindi thought Jarsma was the sole owner, and with him gone, it would be out of business. She wondered if someone was taking care of the animals.

"Lets go see," I suggested.

After I pulled in Kappies' driveway, I saw police cars and deputies walking the property as if looking for something. My car had already been seen. It was too late to turn around,

"Crap," I said.

Sheriff VanBergen saw us and headed in our direction. I lowered the window.

"What brings you out here?"

"We were worried about the dogs and cats Jarsma had and wondered if anyone was feeding them," I said.

"I'm sure we can find room for them at the shelter," Cindi added.

"They're being taken care of, and they'll stay here until we're ready to release them."

"Was he murdered?" Cindi asked.

"What makes you ask that?"

"Just guessing."

"It's still an investigation and this is private property, so I suggest you two leave and not come back." He didn't wait for a response, just turned and strolled back to his buddies.

We speculated on what they were searching for and decided Jarsma must have been murdered. No suicide or accident. I took Cindi to her trailer and then went to pick up my backpack. Time to head to Kalamazoo.

Grams and Cooper were sitting at the kitchen table when I walked in. I told them about the scene at Kappies and then went to my room to get my stuff. Both were silent when I came back downstairs.

"I'm sorry you disagree with what I'm doing," I told them.

"We're worried is all. You be careful," Grams said. She got up and gave me a hug.

I turned and looked at Cooper. "I'll probably be back tomorrow afternoon," I said.

He nodded his head in acknowledgement. "Be careful," was all he said. I felt like kicking him in the shin, but I didn't. I picked up my backpack and left.

I rolled down the window and let the rushing air whip my hair into a frenzy. I cranked up the CD player and Kid Rock's high energy bolstered my spirit. I stayed in the moment for the entire drive; no worries, no what-ifs, no doubts.

Erica was waiting for me as I hauled my backpack up the stairs to her apartment. She greeted me like an old friend, and Webster's tail wagged in agreement.

"Welcome," she said. "Are you ready for the interview?"

"Not really. If anything, I'm too qualified for the job."

"What's your story going to be?'

"The truth. I left Chicago after my son died and my marriage ended in divorce. I'm here visiting friends and decided to stay a while. I'm thinking of attending Western Michigan University to get a master's degree in educational leadership. That I don't want to teach any more. I'd rather be part of the administration. Maybe a principal."

"Sounds believable to me. Who are your friends?"

"Not you," I said. We both laughed. She gave me the name of the people whose apartment I would be staying in and said they would be good friends: Bob and Cathy Harrison.

I filled Erica in on the happenings back home: the beagle disappearing from the shelter only to be found at Jarsma's kennel, Jarsma floating in the river, and how upset Grams and Cooper were about the interview.

Erica said it sounded like I needed a drink. She made a batch of strawberry daiquiris and told me to relax while she made us a snack.

I woke early. I was dressed and ready to be interviewed by 8:00. Erica had already gone to work, but she left me a note listing what she had available for me to eat for breakfast. She asked that I give her a call after the interview to let her know how it went. After devouring a raisin bagel and washing it down with orange juice and coffee, I packed my backpack and left.

I pulled up to the guard shack at 8:45. The guard, an older gentleman with a chocolate brown uniform, found my name on a list of expected guests. He directed me to the visitor's parking and pointed to which door to enter. He instructed me to have a nice day.

Before getting out of the car, I took several deep breaths. I was nervous and didn't want to be. I kept telling myself it was only a job interview. But on a deeper level I knew it was more than that. Secretly, I hoped I wouldn't be hired.

A receptionist greeted me. I introduced myself, and she told me to have a seat. I waited about ten minutes before a woman, dressed in a Hillary Clinton pantsuit, opened a door and introduced herself as Jackie Jones. We shook hands, and she led me to her office.

Jackie's pantsuit calmed me. It was non-threatening. We made small talk about the weather and the ease of which I found the place. She then picked up my resume and started asking questions. Yes, I loved teaching but wanted to move into administration. I hoped to be accepted at Western, but I hadn't applied yet. At the moment my concern rested with finding a job so I could pay bills.

She explained that she didn't know how long the job would last. Linda, the woman I was replacing had gone into early labor, and her baby was born six weeks early. "It'll be at least three months, maybe longer."

"Do you have any questions for me?" she asked after telling me details of the job.

My one question––is my dog somewhere in the belly of this building?––I couldn't ask. Instead I told her she was very thorough and left me with no questions other than when they would be making a decision.

"Soon. When could you start?"

"Monday."

She said she had someone she wanted me to meet. She picked up the phone and dialed an inner-office number. "Hello, Dr. Madden. Are you available to meet one of the applicants for the office job?"

My heartbeat quickened and my entire body felt hot.

Jackie hung up the phone. "I'd like you to meet Dr. Madden. He's our executive vice president and has to approve all hires." She got up, opened the office door and stood back so I could walk through.

"To the left," she said. Madden's office was four doors down from hers. His door was open. Jackie knocked as we walked in.

Dr. Madden stood and reached his hand out over his desk. I shook it while Jackie introduced me. She handed him my paperwork and excused herself. On her way out, she thanked me for coming in.

Dr. Madden stared at me for an uncomfortable amount of time and then smiled. He glanced at my resume and application. I ended up repeating most of what I had already told Jackie.

"I'm sorry for your loss," he said. Jackie must have made notes as I told her about my son and divorce.

"Thank you," I said. I never knew how to respond. Thank you

didn't feel right, but it always came out. "I'm hoping a fresh start in a new town helps."

He then told me about his divorce and how he disliked being single.

I felt uncomfortable hearing of his personal life, but I agreed with his assessment of life after marriage. "It can be lonely."

"Maybe we can do something about that," he said.

"Maybe." I didn't know what to say.

After some small talk, he thanked me for coming in.

"I think I would enjoy working here and hope you consider me for the job," I said.

He got up and shook my hand again. "You're definitely in the running." He led me back to the lobby and told me they would be making a decision before the weekend and would be in touch either way. I thanked him for his time and left.

I waved goodbye to the guard. It was such a relief to have the interview over. I could tell I felt better because I was aware of my surroundings again. A white pickup truck passed by as I was waiting to leave Sweet's, and I realized I hadn't even thought to see if anyone followed me to Kalamazoo. The truck didn't stop or turn around and with my brief glance, it looked like a woman driving.

I called Erica and told her the interview went surprisingly well. "That is until they introduced me to Dr. Madden. I recognized him. He's the one who testified at the Commissioners' meeting on behalf of Gary Jarsma. He said random source dogs were crucial to the work he did."

Erica said she was surprised I met Madden and thought it meant they were seriously considering me for the job.

"It was creepy. I almost felt like he flirted with me."

"He's known for being a womanizer. It might work to your advantage."

"That's a scary thought."

"Scary, yes, but he's the man with all the answers. The man with access to every room in the building. You might want to get to know him better. You'll be needing a new friend with your fresh start." She laughed, but her words held an ounce of truth.

"He told me they're making a decision this week. They have work piling up and need someone to start soon."

"Sounds like there's a good possibility he'll be calling," she said.

As I barreled down the freeway, I made a hasty decision to visit Sara. When I stopped for gas, I studied my Michigan map. All I needed to do was take I96 toward Muskegon and exit at 104. It would take me into Spring Lake and connect to US31. Grand Haven was just a bridge away. I called Sara and woke her. I apologized, but she insisted it was okay. She offered to take me to lunch. An hour later I was knocking on her front door. Sara wanted to go to the Morning Star Café, which was at least a mile away. We opted for walking. I'd had enough of being cooped inside a car.

"I'm craving their oatmeal," Sara said.

"Craving oatmeal? I didn't know anyone craved oatmeal."

"You haven't had oatmeal till you've had it at Morning Star. It has walnuts, dried cherries, wheat germ, sliced apples and is served with fresh fruit. It's absolutely delicious."

We walked on sidewalks the whole way, something that seemed foreign to me. The houses sported manicured lawns trimmed with flower gardens. Squirrels dodged across the walkways and roads playing Russian roulette with cars and bicycles.

The first thing Sara asked about was Cooper. Forever the romantic, she wanted me happy, and her definition of happy included marriage.

"He's becoming a bit possessive. He didn't want me to interview for the job and gave me the silent treatment before I left."

"You what?" she asked, stopping and grabbing my arm.

"It's no big deal. It's just office work."

"What do you think you'll learn by doing office work?"

"I don't know. Maybe plenty. Everything leaves a paper trail, and I'll have access to all the paper."

"When did you apply?"

"A few days ago. I had an interview this morning. That's why I'm in the neighborhood."

"You're crazy. You've gone over the edge," she said.

Her accusations caught me by surprise. I respected Sara's opinions and she made me wonder if I should revaluate my thinking. "Really? Why?"

"I just think you need to face the fact that Blue is gone and isn't coming back. You're chasing a dead end. You know I love dogs, but you're taking this too far."

"I don't know what else to do."

"Go back to Pearline. Find a job. Start living again. Appreciate Cooper."

We reached Morning Star and the conversation ended. Sara ordered her oatmeal and I ordered a BLTA--a bacon, lettuce, tomato and avocado on focaccia bread. We splurged with key lime pie. Conversation was light while we ate--Sara's work, her husband's travels, the weather and the puppies.

On the way home, we walked through downtown Grand Haven. Sara insisted we stop at a specialty boutique, Must Love Dogs. The store carried everything that you could possibly want to spoil your dog. I didn't think Cody or Shadow would appreciate a doggie sweater, so I bought them some bacon and cheese Buddy Biscuits. They deserved a special treat.

We decided to take the walkway along the Grand River to the beach. The river reminded me of Jarsma, and I told Sara about finding him floating in the river. I backtracked and filled her in on the missing beagle who disappeared from the shelter and ended up at Jarsma's kennel.

"Was he murdered?"

"I don't know. Could be. He had enemies. Not many people appreciated him taking pets from the shelter and selling them for research."

The beautiful spring day, the gentle rolling of waves and the people, young and old, strolling the boardwalk, all took backstage to our discussion. We skipped the walk on the pier and the walk along the beach. Instead we walked the sidewalks along the roads.

Back at Sara's house, she let the puppies out of their kennel. They tumbled over each other in play. They were plump and looked like they were ready for homes of their own.

"I have pictures of them on the bulletin board at my vet's office," Sara said. "They're such cuties they should go fast."

I thanked her for taking the puppies and paying for their medical needs, even their spay/neuter surgeries. The adoption fee was $95 for each pup to recoup her expenses.

"When I offer free pups no one calls. Put a price tag on them and the phone starts ringing," she said. "Go figure."

Sara walked me to my car. As we said our good-byes in the driveway, she commented on a black Impala parked across the street and down a block.

"Someone is sitting in that car. I noticed it when we set out for Morning Star. That's odd for this neighborhood."

I didn't recognize the car and could barely make out the form of someone sitting in the driver's seat. I suggested it might be someone waiting for a neighbor to get home from work.

Shortly after I left, Sara called my cell and told me the Impala followed me. It had turned around in her driveway and went in the same direction I did. I looked in my rearview mirror and sure enough, it was behind me.

"Come back to the house," she insisted.

I did as she said and went back. The car stayed on the highway, heading north. Sara met me in the driveway.

"It kept going," I said. "It was just a coincidence."

"Maybe, but you be careful. Call me when you get home."

Chapter 17

The incident with the black Impala worried me. I played it down for Sara, but it had me spooked. Did the driver of the white pickup truck switch vehicles? My eyes constantly shifted to the rearview mirror. I watched every car as it merged into traffic from each on-ramp but never saw the black car again. But then, why would he still be following me? He already knew where I had been, whom I visited and that I was heading home. I needed to be more careful. I phoned Sara as I pulled into the driveway and told her I hadn't seen the Impala again.

Cody and Shadow met me at the door. Grams and Cooper were working side-by-side when I walked into the kitchen. "I'm home," I announced.

Grams gave me a hug and so did Cooper. His first display of affection in front of Grams. It felt normal, comfortable, like wearing blue jeans. He asked how everything went.

"You won't believe it. I was introduced to Daniel Madden, the guy who testified at the Commissioners' meeting. It freaked me out, but I handled it. I don't think he recognized me. He's involved in the hiring. They want someone to start soon so they're making a decision this week."

"If he ever looks at the minutes from the meeting he'll see your name. You're listed as a guest," Grams said.

"Damn, I never thought of that."

"Odds are he won't look at the minutes," Cooper said.

"And if he does, I won't be hired. Have you heard anything more about Jarsma or the investigation into the beagle?"

They hadn't heard anything new. Dinner felt like a peace offering. The criticism disappeared and so did the suggestions on
what I should do.

Cooper kept the wine glasses full. He even made dessert––a
chocolate cream pie made with tofu. I love chocolate cream pie
but one made with tofu made me leery. I was surprised to find it
tasted just like a creamy forget-about-my-diet chocolate pie.

After dinner Grams excused herself to watch TV. She loved
the game shows, and she often took Kal with her to the living
room. She had bought him a clear plastic ball designed for ham-
sters. He could be placed inside, and as he scurried, the ball rolled
around the room. Kal got exercise and the dogs were entertained.
Lucky for Kal, they quickly lost interest in the ball and left him
alone. Cooper and I cleared the table and washed dishes. I felt
tipsy and giddy. I loved being home, and it felt sweet to be back in
the good graces of Cooper and Grams.

Not in the mood for television, I invited Cooper to join me
outside on the porch swing. Cooper grabbed a new bottle of wine
and refilled our glasses again. In the privacy of the night I told
Cooper of my worries of being hired, how Dr. Madden scared me,
and Sara's suspicions regarding the Impala.

"I don't know if I'm paranoid or if it's real. Is someone watching me?"

"I don't know either. All you can do is to keep a close watch
when you're out." He assured me I'd do fine if I got hired. That
working in the office wouldn't be as difficult as the lab.

"I'm sure you'll be able to handle Dr. Madden, too. If you
ignore him, he'll get the message."

I didn't dare tell him Erica's suggestion of taking advantage of
Madden's interest in women. Dealing with his flirtatious behavior
would be a challenge, especially since he could be key to discover-
ing Blue's fate. No sense worrying. I had to get hired first.

"What are you thinking?"

"Just wondering how I got into all this. Sara thinks I'm taking
it too far and should quit looking for Blue. I told her if I didn't get
hired it would be over." Cooper didn't respond.

I heard the TV go off. In a few seconds Grams opened the
screen door, stuck her head out and said good night. The inter-

ruption brought our conversation to a standstill. Good night was on the tip of my tongue when Cooper put his arm around my shoulder and pulled me close. His kiss soft and passionate. "Come to my room," he whispered in my ear.

"I will after Grams is asleep."

"I don't think she would care."

"Probably not, but I care."

He gave me another kiss and said he'd be waiting. We let the dogs out for last call, locked the door and turned out the lights. Cooper went to his room and I to mine.

I took a quick shower, brushed my teeth and slipped into the black lace teddy I bought while shopping in Ludington. I covered it with my tatty terry cloth housecoat. The shower hadn't sobered me. I felt sassy, sexy and alive. Every cell tingled.

I shushed Cody and Shadow and tiptoed into the hallway and down to Cooper's room. It felt odd sneaking around Grams' house. I entered without knocking. Cooper was seated at his desk, writing. He closed the notebook when he heard me, got up and greeted me with a hug and kiss. He untied the cloth belt holding the housecoat shut and took a deep breath when he saw what was underneath. He led me to the bed. I felt dizzy with belonging.

Friday started with a phone call from Jackie Jones asking if I could start work Monday. I heard myself saying yes while my mind flooded with what-ifs. When I gave the news to Cooper and Grams, they pretended to be happy for me, but I felt the riptides, those underwater currents that drag you away from shore. If you panic, you drown. If you keep cool and think, you can tread water until it weakens and then swim back to shore.

After breakfast I called Cindi. She was just heading out the door to go walk dogs at the shelter. She invited me to join her.

She gave me my own dog to walk, a black and white lab mix. She had a German shepherd. We walked the dogs on a trail behind the shelter and then let them loose in a fenced in area. We intended to clean their kennels while they exercised and enjoyed some time outside, but instead of cleaning, we stood by the fence and watched the dogs play––they tussled and chased each other like they were best buddies.

"Did you hear Sam resigned?" Cindi asked.

"No. What was his reason? Was he asked to?"

"I don't know. The police and the commissioners have been asking a lot of questions. He got a lawyer and next thing we knew, he turned in his resignation."

"That's great news. Do you know who's replacing him?"

"No, but Lindsay, who's worked at the shelter part time for years, was appointed interim director. She asked me if I was interested in a job."

"You're kidding. What did you say?"

"That I'd think about it. I have to talk to Charlie and see if I can work at the bar part-time. I don't want to give that up. If he'll let me work only Friday and Saturday nights, I'll do it."

I probed for more details regarding Jarsma, but she didn't have any new information other than the animals at his place would be transferred to the shelter as space became available. I spent the afternoon at the shelter walking dogs and cleaning kennels. I also helped clean the cat cages and played with a litter of kittens that had been brought in the day before.

After I left I headed into Ludington to shop for some work clothes. I didn't want to spend much, but I needed a couple pair of slacks. Shortly after I left the shelter I noticed a black car behind me. My stomach flip-flopped. I turned on a side street and it followed. I swerved into a driveway and it continued on, but then I saw its brake lights pop on as it pulled to the side of the road. I backed out and continued on, passing the car as it sat on the side of the road. It was indeed the Impala, but I couldn't see the driver. I didn't see the car again. I did my shopping and at home told Cooper about it.

He suggested we go for a bike ride and see if the car might be at the farm on Chauvez Road. His hunch was right. The black Impala was parked next to the white truck. Back at home we debated what to do. Call the police? Go to the farm and confront Blair and his girlfriend? Ignore them?

"They probably followed me to Kalamazoo and know I've been to Sweet's," I said.

"Could be, but why does it matter to Blair? He's just an employee at Kappies and now that Jarsma is dead and Kappies is out of business, why would he care what you're doing? I can see why Jarsma would be interested in what you're up to, but why Blair?"

We bounced speculations back and forth and never came up with a theory that fit all the evidence. We couldn't agree on how to handle the situation either. The only plan that sounded halfway reasonable was for Cooper to trail me by a couple of miles after I left for Kalamazoo on Sunday. Instead of traveling down US31, I'd take M37, a back road I had never driven before, and if Blair were truly tailing me, we'd find out.

"And if he does follow me? Then what?"

"You pull into a parking lot. He'll probably park somewhere nearby and I'll go up and confront him."

"What if he has a gun? Maybe he killed Jarsma. He could be dangerous."

"We'll be in a public place. Do you really think he'll pull out a gun and shoot us both? If anything, he'll be scared and leave as soon as he realizes we're on to him."

Grams interrupted our planning session. She had been playing cards with friends and brought in the newspaper when she came into the house. A photograph of Jarsma graced the front page. I read the article out loud, but it only rehashed old information. They still didn't have a cause of death or know how he ended up in the river. The reporter did confirm what Cindi had said--that shelter director Sam Grensward resigned among all the controversy surrounding the beagle and the shelter's relationship with Kappies. Lindsay Cook would be replacing him until a new director could be hired.

"I like Lindsay. She'll do a good job," Grams said.

I told them Cindi had been offered the job and would probably accept it.

Grams liked the idea. "She's compassionate, and that's what is needed at the shelter."

After dinner and dishes, I excused myself to do some reading. I decided to soak in a bubble bath for my reading session. I hadn't had the luxury of a bath since I moved to the farm.

I used to be an avid reader, biographies, mysteries, romances. I loved every genre. When Thomas was diagnosed with leukemia, my brain cells scattered and never regrouped to the point of concentrating on reading. I read the words, but the story never formulated. I'd reread, but to no avail. Books, which had been my favorite form of escape, became a jumble of words without meaning. I missed losing myself in a good story. I desperately needed the change of scenery a book could afford.

But it wasn't to be. There were too many possibilities pulsating through my thoughts. *Who was following me and why? Where was Blue and was he still alive? Who killed Jarsma? How would I do in the job at Sweet's? How would I deal with Madden? Was I falling in love with Cooper?*

The bath wasn't relaxing. I had too much nervous energy to sit still. After fifteen minutes of staring at minuscule holes that make up bubbles, I had enough and pulled the plug.

It was too early to go to bed, so I went downstairs to see what Cooper and Grams were up to. Cooper informed me that Grams had gone to rent a video and would be back shortly. I decided to walk down to the barn and visit Dappy and the other horses. Cooper didn't offer to come with me, but he did say the evening chores had already been done—barn cats fed and horses given grain and fresh water.

I sat in the hayloft petting Maggie and Willow. They were always in need of attention and always appreciative. Willow stood on my lap butting her head against my hand, demanding more head scratching and body rubs. Maggie rubbed against my back and my elbows, waiting her turn for a back massage.

I inhaled the memories of Gramps teaching me how to saddle a horse. I could see him standing off to the side giving step-by-step instructions—first you brush the horse's back making sure there's no dirt or burrs that will cause an irritation under the saddle. Next you put the saddle blanket on, making sure it's draped even on both sides of the horse's back. Place the far side stirrup and straps over the saddle so they don't get caught under the saddle when placing it on the horse. After that, place the saddle squarely on the blanket. Gramps had to lift the saddle in place—I was too short. But the instruction continued. Snug up the front cinch, tighten the back cinch, and tighten the front cinch again.

After the saddle came the bridle. Getting ready for a ride was a ritual that couldn't involve shortcuts.

I watched as Gramps taught Thomas the same things. Gramps glowed with pride whenever he was with Thomas, and there was nothing Thomas loved more than spending time with his Gramps.

Thomas inherited my passion for horses and could ride by the time he was six. I could hear his laughter, his silly jokes, and see his small body sitting straight in the saddle in front of me as we rode the trails. The barn was his favorite place. He'd roll around in the hay with the cats and sneak extra grain to the horses. Of course, Cody and Blue followed him everywhere, all three inseparable.

It was comforting to know Gramps and Thomas were together in heaven. I often wondered if Thomas was the reason Gramps was so willing to let go of his life. His only grandson needed him more than we did.

A new thought crept into my mind. Was Blue with them, too? I could see Gramps telling Thomas stories about the farm with Blue curled up asleep by their feet. It was a comforting image. The only unsettling aspect was how Blue might have died. If he had to go, I wanted it to be peaceful with me at his side. Not in some cold, sterile laboratory where he was alone, confused and in pain. Thinking of how Blue might have died jolted me back to reality.

I was remembering Thomas without tears. Had I accepted his death? At the moment, yes. But the teeter-totter of anger and acceptance was starting to tilt in the favor of acceptance. Maybe that's why I was starting to wonder what the hell I was doing getting a job at Sweet's. I wondered if Thomas had been alive and healthy when Blue was stolen, if I would have broken into Kappies and been so determined to get him back. I'm thinking the answer is no. My thoughts were interrupted by Cooper coming into the barn and calling my name.

"I'm up here," I said, taking a break from scratching Willow to wave to him. He climbed the ladder and sat on a bale of hay. Maggie left my side and jumped onto his lap.

"Grams is back. She's making popcorn and wants to know if you want to come watch the movie with us."

"What did she get?"

"*Little Miss Sunshine.*"

Popcorn and a movie sounded like the kind of mindless entertainment I needed. A movie would also soak up any need for conversation. Something to do together that would allow us to savor our own opinions while keeping them to ourselves.

Chapter 18

I left the window cracked open when I went to bed and woke to the whimsical sounds of birds chirping. I snuggled under the covers, listening to their peaceful coos and warbles. Sometime in the night Cody and Shadow snuck onto the bed and now cuddled together, keeping my feet warm. Nights were still chilly, but the morning air tasted sweet and healthy. I heard Grams go downstairs and knew coffee would soon be brewing.

"Come on guys, let's get up," I said, nudging my foot warmers. It didn't take much to get them excited and ready to go. I opened my bedroom door and sent them downstairs, knowing Grams would let them outside for their morning business. What would I do without my dogs while in Kalamazoo? Hopefully, I wouldn't be there too long, and if I were, I could always retreat to the farm on weekends. I took a quick shower. The sharp aroma of coffee lured me to the kitchen. Cooper had just come in from morning chores with the dogs while Grams flipped buckwheat pancakes on the griddle. I poured us orange juice and put the syrup on the table. Then I checked on Kal and fed him.

"What's on the agenda for the day?" Grams asked.

I didn't have any plans, neither did Cooper. Grams had a garden club meeting. She kept busy with clubs, ladies groups, dog boarders, church and friends. It showed how much Mother didn't know about her. Grams would be fine living alone because she was seldom alone. Her circle of friends watched out for one another. It made me wonder–– *did anyone miss me in Chicago?* I had withdrawn and closed out my friends, and they let me.

Grams suggested we go kayaking on Hamlin Lake. A son of one of her friends opened a kayak and canoe rental business and needed customers.

"I've never kayaked," I said.

"Have you canoed?" Cooper asked.

When I said I had, he assured me I'd have no problem with it. "They'll give you some basics when you get on the water."

Anything that involved soaking up the sun and breathing fresh air sounded good to me. By nine o'clock we were heading toward Ludington on US 10. Grams' directions were to take 10 to Lake Shore Drive and follow it to the east side of Hamlin Lake. Then watch for signs, freshly painted since Bob just opened for business last week.

We debated taking Cooper's bike but decided to take my car. Cooper wanted to grocery shop on the way back. At a traffic light in downtown Ludington, I spotted a white truck parked on the side of the road. It pulled into traffic a few seconds after we passed. I saw a passenger in the front seat and it looked like a woman.

"Pull into a parking lot where there are people," Cooper said.

I followed his instructions and turned into a lot for a restaurant. We got out of the car and casually went in the front door. The truck pulled into a parking lot across the street. We sat by the window where we could see the truck and ordered only coffee. The driver and passenger didn't get out.

"Let's go talk to them," Cooper suggested.

I wasn't keen on the idea, but it was a public area and hopefully someone would come to our rescue if we needed help. We went out the side door, following a family with a noisy bunch of kids. We stuck close to them as they headed down the sidewalk toward the beach. After a block we jaywalked to the truck's side of the road and snuck up behind it. The truck's windows were open, and I could hear the radio blaring rock music. We were almost in touching distance of the back bumper when the driver spotted us in his mirror. For an instant I made eye contact with him. The driver's door opened and I stopped, my heart thumped so loudly that I suspected that's what drew his attention to us. I clutched Cooper's arm.

The young man got out of the truck but didn't close the door. He looked about 20 years old, dressed in blue jeans and a tucked-in black muscle shirt that showed off tanned well-developed arms. Crew-cut hair gave him a military look or maybe a radical skinhead look. He stared at Cooper and then his face broke into a huge smile.

"Cooper?"

"Taylor?"

The next thing I knew they embraced in a bear hug. The passenger, a young woman with sun-bleached blond hair, slid out of the driver's side of the truck. She greeted Cooper like a long-lost friend, too.

"What are you doing here?" Cooper asked.

"We need to talk, but not here," the young man said. "Follow us."

Cooper and I headed back to the car. "What the hell is going on?" I whispered when we were out of hearing range of the couple.

"I don't know. I met Taylor and his girlfriend in California last year at an animal rights conference. They're friends of a friend. I have no idea what they're doing here."

"Is he Blair?"

"I don't know."

"Is it safe for us to be meeting with them alone in the middle of nowhere?"

"I think so. I don't think we have much choice."

When the white truck headed west on US 10, I pulled out behind it. It turned north on Lake Shore Drive and headed toward Ludington State Park. Lake Shore is a scenic drive with miles of paved road that runs just yards from the Lake Michigan shore. Small parking lots dot the roadside, giving ample place for people to park and enjoy the sandy beach and spectacular views. The truck pulled into a deserted parking lot. I pulled alongside it.

Taylor suggested we sit by the lake. We walked a trail between two sand dunes and found a private place behind a dune where we had a beautiful view of the Great Lake. We sat in the sun-warmed sand. Waves gently lapped at the shore and seagulls squawked as they searched the waters for food. I introduced myself to Taylor and his friend, Ashley. Cooper broke the small talk with a simple question.

"What the hell is going on?"

"After seeing you, I'm not sure," Taylor said.

"Let me ask a question," I said. "Is your name Taylor or Blair?"

The young man hesitated. Instead of answering me, he asked Cooper what he was doing in Michigan.

"Alison's grandmother is a family friend, and I'm working for her for the summer. What are you doing here?"

"The group I've been working with in California got a couple calls about dogs disappearing in this area, and they talked me into coming out and snooping around to see what I could find. I talked Ashley into coming with me. As luck would have it, Gary Jarsma had an ad in the *Ludington Daily News* for kennel help, and I got the job. I've been working for him for a couple months."

He then turned to me and said they rented a room from Blair who also worked at Kappies. Blair was as corrupt as Jarsma, and he often kept dogs whose owners might be looking for them in his barn.

Taylor said Jarsma suspected me of breaking into his kennel and letting the animals lose. He also thought I set the fire.

"He asked me to find out everything I could about you."

"So you've been following me? In the black Impala, too?"

"That's my car. The truck belongs to Jarsma, or I should say to Kappies?" Ashley said.

"Jarsma is dead. Why are you still following me?"

"You had me intrigued. I wondered what the hell you were up to," Taylor said.

"My dogs were stolen. One came back after the break-in at Kappies, but the other is still missing. A blind beagle. Do you know what happened to it?" I got excited as I realized Taylor might have an answer to the mysteries surrounding Blue.

Again he hesitated, but then he admitted remembering a blind beagle with odd eyes. "I'm sorry," he said, his voice breaking with emotion.

Ashley rubbed his back and explained how difficult it was for Taylor to work at Kappies knowing the dogs and cats that were being sold were being sent into research. But he had hoped to build a case against Jarsma and get him closed down.

"He definitely bought stolen dogs, and he had a key to the animal shelter. He would go in the mornings before the shelter opened and take any animals he wanted. He paid off the shelter director with cash. The director destroyed the paperwork on the dogs he took before their legal holding time was up," Taylor said. "Most of the dogs he got from the shelter he got legally. The county has a contract with him."

He added there were a couple young guys who brought dogs to Jarsma a couple times a month. No questions asked. He paid them $25 cash for each one. They took Cody and Blue into the kennel.

"Do you know their names? I'd like to get my hands on them," I said.

"I don't. They only dealt with Jarsma, and he always took them into his office and closed the door. But then I'd see them unload dogs from their van."

"What else was going on?" Cooper asked.

"When the USDA did an inspection two weeks ago, I secretly recorded the inspector's conversation with Jarsma. They argued on a payoff amount for a clean inspection," he said. "They agreed on $5,000 cash. Can you believe it?"

"Do you know who killed Jarsma?" I asked.

"No. He had a lot of enemies. The guy who found his beagle at the kennel wanted to strangle him, but I don't think he did. Sam lost his job because of Jarsma, and he was pissed. Even the inspector had a reason––if the bribery came out in the investigation he would most likely lose his job and probably more."

"What about Blue?"

"He's a hard dog to forget. Friendly, researchers like that."

"Do you know what happened to him?"

"He was sold. I don't know where, and the kennel records were destroyed in the fire, so it would be impossible to find out."

"You must have an idea."

"I can tell you the places Jarsma sold animals, but I don't know which one he went to."

Cooper took over the questioning again and Taylor admitted

he was responsible for the fire. Friends from Chicago came and got the cats and dogs in a cargo van and were four hours on the road before the fire started.

"I couldn't handle it any more and needed a way to put him out of business for awhile," Taylor said. "I would have killed him myself if I had to watch one more dog shipped to a damn lab. I hoped Jarsma would take the insurance money and retire. I couldn't believe it was business as usual a couple days later."

We spent two hours talking and learning of the unscrupulous ways of Gary Jarsma. I still couldn't grasp that the guy following me turned out to be someone Cooper knew. I was disappointed he couldn't give me more information on Blue, but at least he confirmed what I already knew, that Blue had been there. And we did have copies of the paperwork showing a shipment of dogs going to Sweet's right before my midnight visit. A detail we didn't share with Taylor.

Before we said our good-byes, we agreed it wouldn't be a good idea for anyone from the sheriff's department to know we knew each other. We'd keep contact to a minimum. Cooper and I watched the truck drive away and then went back to the beach.

"Let's walk," Cooper said.

We had the beach to ourselves. We took off our shoes and walked on the water-soaked sand where the waves rolled in. The water chilled my feet while the sun toasted my back.

"What do you think?" I asked.

"I'm stunned. I believe what he says, but I still can't believe Taylor is here and working at Kappies. I guess it makes sense that someone on the inside was connected to the fire. It was organized with the animals taken before the fire started."

We rehashed all our theories regarding Jarsma and Blue. At least we had one piece of the puzzle.

I asked Cooper if he still wanted to go kayaking, and he did. First, we stopped at a small sandwich shop and devoured veggie subs and chips. We reverted to Grams' directions and soon found Bob's Lake Rentals. Bob himself gave me a 10-minute kayak lesson. How to get in. How to get out. How to paddle and what to do in case I tipped over. What more did I need to know? He insisted I wear a life jacket, for insurance purposes, of course.

Bob also gave us the history of Hamlin Lake. It was more than 12 miles long and covered 5,000 acres. Surrounded by undeveloped wilderness, it touched Manistee National Forest on the north and towering dunes in the west. The lake was made during the logging heyday when lumbermen dammed the Big Sable River to make an enormous holding pond for trees felled upstream. It looked natural to me. No way could we see the entire lake during our two-hour rental time.

I fell in love with kayaking that day. It was peaceful, relaxing and a gentle way to experience nature. We paddled close to the shore, often stopping to float in the shade of the shoreline trees and watch the fish swim in the shallows. Turtles sunned themselves on logs along the shore and a variety of birds flittered and fluttered about. Relaxing. We barely spoke.

I experimented with paddling techniques, and it didn't take long to learn how to change directions and stop, or a least slow down. Two hours rushed by, and before I knew it we were heading for home. We stopped for groceries. Cooper gave me a list of what he needed and asked if I minded shopping without him. His endeavor to be invisible in the community apparently was working. If Taylor, who had been following and snooping into my business, didn't know Cooper was around, then probably no one knew Grams had a hired man working for her. It took me a good half hour to get everything on Cooper's shopping list. I had no idea where tofu was and spent too much time wandering the aisles searching for his vegan ingredients. I hid my irritation when I got back into the car. A little frustration with shopping was a small price to pay for home cooked meals, even if they were without meat.

Grams was watering the garden when we got home. She was stunned and relieved when we told her about Taylor and Ashley.

"Good for him," she said, when told he started the fire at Kappies.

Cooper headed to the barn to take care of the horses, and I hung out with Grams as she continued to water her seedlings.

"Did Taylor have any information on Blue?"

"Only that he had been at the kennel and sold. He didn't know where and the records burned in the fire." I told her what

Taylor had said about the young guys selling dogs to Jarsma for $25, no questions asked. She wondered who they were and hoped they were out of business now since Kappies closed.

Our conversation screeched to a halt when she asked if I still planned on going to Kalamazoo.

"At this point, I have to."

She didn't say anything more. I excused myself to take a shower as I felt sun drenched, sweaty, full of sand and mad at being asked the same question again. When I came downstairs, Grams and Cooper were in the kitchen cooking. It was definitely a favorite pastime of theirs. I would miss their meals and didn't relish cooking for one again.

Red wine was again the beverage of choice for dinner, and afterwards it was a repeat of Thursday evening's entertainment. Grams watched TV and Cooper and I relaxed on the porch swing drinking. And just like Thursday night, Cooper invited me to his room. I went to my room and pulled out my suitcase. Cody and Shadow watched as I loaded it with clothes. Where would they sleep tomorrow night? And the next? I'd have to move their bed to Grams' room before I left in the morning. I truly didn't want to be packing for another move. I kept telling myself I'd be back soon with an answer to my obsession. But part of me was beginning to accept that I might never know all the details regarding Blue's fate. Odds were he was dead.

When I finished packing, I tiptoed to Cooper's room. He sat in a comfy chair with his legs resting on a footstool. When I entered, he stood, placing the book he had been reading on the dresser. Soft music danced in the background and a night breeze drifted through an open window, filling the room with spring scents. Cooper greeted me with a hug and kiss.

I pulled back. I needed to talk. "What a crazy day," I said.

"Crazy in a good way. You're going to miss the excitement when you start a nine-to-five office job."

"It might just be what I need to start feeling normal again. All this intrigue is getting to me. I want an everyday life again."

He pulled me close and whispered, "I think I have what you need." So much for talking.

Chapter 19

The day flew by, and before I knew it I was driving back to Kalamazoo. Habit had me watching for white pickup trucks, black cars and any other vehicle traveling too close or at the same speed I drove. But I was alone. Truly alone.

That morning Cooper and I had ridden the horses on old logging trails in the Manistee National Forest. He packed one of his fabulous picnic lunches, and we stopped in a meadow to eat. We avoided talk of my leaving, stayed in the moment, and appreciated nature and each other's company. We made love in the sun with long slow passionate kisses. Another cherished moment. If I didn't come home Friday night, he planned on coming to Kalamazoo Saturday morning. Sounded excellent to me. One of the reasons I dreaded moving forward with my plan was it meant being away from Cooper. He wormed his way into my life, and I knew I would miss his company, his advice, his arms around me and his cooking. He and Grams packed a cooler full of meals--enough to last the entire week. Enough to share with Erica and still have leftovers.

Erica awaited my arrival and helped carry my suitcase and the cooler up the two flights of stairs to my borrowed apartment. She unpacked the containers of food, reading every label, and stocked the refrigerator.

"How long are you staying?" she joked.

"I think they planned on you joining me for dinner every night."

"It's good by me. I'm not fond of cooking."

Erica invited me to join her and Webster for a walk. We strolled the sidewalks in her neighborhood with no set destination. The summer air was filled with the earthy scent of fresh mowed grass, and early summer flowers were in full blossom. I loved walking in older neighborhoods, seeing the architecture of days gone by and the creative landscaping of city yards. Squirrels darted about, scaling trees and scampering across yards and roads. I held my breath more than once at close calls between a squirrel and a speeding automobile. There wasn't a shortage of the bushy-tailed rodents.

I filled Erica in on the latest happenings surrounding the animal shelter and Kappies. She stopped walking and gave me a huge hug upon learning the animal dealer was out of business and the shelter under new management with people who cared about animals running it.

"Such good news. One-by-one the Class B dealers are disappearing. I can't wait until they're all closed."

She remembered me talking about Cindi, and she had confidence in her without ever meeting her. "I'm sure adoptions will increase as the public becomes aware that nice people are running the shelter. She'll get more volunteers and donations."

The walk relieved the tension I had accumulated on the drive, but I knew I would still have a restless night. Erica invited me to her place for a bedtime drink, and I gratefully accepted. She surprised me with hot chocolate with Kahlua.

"It'll help you sleep. I know the night before I started at Sweet's I didn't get much sleep. I didn't sleep much the whole time I worked there."

"Any idea what I should be looking for?"

"Just scan any paperwork or computer files you come in contact with, and if they look interesting copy them, if you can. Look for an opportunity to get into the labs. Maybe you could even ask for a tour."

Erica and I exchanged life stories till after midnight. I didn't mind the late hour as I knew sleep would be elusive. The common bond of Sweet's and the alcohol made us instant buddies, and we swapped intimate details of soured relationships and heartbreak. We hugged when I got up to leave, and she wished me luck.

"I'll be sending you positive thoughts all day. Smile, they'll love and trust you."

At 7:50 the next morning I pulled up to the guard shack at Sweet's. I introduced myself, and the guard congratulated me on my new job. His name tag read Stewart. He pointed to the parking lot on the south of the building. I spotted a sign saying 'Employee Parking.' I thanked him with as much gusto as I could manage. The Kahlua had helped me fall asleep, but it didn't keep me asleep. I tossed and turned most of the night and finally got up and watched reruns of sitcoms.

Jackie sat working at her desk when I walked in. She smiled when she saw me and welcomed me with a vibrant "good morning." She then handed me a packet of papers to fill out. I answered the questions with half-truths––I didn't want them having emergency contact names and numbers. Jackie gave me a seat at a computer and pulled over a stack of file folders. She explained how to get to the program I needed and gave me a password. Data entry––and it looked like an all-day project.

"This is the most tedious part of the job. Once you get it caught up, you'll only have to do it a couple hours each week. Nobody has entered this stuff since Linda left three weeks ago."

Jackie was right. I was probably more bored than the security guard stuck in his outhouse-sized shack watching cars come and go for eight hours.

For the last hour of the day, I filed the papers I had just worked on. It felt good to be on my feet and moving. I never saw clock hands move so slowly. It reminded me of being stuck in rush-hour traffic back in Chicago. Stopping, then rolling ahead a bit, just to be at a standstill again. At 5:00 I punched out and mentally said goodbye to day one. Jackie nailed it––tedious was the word for the day. I went home exhausted and cross-eyed from staring at a computer screen. My butt ached, and my neck felt permanently kinked. I don't remember ever having sat for so long. It left me more exhausted than a day of farm work. None of the information I entered had anything to do with Blue. So, on top of being tired, I felt dejected and kept asking why I put myself through the agony of a job that kept painful memories alive. Maybe Sara and Grams were right––I would be better off if I moved on and let go of the past. I realized the negative thoughts sprang from my weariness and blocked them. I intentionally chose this path and would stumble along until I found answers.

Erica met me at my apartment door. "How was it?"

I invited her to dinner. We rummaged through the refrigerator and had a scrumptious assortment of Cooper's homemade fare––oatmeal walnut loaf, pasta salad, hummus with raw veggies and crusty wheat bread. We celebrated my first day by popping the cork on a bottle of champagne and toasting to my unproductive success.

The animals at Sweet's held a special place in Erica's heart. She thanked me over and over for getting the job and poking around to see what I could find. "I didn't know what to do next. Then Cooper and you walked up and started asking questions," she said.

After we stuffed ourselves into relaxation, we took Webster for a walk. The fresh air revived me. When we got back to the apartment, I excused myself and decided to soak in the tub in hopes of relaxing my newly-found aching muscles. I hoped to get a better night's sleep than the night before. And I did.

At 7:50 I pulled up to the guard shack for day two. I had the urge to point my car north and drive, but I didn't. I waved to Stewart and he waved me through. Jackie welcomed me with open arms and praised me for the work of the previous day. She reviewed my entries after I left and my accuracy impressed her.

"Have you ever done any transcribing?" she asked.

I told her I used to record lectures in college, transcribe the tapes and sell the written notes to students who missed the classes. Jackie laughed at my inventiveness.

"Usually I transcribe the doctor's tapes, but I'm behind in my work thanks to Linda. Do you want to give it a try?"

I felt a rush of adrenaline. What better way to learn what the researchers were doing? "I can try. I'm sure I can type fast enough, but it's always a trick understanding the words. If they speak with an accent or use words I'm not familiar with, I might have a hard time."

"Go slow, as you learn their speech patterns and terminology, you'll get faster." Jackie moved the transcribing gear to my desk and showed me how to work it. The high-tech equipment didn't compare to my old hand-held mini cassette player. It had a headset and a foot pedal for stopping and rewinding. It left both hands free for typing. Jackie explained how it worked and gave me her pass code for getting into the program I needed. She trusted me completely.

It didn't take long to get the foot-hand coordination perfected. I found myself paying so much attention to the words that I couldn't comprehend the meaning. I planned on copying all the work I did onto a travel drive to study later.

About the time my stomach began to growl, Dr. Madden strolled into the office and asked how I liked the job.

"It's not bad. There's a lot to learn, but I'm catching on." I called him Dr. Madden and he insisted I call him Daniel.

"We're informal here." He then asked if I had plans for lunch. "I'm going to Cheryl's Roadhouse for a burger. Why don't you join me?"

"I brought a sandwich, but I can save it for tomorrow. I'd love to join you."

He suggested I stop work early so we could miss the noon rush. He informed Jackie of our plans, and she nodded okay. She didn't seem fazed. I wondered if he often took office workers to lunch.

Cheryl's Roadhouse looked more like a bar than a restaurant. "The burgers here are exceptional," Daniel said.

I took his advice and ordered a mushroom burger with fries. He ordered the same, and told the server to bring two beers.

"I hope you don't mind."

"I like beer, but I shouldn't drink while I'm working."

"One beer won't hurt anything. If Jackie says anything, tell her I insisted. We have an understanding."

We made small talk about my work, and I told him Jackie had me transcribing tapes. "The terminology is difficult, but I think I'm getting it."

He offered to show me some of the work being done at Sweet's and assured me it would help in my understanding the tapes.

I told him I would love to learn more about what they did.

"A lot of it is routine third-party product testing. The government requires products with new ingredients be tested for safety before they are put on the market," he explained. His passion was medical research, and he bragged that he had received hundreds of thousands of dollars in grants to study heart disease.

"Heart disease is one of the leading causes of death in the United States," he said. "It's the number one killer of women. Most people think it's cancer, but it's not. Cancer just gets more publicity." He added that heart disease ran in his family and his father died of it three years ago.

I offered my apologizes. I understood the pain of losing someone close––that my grandfather had recently died and my son passed away from leukemia. I wasn't sure why I shared that with him. I blamed it on the beer poured into an empty stomach.

"I'm so sorry. Losing a parent or grandparent is inevitable. But one should never have to suffer the loss of a child."

I thanked him for his concern and before I melted into tears, I asked about research for children's leukemia.

"We're not working on it, but I know it's the subject of research at several leading hospitals and research facilities."

I thanked him for the work he did and praised him for helping to cure such a devastating disease. He glowed with pride, and I knew I had his trust.

When we got back to the office, Daniel said he would be out of the office on Wednesday and would plan on giving me a tour Thursday. I thanked him and told him I would be looking forward to it. He also asked me to dinner Saturday night.

"I don't usually date co-workers, but you're an exception. You're only here temporarily," he said with a wink. He stared into my eyes waiting for an answer. My pulse quickened. I felt an electricity pass between us, and it wasn't static from the carpet. I kept my cool.

"If you think it doesn't violate any company policies, I would love to have dinner with you Saturday," I said. What would I tell Cooper?

"Wonderful, until Thursday," he said with another wink. With that he left the office.

Jackie sat at her desk pretending to ignore us. When Daniel left, I turned to her. "I'm not sure how to handle this. I've never had a boss ask me for a date. He said it's okay because I'm here temporarily. What do you think?"

"Do what you please, but be aware he's a ladies man. He's been known to break a few hearts."

"It's hard to say no to him."

"I know. Just know he's not the marrying type. Have fun and don't make long-term plans for him."

I thanked her for the advice and told her I already regretted accepting his invitation.

"Go out. Enjoy a free meal. Nothing wrong with that. Just don't think it's going to turn into a relationship. Romance, maybe. Relationship? No. Daniel is a loner."

I settled back into my chair and started the afternoon stint. The second tape I worked on belonged to Dr. Madden. I instantly recognized his voice. I didn't understand the research he performed, but it involved dogs. The next two tapes were also his, and I would work on them tomorrow.

Jackie left the office a few minutes before quitting time. I took her absence as an invitation to transfer my day's work to my flash drive, which I did. She came back after I had turned the computer off.

"I think I'm getting it," I told her. "I'm so focused time flies by. Thanks for letting me give it a try."

"I'm the one who needs to be thanking you. I appreciate your willingness to try transcription. Not everyone is up to it."

"I enjoy it, so I guess it's a win-win." Little did she know how much of a win it was for me, and for Blue, too.

I waved to Stewart as I left. He gave me a thumbs up. I took it as congratulations on surviving another day.

Erica and I were settling into a pattern of a shared dinner, followed by a walk and talk. It was easy with a refrigerator stocked with Cooper's scrumptious cooking and a dog who laid his leash at Erica's feet as soon as she finished eating. We loaded the dishwasher and headed out to enjoy the Michigan summer evening.

I waited till we were out for our walk before telling Erica about my new job of transcribing tapes.

"Unbelievable! Do you realize what you're going to glean from hearing those tapes?"

"Not much. I can't comprehend what I'm hearing because I'm typing so fast. But I think I'll be able to copy the files once I get them done."

Erica stopped and gave me a hug. "Fabulous. Fucking fabulous."

It did me good to see Erica so happy. After we said our good nights, I called Cooper. He had been waiting for me to call ever since I had left Sunday. I apologized for not calling sooner. He found it unbelievable the job included transcribing tapes and that I planned on making him copies. He sounded surprised that Daniel offered to give me a tour on Thursday. He was silent when I told him I went to lunch with him.

"It's the best way to get information," I said, trying to ease his concern. I didn't dare tell him about the dinner date with the boss.

I told him I probably wouldn't be coming home Friday night, so maybe he should plan on driving down Saturday. "By then I'll have a lot of files for you to sift through."

"Maybe I should come sooner. Like tomorrow. I could pick up what files you have and bring them back to the farm to study."

"Great idea." I told him I looked forward to seeing him when I got out of work the next day.

Chapter 20

The thought of Cooper put a smile in my heart; not only had he become a lifeline to reality, he was my salvation from the eight-to-five workday, which was a jumble of boredom and intrigue. The morning sparkled, much too beautiful to be cooped inside for hours. The gentle blue sky offered a promise of a stunning day.

I waved to Stewart as I sped into the parking lot. The punctuality that comes with a new job had already slipped away; I rushed to be on time. Stewart waved back and then pointed a finger at his wristwatch. Cute. He had fun with my tardiness. But I wasn't late. I just wasn't early. I parked in the closest parking spot, grabbed my lunch and hurried to the front door.

"Good morning Jackie," I said. She stood by the sink in the break room pouring a cup of coffee. I tossed my lunch into the refrigerator.

"Good morning. How did transcribing go yesterday?"

"It started slow, but I'm picking up speed."

"Good. We need hard copies of everything. Could you print all the work you did yesterday?"

I made the copies Jackie requested and asked where they were to be filed. She told me to put them in a folder and place them on Dr. Madden's desk. She showed me where to find the key to his office door—in a key box in the office supply closet. She kept the key to that box on the top shelf of a bookcase next to it. The revelation stunned me.

"Just make sure you replace the key when you're finished. It's the only one I have to his office."

I assured her I would. Returning the key to its proper peg, I noticed tags on all the other keys in the box. I took a few seconds to read the labels; they were keys to all the rooms in the building. Crazy luck! They didn't even lock the supply closet door. Unbelievable. My winning streak continued.

Back to transcribing. Yesterday some of the tapes had been from someone I hadn't met and were about suntan lotion toxicity tests. Kal had probably been part of the test group. I wondered if they missed the little guy, and if they did, what did they think of one of their test subjects disappearing?

Jackie gave me more of Dr. Madden's tapes to transcribe. Knowing his work with heart disease involved dogs made transcription more interesting.

After four hours of focused work, I grabbed my lunch and went outside to eat. I sat at a picnic table usually inhabited by smokers. I munched down my sandwich and apple within minutes and grew restless. I took a walk for some much-needed exercise and found myself closing in on the guard shack and Stewart. I interrupted his reading.

"It's such a beautiful day, I thought I'd get some fresh air during my lunch break," I said. "Don't you got bored sitting here all day?"

"Sometimes, but I read. Makes the time go faster."

"You must go through a lot of books. Do you work full time?"

"Full time, plus some. I usually work days, but when Hank or one of the other guys goes on vacation or calls in sick, I fill in for them."

"You mean there's someone sitting out here around the clock?"

He laughed. "No. The gate is shut at 5:30 and a pass card is required to get in or out. After hours and on weekends there's a security guard inside making sure everything is secure."

"That must be as boring as this."

"Not really. Inside we can watch TV. We just have to make rounds every hour."

"Paid to watch TV, not bad."

"I don't mind it at all. So how are you liking your job?"

"For temporary work, it's fine. I'm filling in for Linda who's on maternity leave, but I bet you already knew that."

We made small talk for about a half hour, and then I excused myself to get back to work.

In the afternoon, I started to transcribe Dr. Madden's tapes. It made things a heap more interesting. The tapes were from his heart research. He was testing the long-term effects of a new cholesterol-lowering drug. The results had been excellent in rodents, and he was starting to test CL108 on dogs. At the start of the tape, he explained the research protocol. From what I could decipher, the dogs would be given the drug daily for 120 days. Blood tests would be performed once a week. At the end of the test period the dogs would be sacrificed and their organs studied.

I felt hopeful. If Blue was in this study, he was alive and would be for several more weeks.

At the end of the day, I printed copies for Dr. Madden and copied the files onto my flash drive. I placed the printed files in a folder and told Jackie I was taking them to Dr. Madden's office. I got the key from the supply closet. This time I took the time to inspect Dr. Madden's personal space. I could smell his presence in the room—a husky scent from a bottle. Definitely a man's office: dark woodwork and Ducks Unlimited artwork—a wood duck drifting on a stream, a drake mallard stretching his wings and a flock of Canadian geese flying in formation. One wall held a built-in bookcase, its shelves filled with medical books and carvings of ducks. I noticed an absence of personal photographs. No wife, no children, no grandchildren, not even any pets. Did a man who spent his day doing research on animals have pets?

I left the quiet retreat of Daniel's office and returned to clean my work area. I said good night to Jackie, waved to my new friend Stewart and raced home, tickled at the prospect of Cooper.

He waited for me on the porch steps and met me as I opened the car door. When I stepped out he greeted me with a bear hug.

"I missed you," he whispered. And I believed him.

"I missed you, too." We kissed. I led him inside, up the stairs and to the apartment.

"Does Erica know you're here?"

"She does. We had a long visit this afternoon."

I started to tell him what I had found out, but he smothered me with kisses.

"Later. Tell me later."

We made love like we hadn't seen each other for months instead of three days. After our passion we showered––igniting our love one more time. When we were finally satisfied, Cooper opened a bottle of wine and started to prepare dinner. We talked as we chopped vegetables and sautéed them with tofu in olive oil. Cooper had arrived at noon and had read the files I had left for him.

"They weren't what we were looking for," he said.

"I know, but today I hit the jackpot. I transcribed Dr. Madden's tapes and he's testing a new drug for cholesterol on dogs. The timing is right. If Blue is here, he has to be in this group. And the good news is, if I understood it right, the testing is going on for 120 days. That means Blue is alive, and we have time to rescue him."

"And how do you plan on doing it?"

"We have to break in again. But I have more good news. The keys to all the labs are kept in the supply closet, which isn't locked. Plus, I talked to the security guard, and he told me there's one guard inside after hours who does rounds every hour."

"All good information."

"Now we just have to figure out when."

"This weekend. But I don't want you involved. It might be suspicious that someone breaks in days after you were hired. I'm considering asking Taylor. I've met with him twice since you've been gone, and I think he would help. He's out of work, so he can head west as soon as he's done here."

Cooper's suggestion stunned me, but he was right.

"If you do it Saturday night, I have the perfect alibi," I said. I hated to tell Cooper I had accepted a dinner date with Dr. Madden, but I didn't want to keep it a secret.

"What?"

"Well, Dr. Madden has been flirting with me and asked me to dinner Saturday night. I thought it would be a good opportunity to learn more about him and the company so I said yes."

"You what?"

"It's just dinner." The silence that followed penetrated our cozy cocoon. The intimacy vanished. I considered offering to break the date, but then Cooper spoke. He agreed dinner with the boss would be a perfect alibi for me, and it would keep Dr. Madden occupied.

"It really is working out for the best," I said. "He asked me in front of Jackie so she knows we'll be together."

"What's he doing asking his employee on a date?"

"Because I'm temporary he says it's okay."

Cooper didn't have much good to say about the doctor. I ignored his contempt and invited him for a walk around the neighborhood. We invited Erica and Winston, but they had already gone for their evening jaunt and declined the offer.

We held hands like teenagers while we walked the city sidewalks. I asked about Grams, and Cooper said she kept busy and pretended not to worry about her wayward granddaughter. The dogs were fine too. Cody and Shadow had taken to sleeping in Cooper's room and even slipped up onto his bed after he fell asleep.

"Doesn't leave much room for me, but I don't have what it takes to break them of the habit. And I'm sure you wouldn't want me to change their routine."

I loved waking up every morning to the dogs cuddled at my feet. "I can't wait to get back home. I miss everything––Grams, the dogs, riding, and mostly you."

"Really? You miss me?"

"I do. You've wormed your way into my life. I miss you."

"Ditto. I didn't plan on falling in love, but I think I've loved you since the first moment I saw you."

"The first moment?"

"The first moment!"

Our declaration of love left us speechless and we walked in silence for several blocks. Then all we could do is small talk about the landscaping, the houses and the countless number of squirrels that peered at us from the trees.

"I feel like I'm being watched," Cooper joked as he started to count the bushy-tailed critters that seemed to track our every move. He quit counting when he reached eight.

170

Back at the apartment I showed Cooper the files I had copied. I took a candle-lit bubble bath to give him alone time to concentrate on his reading. It didn't take him long to knock on the bathroom door and ask if he could join me. He didn't wait for an answer. Instead he came in and set two glasses of wine on the ledge next to the tub.

"I think you got it right when you said there is a good chance Blue could be part of Dr. Madden's research. The timing is right and so is the breed."

Cooper disrobed as he talked, making it difficult to concentrate on what he said. He pulled his T-shirt off over his head revealing his muscular tan chest. It looked ripped in the flickering candlelight. He unbuckled his belt, unzipped his jeans and shimmed till they were around his ankles. He bent over to tug at the bottom of each pant leg to pull them off. Next he peeled his socks off. Then his black briefs.

He finally noticed I paid more attention to his disrobing than to what he was saying.

"You like the show?" he asked.

I nodded. "Very much."

He stepped into the tub and slowly settled himself into the steaming water. "It's a little hot, don't you think?"

"I like it hot," I said, flicking some water at his chest.

After he immersed himself in the bubbles, I asked him to repeat what he had been saying.

He planned on heading back to Pearline in the morning and returning with Taylor. While I was on my date, they would pay a visit to the lab.

"Hey, I forgot to tell you. Dr. Madden offered to give me a tour of the labs tomorrow. I'll find out which labs the dogs are in."

"Do you think you're up for a tour?"

"I'm not looking forward to it, but I can handle it."

"You'll make our visit a lot easier."

"I'll draw you a map so you know where the supply room is. Or maybe I can just borrow the keys you'll need for the weekend. I don't think anyone would miss them."

"You can play it by ear on Friday. Having the keys ahead of time would be nice."

After our planning session we took turns washing each other's backs. Maneuvering in the tub built for one was tricky and kinky. We finally found comfort in me leaning back against Cooper's chest–a position made for sipping wine. I felt safe and content. The lilac scented bubble bath and candles gave the room a sweet, romantic fragrance. I closed my eyes and transported my thoughts to Gram's farm where the lilacs were sure to be in full bloom.

When our glasses were empty and the water cold, we finally left our private sanctuary for the comfort of a queen-size bed with silk sheets––complements of the real tenants of the apartment.

Our lovemaking was slow, deliberate and passionate. Not the secretive quiet variety of sneaking behind Gram's back.

I woke up at 3:00 with all the possible scenarios of the next few days running through my head. I wasn't looking forward to the tour with Dr. Madden or the Saturday dinner date. Although he meant nothing to me and Cooper knew everything, I felt a tinge of guilt. I felt nervous and worried about being alone with him. I sensed his intentions weren't honorable and didn't want to upset him when I said no to his advances.

I would be glad when this was all over, but I pondered the future, especially with Cooper. *How long would he be in Pearline? Would he move back to California and face the questions law enforcement had for him? Where did that leave me?* I lay awake until the alarm went off at 6:30. We showered together, had a quick breakfast and said our good-byes. Saturday would be the day, but I had Thursday and Friday to get through.

Chapter 21

Day four. It had started with the pure joy of sharing a bed and a morning with Cooper. The anticipation of another day of work fouled my good mood. Stewart's smiling face and friendly wave as I cruised past the guard shack shifted my outlook up a notch.

Dr. Madden's car was parked in his personal parking space. I noticed the sign with his name on it for the first time yesterday when I ate lunch outside. Of course, it was the closest spot to the door. Ironically, the doctor studying heart disease walked the shortest distance in the parking lot. Maybe he should be studying exercise as a preventative measure instead of drugs. I focused my thoughts on Cooper to change my attitude.

Jackie gave me more tapes to work on and said she would be in a meeting for a couple hours. I found a handwritten note on my desk from Dr. Madden saying he would be in meetings until early afternoon and planned on giving me the tour at 3:00. He signed it Daniel and then drew a little heart with an arrow through it. My eyes involuntarily rolled and my dread intensified.

The tapes were from the toxicology department. I put my mind on autopilot and did the work without comprehending the words. I really didn't want to know what tests were being performed on hapless little creatures. I had filed the invoices for dozens of mice and rabbits. What would Daniel show me this afternoon? And how should I react?

Jackie wasn't back by noon. I repeated yesterday's routine for lunch. Stewart seemed pleased to see me. I asked how long he had been a security guard. Everyone loves to talk about themselves, and Stewart was no exception. I learned he was a retired police officer and took the job at Sweet's after his wife died.

"I needed to get out of the house. I was going crazy being alone and found myself watching way too much TV."

"Isn't this boring after the excitement of being a cop?"

"Boring can be good. I don't worry about being shot here or having the need to shoot anyone."

"Did you ever shoot someone?

"Only once, during a convenience store robbery. The guy was high on meth and pulled a gun. I had no choice. Luckily, I didn't kill him."

"That's good."

I hesitated, but I had to ask. "Do you carry a gun?" Stewart was always in his guard shack with its door closed, and I couldn't tell if he had a gun somewhere.

"I do. That's one of the reasons I got the job. I have a permit to carry a gun."

"That's crazy. Why do you need a gun here? What are they scared of?"

"Animal rights fanatics. They picket here every once in awhile."

"Really? I guess I never thought of it."

"Everyone is entitled to their opinion, but in the last few years they've become brazen. So it's a concern."

We spent the rest of my lunchtime comparing life in Kalamazoo to Chicago, which gave us a couple of laughs. I watched the time and soon had to say goodbye to get back to the office. I didn't like the fact that the security guards carried guns. I had thought they were wanna-be cops who carried radios to call for help, and maybe a billy club and mace. Or a stun gun.

Back at my desk I watched the clock in dreaded anticipation. I did a New Year's countdown but with five minute segments instead of seconds.

Dr. Madden––Daniel––was punctual. As the little hand hovered at 3 and the second hand swept past the 12, he strolled into the office. He was impeccably dressed in a dark blue suit with a white shirt, his silk tie a swirl of different shades of blue.

"I didn't forget," he said.

"I didn't think you would. I found the note."

He waited while I put the computer to sleep and untangled myself from the headset.

"Ready?" he asked.

"I am."

He led the way down the hallway past his office. After several offices, a locked door blocked the hallway. Daniel pulled a set of keys from his pocket and unlocked the door. Behind the door the hallway continued.

Daniel talked about the testing Sweet's did for various companies, all of it required by the U.S. Food and Drug Administration. Any new drug had to go through rigorous research to ensure its safety for human use. He gave me quick peeks at unoccupied labs that smelled sterile and were filled with stainless steel counters and tables that reflected the fluorescent lights. He introduced me to the head of the product testing division. I recognized his name from the tapes. I smiled and offered platitudes and asked questions. He answered with short simple answers. I noticed several closed doors that Daniel ignored. I wondered if my tour was going to be as sterile as the labs were.

One of the labs was devoted to a long-term study of the causes of skin cancer, a subject Daniel knew quite a bit about.

"Skin cancer is increasing each year. Statistics indicate one out of seven people in the United States will develop some form of skin cancer during their lifetime," he said.

He added that most dermatologists believed in a link between childhood sunburns and skin cancer later in life, and cancer was often the cumulative effect from sun exposure.

"But some scientists are looking into the effects of chemicals that go into commonly used cosmetics and what effects, if any, they may have on the skin when it's combined with sunlight."

"You mean it could be the combination of my makeup or moisturizer with the sun that might cause skin cancer?"

"That's what we're trying to find out."

He said we weren't allowed in parts of the lab because lighting was strictly monitored and at the moment lights were prohibited. I felt for whatever animals were living in darkness.

The next two labs were vacant.

"We're between two big jobs right now so it's a little slow," Daniel said as I followed him into an empty lab. With no one around, he slipped his arm around my waist and pulled me toward him. Before I knew it, he was kissing my lips and slipping his tongue into my mouth. Surprisingly my brain calculated the results of any possible reactions while I kissed him back. Getting upset would most likely end the tour. Pushing him away might anger him, resulting in an abbreviated tour. Pretending to appreciate his advances might mean an extended tour. The kiss lasted until I realized he wanted more than a kiss. When he unbuttoned the top button on my slacks and started to unzip the zipper I pulled away.

"Not here," I said.

"We're alone. No one will catch us."

"I can't. Not here," I repeated. Luckily he respected my wishes. He even zipped my pants back up and fumbled with the button until I interceded and took care of it. He was more adept at undressing than dressing. He gave me another kiss and smiled.

"Until Saturday night."

I couldn't tell if it was a question or a command. I nodded.

The tour continued. After passing several doors, which Daniel said were all unused labs, we reached an area I was familiar with, the loading dock. It, too, was empty. We headed up the hallway Cooper and I had explored. The lab where we had seen the rabbits was empty, but it still had a chemical smell fused with a primitive odor. I had all I could do to not gag. Daniel didn't seem to notice it.

"We just finished a big project here," he said. The entire room, floors, walls, equipment will undergo a thorough cleaning before it's used again."

"Why is that?"

"To keep the results clean. We don't want the possibility of contaminating the results of new projects."

The next few labs were where Erica said dogs were used. Cooper and I hadn't had time to investigate them.

Daniel stopped in front of one of the doors and turned to me before opening it. "This is where I do my work," he said. He was like a kindergartner at show-and-tell time. He was proud and pleased with himself and assumed I would be, too. He opened the door and stepped aside. I could see desks, computers and filing cabinets. As soon as I entered I could smell dog, or a least a kennel that hadn't been cleaned.

Daniel pulled out a notebook and showed me his application for a government grant of $1.5 million.

"It's for a two-year project studying heart disease. We've had good luck with a new drug we tested on mice. We were approved to study it on dogs. If it passes that stage, it'll go on to human clinical trials."

"That's great. I'm impressed," I said.

"I'm excited. It's going well."

"This is all new to me. How do you test a new drug?"

"After months of analyzing cholesterol, we arrived at a new drug––CL108. Actually it's the eighth version of the drug, and it's the most promising. We give the dogs various amounts and then draw blood weekly and see what impact it is having."

"It sounds simple."

"That's because I'm giving you a simplified version," he said.

He failed to mention the dogs would be sacrificed at the end of the study. I waited for him to take me in to see the dogs, but he didn't. When he shelved the notebook and turned towards the door, I had to act, but I didn't know what to do. I blurted out, "Can't I see the dogs?"

"They're just dogs. Nothing special to see."

"Please?" I said with my biggest saddest puppy-dog eyes as I took his hand in mine. He was a sucker for a caress.

He stared at me for a couple seconds then said, "Whatever you want." It came with another one of his sweet smiles and a devilish wink.

My heart started pounding and the adrenaline flowed. Not from Daniel, but from the thought of seeing what was on the other side of the door. Could this be it? He opened the door and stood back so I could enter first.

The dogs, each in their own kennel, were frantic with excitement at our presence. They barked, but what came out was a hoarse raspy sound, almost like a cough.

"What's up with their bark?"

"They've been debarked."

"Debarked?"

"It's a simple procedure of cutting the vocal cords. Their howling would drive everyone nuts. This is much quieter."

"I never heard of it."

"It's routine. I apologize for the stench. The cleaning crew comes in at night," Daniel said.

"The room needs a window you can open."

"Open windows could contaminate results," he said.

Daniel's cell phone rang, and he excused himself to answer it. While he chatted I strolled around looking each dog in the eyes. The dog in the last kennel, maybe it was my imagination, seemed a tad more frantic than the rest. Was it Blue? Had he recognized my smell? Maybe my voice? His bark was pitiful. Then I saw his eyes. *Blue. It was him!*

Daniel had his back to me. I got down on one knee and put my hand up to Blue's kennel and whispered, "Blue, how you doing? Mama misses you." I knew he would go crazy, but all the dogs were spinning, jumping and acting like dogs who had been penned up too long. I continued to sweet-talk Blue until Daniel turned around. Then I deserted him and started paying attention to the other dogs.

"Ready to go? Or do you have more questions?"

"How long does the study continue?"

"It started three weeks ago. It'll go about three more months."

I couldn't concentrate on what Daniel said the remainder of the time. My thoughts were spinning like a milkshake in a blender. They were jumbled and unfocused. *I found him*, was the only concrete thought I had. *I found him!*

Daniel walked me back to the office. Jackie sat at her desk, so his goodbye was simple and professional. I thanked him for taking the time to show me around and said I looked forward to dinner Saturday night. He gave me a slight nod and left.

I had an hour left to work. I did transcription for half of it, then printed the hard copy and copied the files for Cooper. When I got the key from the supply room, I looked for the key to the lab room where Blue was being housed. I took it off the key ring, pocketed it, then randomly selected another key and switched tags with it. When I took the paper copies to Daniel's office, he wasn't there. I was thankful I didn't have to see him again. I left the folder on his desk.

Cooper, Taylor and Ashley were waiting for me in my apartment when I got home.

"He's there," I blurted out. "I saw Blue." Tears streamed down my face as I tried to explain how I had seen him. Cooper got up and gave me a hug. He excused us and led me to the bedroom, leaving Taylor and Ashley alone in the living room.

"How did he look?"

"Okay. I think he recognized me, but I don't know for sure. All the dogs were crazy with excitement at having company. I only had a few seconds alone with him."

"We'll get him. Don't worry."

Then I remembered my conversation with Stewart. "The security guards carry guns," I said. "I had another chat at lunchtime with the guard and he told me."

"I don't plan on any security guards knowing we're there."

After I was calm, we returned to the living room. I apologized to Taylor and Ashley.

"No need. It's totally understandable," Taylor said. He was tan and his hair a bit sun bleached. No doubt he was taking advantage of the Lake Michigan beaches in his off time. Ashley, dressed in short shorts and a halter top, looked so young. Even though our ages were less than a decade apart, I felt eons older.

Cooper had prepared dinner before I came home from work. I went and knocked on Erica's door, told her the good news and invited her to dinner. After we ate, the five of us sat around the table and planned Cooper and Taylor's Saturday night visit to Sweet's.

I drew them a map and gave them the lab key. Cooper would have to pick the loading dock door and hope the security code Erica had given us still worked.

"I've been keeping my eyes open for a list of security codes but with no luck," I said.

"I think they rely on the security guards too much and don't worry about things like keys and codes," Erica said.

"That's what it looks like to me, too," I said.

Cooper and Taylor memorized the layout of the inside and outside of the building. They calculated their every step and movement.

"How many dogs will you be able to get?" I asked.

"We talked about that," Cooper said. "And we decided that with a guard in the building, it would be too risky to take more than one."

Now I felt guilty. "Only one? You're leaving the rest?"

"It's too time consuming, and the dogs will be too noisy. We'll need to give Blue a sedative to get him out."

"I hadn't thought of that. Do you have a sedative?"

"Grams gave us a half pill. She had some from a hyper dog she boards that needs a little help sleeping."

"Maybe you could give it to the security guard," I said jokingly. Everyone laughed. I'm sure they felt as bad as I did about leaving the rest of the dogs behind.

We reviewed the plans one more time before going to bed. Erica said good night and Taylor and Ashley retreated to the guest room. Cooper and I went to our room but stayed up talking.

"Once you get Blue I'll work another week and then find an excuse to quit," I said. "I could even blame it on Dr. Madden––how I don't feel comfortable around him."

"I can't wait till you're back at the farm. It's not the same without you. Everyone misses you."

We finally turned out the lights and let our bodies do the talking. It was a good night, except I woke too early and started playing the what-if game. What if they got caught? What if one of them got shot? What if the sedative didn't knock out Blue? I kept reminding myself––one more week and waking next to Cooper would become routine. No more hiding our love from Grams

I ate breakfast and kissed Cooper goodbye. Two more days.

Chapter 22

It was another clock-watching day. At 4:00 Dr. Madden stopped by to confirm our dinner date.

"I'll pick you up at 7:30––I need directions to your place."

"I'll just meet you at the restaurant." I didn't want to be dependent on him for transportation. I also didn't want him knowing where I lived, which was a moot point since I used the apartment's address on my resume.

"No date of mine drives herself to dinner."

"Can't handle an independent woman?" I teased.

He laughed and asked for directions again. I relented. After all he was my alibi, and I needed to be with him as late into the night as possible. I just had to play the cards right and not put myself in a compromising position. I was determined we would stay in public, no going back to his place. I knew one thing––my feet would be sporting comfortable shoes in case I needed to walk home.

"You're going to love the restaurant I've chosen. It's quiet and quaint and the food is superb. Reservations are at 8:00."

"I can't wait."

Cooper, Taylor and Ashley were watching TV when I got home. I attributed it to nerves. They needed a mindless diversion.

"Everything under control?" I asked.

Cooper greeted me with a hug and kiss. "It is. We're just playing the waiting game."

They were in hiding until time to go to Sweet's. Security cameras were everywhere, and they didn't want their faces inadvertently recorded. They had another day of being holed up in the apartment.

"Dr. Madden is picking me up at 7:30 and we have reservations for 8:00." The announcement was greeted with silence. "What time are you going in?"

"We were hoping to wait till after dark or at least dusk, but the sun doesn't go down until after 9:00 this time of year. But we think earlier will be okay. Game five of the Stanley Cup Finals starts at 8:00. The Detroit Red Wings are playing and it's a big thing around here. Most people will be glued to their televisions. Hopefully the security guard is a hockey fan."

"Most guys are," I said.

"Remember this, I'm missing the game for you," Taylor said with a laugh.

"If you're fast, you could be back in time to catch the end," I said as I headed to the kitchen. "What's for dinner?"

"Erica is cooking. She's bringing the food down here at 7:00."

"I'll go see if she needs help."

Erica had things under control. The water for the spaghetti was near boiling and the aroma of garlic filled the small apartment. Erica wore a plaid green and yellow apron and looked like a domestic goddess. She greeted me with a hug.

"How are things going?" she questioned.

"As well as can be expected. It's going to be a long wait until tomorrow evening. Cooper doesn't appreciate me going out with Dr. Madden. I'm worried about them going back to Sweet's. Yet I can't wait for them to get Blue. But I feel bad they can't get all the dogs."

She opened the refrigerator and handed me a bottle of wine. "It's open. I love to sip as I cook. Join me."

I poured myself a glass and topped hers off. Webster came and sniffed my hand. I missed Cody and Shadow. I refused to think too much about the possibility of Blue coming home. It didn't seem real. As Erica checked the pasta, kept an eye on the garlic bread and ripped lettuce for a salad, my mind wandered to the past year. It was too much change to comprehend.

Erica added chopped tomatoes, green peppers and cucumbers to the lettuce and handed me the bowl, along with two bottles of dressings to carry to the apartment. "Everything else will be done by the time you get back."

Ashley and I set the table as Cooper and Taylor helped Erica carry the food and wine. She had four bottles. Dinner was scrumptious. The merlot eased everyone's tension and conversation flowed. I listened as Cooper, Taylor and Erica discussed the status of animal rights in the United States. I had turned off the TV and put The Best of Sheryl Crow in the CD player. As the alcohol eased the anxiety, my listening switched from the conversation to the upbeat tempo of *A Change Would Do You Good*. The title line repeated itself like an affirmation ... *A Change Would Do You Good, A Change Would Do You Good.*

A change had done me good. It wasn't the change I would have personally selected, but it was the change I got, and it was good.

I drank the last bit of wine from my glass and got up to get another bottle. I did a little dance on the way to the refrigerator. Cooper got up and joined me. We had never danced before. His moves surprised me, but they shouldn't have. I knew he had moves. The next song was the slow melodic *Home*. In the kitchen Cooper wrapped his arms around my waist, and I rested my head on his shoulders. We held each other tightly and slow danced.

This is home, home
And this is home, home
This is home.

The song ended and we kissed. Without a word I got the bottle and we returned to the dining room. We talked, drank and ignored tomorrow. It was after midnight when Erica excused herself to go to bed.

"I'll come over in the morning to help clean," she said. Dirty plates and silverware still sat on the table.

The room was spinning when I lay down in bed. The last thing I remembered was Cooper giving me a back rub. In the morning we were all sporting hangovers. Another diversion. Nobody wanted breakfast, only coffee. Erica came over and we loaded the dishwasher and cleaned the table.

During our confinement, we learned Taylor was a news junkie. He spent the day watching CNN. I called Grams. I worried about her being alone, but she sounded fine. I told her Cooper would be back Sunday, and I hoped to be home the following week. I didn't want her to worry about us, but I had to tell her the news.

"We found him, Grams."

"Blue?"

"Yes. I got a tour of the lab and saw him."

"Now what?"

"Cooper is going to get him." She told me to tell him to be careful, and she would be praying. I thanked her and told her I loved her.

By mid-afternoon the guys were starting to think of food. Cooper made sandwiches, but I couldn't even stomach the thought of eating.

At 6:00 I started getting ready. The atmosphere in the apartment was subdued. I wore a sleeveless knee-length black dress with black leather flats. Erica loaned me a pearl necklace and matching earrings.

"You're wearing that?" said Cooper when I walked into the living room where the TV was still on CNN.

I ignored him. "You guys need to go to Erica's now, in case he comes early." Taylor turned off the TV and left with Ashley. They both gave me a little wave as they left. I turned to Cooper.

"Please, don't make this harder than it is. It's nothing. Just part of the plan." I gave him a hug, and he apologized.

"You know my thoughts will all be with you. I truly appreciate you doing this for me," I said.

"I love you." That was all he said. He turned and left. I watched him go and felt like putting on my blue jeans. Maybe I was wrong to wear a sexy dress. Dr. Madden didn't need any encouragement. I changed into black slacks and a white cotton blouse. Simple and uninviting. I rushed to Erica's apartment and knocked on the door. She answered, and I said I needed to see Cooper. He came to the door. I twirled like a model.

"Is this better?"

He laughed. "Much better."

I gave him a quick kiss. "See you tonight."

Back at the apartment I watched out the window for Dr. Madden's black Mercedes. At 7:30 it pulled up. I grabbed my purse, started down the stairs and greeted him at the front door. We exchanged hellos and walked to the car. He opened the door and I got in. I felt Cooper watching my every move from the upstairs window.

"How are you doing this evening?" Daniel asked.

"Fine, thank-you. And you?"

"Excited at the prospect of being with you tonight."

I wondered what he meant. "I've been looking forward to our dinner, too."

He laughed. "Ever the little vixen, aren't you."

"No, just a woman looking for a night on the town."

"That you shall have."

I expected the restaurant to be downtown Kalamazoo, but he drove in the opposite direction of the business district. "Can I ask where we're going?"

"You can ask, but I won't tell. I want it to be a surprise."

My concern increased the farther we got from town. There were so many turns that I lost track of where we were. I was lost. I started watching for street signs, but before I spotted one, Daniel put on his turn signal and turned onto a narrow driveway with no house in sight.

"Where are we?" I demanded.

"Home. I've worked all day to prepare us a three-course meal. You didn't know one of my hobbies was cooking, did you?"

"I had no idea."

The driveway was at least a half-mile long. Daniel parked the car and like a gentleman he walked around and opened my door. He took my hand and helped me out. I stared in disbelief. It was a log home. A wrap-around porch hugged the entire outside. At the back of the house, the porch was at ground level, but in the front, it rested on wooden pillars. The house sat on a bluff overlooking a lake, and as far as I could see there was nothing but water and woods.

"It's beautiful."

"It is. It's my sanctuary. It's where I come when I need solitude."

"I feel like I'm in the middle of nowhere."

"You almost are. It's a private lake, and I own the surrounding 200 acres."

I felt doomed.

The inside was as spectacular as the outside. The great room had a cathedral ceiling with crisscrossing beams. A massive stone fireplace filled one wall, and nestled in a corner was the kitchen. It had stainless steel appliances and a stone island with a granite counter top. An antler chandelier hung above the dining table.

"Let me give you a tour."

"I'd love one."

Also on the main floor was a laundry room, bathroom and guest bedroom. In the lower level, which had a walkout facing the water, was a recreation room complete with a bar, big screen television and a pool table. Upstairs, a loft office overlooked the great room. There were two bedrooms, which Dr. Madden quickly bypassed. He led me into the master suite. Four skylights in the vaulted ceiling filled the room with natural light. A king-size bed dominated the room. Its massive headboard matched a wardrobe and dresser. A sitting area was tucked in one corner. French doors led to a covered balcony overlooking the lake. The master bath had a walk-in closet that was larger than my entire bedroom back home. The floor was gray tile, and a whirlpool tub sat on a deck made of the same gray tile as the floor. There were two steps to get up to the deck and another step to get into the tub. A huge window overlooked the woods. I could only imagine what it would be like to soak in a tub, with jets of water massaging my body as I relaxed among the treetops and watched the clouds drift past.

"It's built for two," Daniel said, as he put an arm around me and pulled me close. "Dinner can wait."

"It's beautiful, almost beyond words." I ignored his arm on my waist and his suggestion and walked back into the bedroom. I opened the French doors; from the balcony I could see the lake and what looked like a boathouse.

"Do you have a boat?'

"A fishing boat and a couple kayaks."

"Are we having fresh-caught fish for dinner?"

"Fish, but not fish I caught. Salmon."

Back downstairs he showed me the outside patio where he had a table set for two, complete with a white linen tablecloth, bone-white china and candles. He pulled out one of the chairs and motioned for me to take a seat.

"I'll be back in a moment with our appetizer."

He returned with a bottle of wine in a tub of ice. On his second trip he carried a platter of toasted sliced baguette and a bowl of seasoned diced tomatoes.

"Bruscetta," he said as he pulled his chair close to mine. "And pinot noir." He filled two glasses of the red wine and then topped a baguette slice with a scoop of the tomato mixture and handed it to me. I took a careful bite. I didn't need diced tomatoes tumbling down my chest. It tasted wonderful.

"It's the best I've ever had," I said. And I didn't lie.

It was a beautiful evening. The only thing wrong was the company. How I would have loved it to be Cooper serving me food and drink instead of Dr. Madden. The thought brought me back to the reality of the situation. What was Cooper doing at this exact moment?

Daniel interrupted my thoughts. "For the main course we're having lavender honey-glazed salmon with arugula and fresh berries."

"Sounds delicious. Can I help?"

"No, but you can come in the kitchen and keep me company while I prepare it." He sat me on a bar stool next to the island. I felt like a child watching a parent cook. He glazed the salmon with a mixture of honey and dried lavender. He then seared the salmon in hot oil until the glaze caramelized.

While he kept an eye on the salmon, he tossed a bowl of arugula with a homemade vinaigrette he had made earlier in the day. He flipped the salmon in the pan and then put mounds of arugula on two plates. When the salmon was cooked, he put a slice on each pile of greens. He sprinkled homemade focaccia croutons over the top, along with fresh red raspberries and blueberries.

"Isn't that beautiful? Almost too pretty to eat," he said.

"I'm impressed."

He carried the plates to the patio, filled our glasses and surprised me by saying a short prayer. I thought of Cooper as I sank my fork into the salmon. He would definitely disapprove of eating fish, and I felt a little twinge of wrongdoing. His life philosophy had rubbed off on me one bite at a time. But I have to admit the salmon tasted wonderful, tender with a sweet crunch to every bite.

"This is absolutely fantastic. You could be a chef in your next career," I said.

"It's one of my favorite meals. Very heart healthy."

I tried to go easy on the wine, but Daniel refilled my glass every time I took a sip. I tried to stop him, but he ignored my pleas. I began to worry about what would happen after the meal, so I quit drinking. The full glass could go to waste. When I finished my salmon, Daniel picked up both our plates.

"And for dessert, chocolate mousse," he announced.

"I'm so full, I'm not sure I can eat any more."

"It's light. You always need a touch of sweet to top off a meal."

Daniel was on his way back with the mousse when his cell phone rang. He sat the mousse down and looked at the called ID. "Excuse me, I have to answer this," he said. He went back into the house, and I couldn't hear his conversation. I prayed that nothing had gone wrong at the lab.

A few minutes later he returned and apologized for needing to cut the evening short. "Something has come up that needs my immediate attention. I need to go to the office. I can drop you off at home on the way."

"What is it?"

"There's been a break-in at the lab, and the security guard shot someone. The police are on their way, and I need to get there as soon as I can."

"Oh my," I said. I didn't know what else to say, and that was probably the perfect reaction to have to his news.

He ushered me to the car, and we were soon speeding back to town. All I could think about was who had been shot? Cooper? Taylor? How bad? I refused to entertain the thought that one of them may be dead. Not possible.

When we got back to my apartment, Daniel walked me to the front door and kissed me good night. "I'm so sorry," he said. "I hope you'll take a rain check and let me make it up to you."

He was gone before I could answer.

Chapter 23

I watched the taillights of Daniel's Mercedes disappear into the night and then raced inside. My apartment was empty, so I rushed to Erica's.

"Alison, I'm glad you're here," Erica said.

"What happened? Daniel got a call saying someone was shot."

"It's Cooper. He's okay. We don't think it's serious."

Taylor and Ashley were sitting beside Cooper who was lying on Erica's bed. I hurried to his side. "What happened?" I asked.

"The guard apparently isn't a hockey fan."

I heard a whimpering coming from the corner of the room. It was Blue waking from his tranquilizer. Beside him lay a second beagle, "You got two?"

"We didn't want them to focus on one missing dog. They could trace it back to Kappies and possibly to you," Taylor said.

"Smart," I said, turning my attention to Cooper. "How are you?"

"I don't know," he said pulling the blanket back that had been covering his legs. He had a blood-soaked bandage on his left thigh.

"We need to get you to a doctor."

"That's what we've been trying to tell him," Taylor said. "But he refuses. He knows they'll be watching for him."

I held Cooper's hand and looked him in the eye. "You need medical help."

"I can't risk it."

I thought for a moment, and an idea popped into my head. "I can take you to Sara, she's an emergency room nurse. She'll know what to do."

"Where is she?" Erica asked.

"Grand Haven. It's a two-hour drive, maybe three."

"Are you willing to go there?" I asked Cooper.

He nodded yes.

"I'll go with you," Erica said.

With a plan in place I turned to Blue. He lay on his side, his eyes slightly open. I sat on the floor next to him, cradled his head in my lap and stroked his head and body. I could feel every rib. He had been plump when he disappeared. "You're going to be okay, Baby Blue. Cody is waiting for you," I whispered in his ear. I could feel his body relax at my touch. The other beagle started to wake too. I patted his head and told him he was in a safe place. I turned to Taylor and Ashley and asked if they would drive Blue to the farm on their way back home to California.

"He needs to be kept hidden. His eyes will be a giveaway if they look for him," I said. "You can break the news to Grams about Cooper too." The second beagle would go with them to California.

Taylor helped Cooper to my car. We put him in the back seat with pillows and blankets. I carried Blue to Taylor's car and kissed him goodbye. "See you soon, bud."

I hugged Taylor and Ashley goodbye and thanked them for their help. I promised I would call when we knew more. Taylor asked if he could talk to me for a minute before they left.

"I just want you to know we also took a laptop computer. It was sitting on the desk asking to be taken," he said.

At the moment it didn't matter to me. I acknowledged the information and asked what he would do with it.

"When we get back to California I'll give it to someone who knows more about computers and research, and we'll see what they can find."

We gave Cooper two Tylenol PMs to ease the pain and help him sleep. I crawled into the backseat with him and put a pillow on my lap for his head. Erica played the chauffeur. Before Cooper drifted off he told me a bit of what had happened. Getting in was uneventful; they were in the lab when the security guard made his rounds. They assumed they had an hour before he came around again.

"But we assumed wrong. For some reason he came back in less than fifteen minutes, maybe he suspected something. I don't know. Anyway, we were by the back door when he spotted us. He ordered us to stop, but we ran. Luckily Taylor was carrying the dogs—we had them in a backpack. I heard shots and felt something hit my leg. I kept running, adrenaline I guess. I made it back to the car before I collapsed." He asked about my evening.

Cooper was asleep before I finished telling him about my date. I kept close tabs on his breathing. I didn't know the extent of the injury. When we were about a half hour from Sara's, I called and asked for a favor.

"It's not more puppies," she said.

"No, but when you find out you might wish it were puppies."

"What is it?"

"Cooper. He's been shot. We don't know how bad it is, and he refuses to go to a hospital. You're the only person I know who has any medical training."

"How long before you're here?"

"Thirty minutes or less."

"I'll be waiting." I thanked her. I owed several people an awful lot. How would I ever repay them?

I directed Erica to Sara's house. Sara opened the garage door, so we could pull the car inside. No need for neighbors seeing us carrying an unconscious man into the house. She directed us to put him on the bed in the guest room. She had towels, hot water and a first aid kit sitting on the dresser.

Sara tried to wake Cooper, but he was groggy.

We told her we had given him Tylenol PM for the ride. "It's just as well that he's sleeping. This isn't going to be pleasant." We removed his pants. Taylor had cut the pant leg open to bandage it. Sara removed the bandage while I looked the other way. I wasn't good with blood. Erica handed Sara what she asked for and didn't hesitate to stand at her side, watching her every move. After cleaning and probing the wound for a few minutes, Sara announced that it looked like the bullet was still in the leg.

"I hoped it had passed straight through, but there's no exit wound. He needs to see a doctor. The bullet needs to come out, and I can't do it."

"Are you sure? Odds are they'll be on the lookout for someone with a bullet wound, and he'll end up in custody. They'll figure out who he is and discover he's wanted in California, too."

"I don't see any other way."

"Okay then, how do we get him to the hospital without being asked questions or even being seen?"

"There are no cameras on the south side of the hospital. You can drop him off and call the police. Or we can wait till he wakes up, and maybe he'll be able to walk himself in. If we wait till morning, I'll be there. I go in at 6:00 on Sundays."

"Is it safe to wait that long?"

"It's not bleeding any more, so it's okay to wait a few hours."

Cooper seemed to be resting comfortably, so Sara decided to get some sleep. She gave Erica a pillow and blanket so she could sleep on the couch. I pulled a rocking chair next to the bed and didn't sleep for one minute. A desk lamp cast a dim light throughout the room. In the quiet of the night I could hear Cooper breathing. I watched his chest rise and fall with every breath. In my mind I replayed our times together–our first meeting, riding to the lighthouse, kayaking, picnicking, helping Grams plant the garden, falling in love.

I heard Sara get up a 5:00. Cooper shifted his body and winced. He opened his eyes.

"Where are we?" he asked.

"At Sara's in Grand Haven."

"What's the verdict?"

"The bullet is still in your leg, and she can't get it out. You need to go to a hospital."

"Is she sure?"

I held his hand and nodded yes, tears trickling down my cheeks. "I'm so sorry."

"Don't worry. It'll be what it is."

Sara came in to check on him. Cooper tried standing and was able to take a few steps. We decided I would drop him off where there were no cameras.

"Wait till after 6:00; I'll be at work. I'll be able to assist the doctor with the initial diagnosis and make sure they take good care of you."

We had one hour. Sara left us alone.

"I'm so sorry I got you into this," I said.

"It's not your fault. I knew there was a chance of getting caught. At least we got Blue out. If we hadn't gotten him, this would be harder to take."

"What do you think will happen?"

"At the least, they'll figure out who I am and send me back to California. I'm not sure what will happen there. As far as Sweet's, I don't know what will happen. Cross our fingers, say a prayer and hope for the best. That's all we can do."

He made me promise not to contact him. "I don't want you getting caught or even questioned. They could charge you with all sorts of things if they knew you were involved. When I feel it's safe I'll call you. We can keep in touch through my grandmother and Grams. They write each other."

The hour seemed like a minute. Sara knocked on the door and said she was ready to leave. She helped Cooper sit on the side of the bed and helped him put on his ripped, bloody blue jeans. Although in pain, he could walk. We helped him to the kitchen where he could rest before making the short walk to the car. Before she left, Sara told Erica and me to come back to the house after we dropped Cooper off and to put the car in the garage again. She doubted if she would dare call with an update but would be home around 3:00.

Cooper and I said our good-byes before getting to the hospital. The main entrance to the hospital was on the east side, the south side had a sidewalk and landscaping. Cooper got out, and Erica and I watched him limp along the sidewalk to the front of the hospital. Then I drove away. We both cried. Back at the house, Erica made a pot of coffee. Neither of us could stop crying. We watched TV, drank coffee and waited for word from Sara. I called Taylor and updated him. Then I called Grams. She said Taylor and Ashley spent the night and left at dawn. Blue and Cody were doing great. They sniffed each other and then acted like they had never been separated. Shadow acted jealous but accepted Blue.

"Whenever Cody lies down, Blue and Shadow both have to be next to him, touching him."

"I wish I could see it."

Before she asked, I told Grams about dropping Cooper off at the hospital. "We're waiting to hear from Sara on how he's doing. I can't even go see him." I tried not to, but I started crying again.

"It'll be okay. It'll all work out."

"I know it will, but this isn't the way it was supposed to be." She would have none of my whining.

"You knew the risks, so did Cooper. Now you live with the consequences."

She was right. I quit feeling sorry for myself and told her I'd call when we knew more.

We greeted Sara at the door. "What happened?" Erica and I both asked before she could say a word.

"He's fine. They did surgery to remove the bullet shortly after he arrived. There was already a bulletin out, asking the hospital to be on the lookout for a gunshot wound. Before the surgery Cooper denied any involvement to the break in. He did give them his real name, so it's just a matter of time before they realize he's wanted in California." She held out her hand to me.

"What?"

"It's a present."

I held out my hand, palm up. She dropped something into it, but I didn't recognize it.

"It's the bullet they removed from Cooper's leg," she said with a chuckle. "The damn thing disappeared and no one could find it."

I was speechless.

"They won't be able to tie him to Sweet's without it," Erica said.

"Does he know you have it?"

"He does. I checked on him before I left. He was awake and I told him. He said to tell you not to worry and that he loves you."

"I don't know what to say." I started crying again.

Sara made us sandwiches and promised to keep an eye on Cooper and give me daily updates.

"I can't believe we're leaving him here," I said.

"You have no choice. They don't believe him––they have a guard outside his door. It's not like you can break him out. You can't visit him either. You'd be asked a ton of questions. They'd figure out who you are and you'd be in jail, too. He needs to quit running."

Soon Erica and I were heading back to Kalamazoo. This time I sat in the passenger's seat.

Silence devoured most of the trip. What more was there to say? Before I knew it, I was alone in my apartment. How I missed the camaraderie of the friends I hadn't even known two months ago. This change I didn't need. I sat on the couch and sobbed.

When I got up to grab another handful of tissues, I saw a police car roll to a stop in front of the house. My heart started beating double time. I froze in place and stared out the window. Two officers got out of the car and headed toward the front door of the house. I waited for a knock on my door, but it never came. Instead I heard footsteps walk past my door. They were going to Erica's apartment. My knees were shaking as I sank to the floor. I stayed there repeating over and over in my head, "be safe, be safe, be safe." It seemed like forever, but finally I heard footsteps going past my door again, this time in the opposite direction. I pulled myself up to the window and waited for the officers to come into view. They were alone. After they drove away I hurried to Erica's. She looked calm, almost in a trance.

"I saw the police car pull up. I almost died," I said.

"They were just fishing. They don't know anything. I'm on their list of animal rights sympathizers. I'm not surprised they showed up."

"I didn't expect it," I said. She gave me a hug and told me to be strong.

"The only thing they will be suspicious of is if they figure out you live in the same house that I live in, and I'm betting they might. We have to say we don't know each other. It's just a coincidence that we live in the same house."

"Got it."

"You found the apartment on Craigslist. And don't call or e-mail me. They can easily trace calls and read personal mail."

I rehearsed my story until it was ingrained in my brain. With the new facts straight I returned to my apartment. When I remembered I had to go to work the next day, I popped two Tylenol PMs. They knocked had Cooper out, and I hoped they would do the same for me.

I woke to the alarm and was so groggy I didn't remember where I was, but then it all seeped into my brain, and I didn't want to wake up. It took a force to drag myself from the bed.

I drove to work and instead of Stewart waving to me from his booth, he stepped into the driveway and motioned for me to stop.

"What's up?" I asked

"There was a break-in Saturday night, and the police want the building closed to staff till at least Wednesday."

I couldn't formulate a reply. I just stared at him.

"You can go home. You have two days off work," he said.

Finally I mustered up a simple "What happened?"

"I've been ordered not to discuss it, but a news crew was here yesterday, so if you watch the news you should see something about it—can't say if it'll be accurate."

"Okay then. I guess I'll see you Wednesday." With that I turned the car around and went home. Erica had already left for work. I got my lap top computer out and found the online version of the local news. One of the top stories was the break-in and shooting. The report gave background information on Sweet's and showed old footage of the lab being picketed by animal rights extremists. A female reporter stood in front of Sweet's and said the owner of the research company confirmed animals were stolen, but wouldn't specify what kind or how many. It ended with the reporter saying the police didn't have any suspects. She gave a telephone number to call if anyone had information on the case.

It took 30 minutes of sitting alone in an empty apartment for me to decide to drive home. I considered leaving Erica a note on her door telling her where I had gone, but I worried the police would return and find it before she did. She had a key to my apartment, so I left her a note on the kitchen table. I said I'd be back Tuesday night.

Chapter 24

I called Grams before I left and warned her that her wayward granddaughter was returning to the nest. I worried about the welcome I'd receive after the shenanigans I had being pulling. I vowed to reform my ways. What choice did I have? My mission had been to rescue Blue; mission accomplished! Too bad the consequences were so damn high.

I drove straight north up US 131, through Grand Rapids, to US 10. From there it was a straight shot west. I worked hard to keep my speed at 70 mph on the expressway, knowing I'd have a heart attack if I heard sirens and saw red and blue strobes in my rearview mirror. With the windows rolled down, I inhaled the fresh air, and all was good until Cooper popped into my thoughts. I imagined him lying in a hospital bed alone. No visitors. Tears filled my eyes, making it hard to see, hard to drive. I turned on the radio and picked up an AM station, WOOD 1300. Talk radio with a local show, Mouth 2 Mouth with Scott and Michelle. It was the distraction I sought--entertaining and absorbing chitchat. I cranked the volume to loud to drown out my thoughts. No more tears. No more second guessing decisions and choices.

Ninety minutes later I pulled into Grams' driveway. She sat on the porch swing waiting for me. The dogs, except for Blue, romped in the yard, chasing and wrestling with each other. They almost knocked me off my feet with their rambunctious greetings. Blue lay at Grams feet. Grams and I hugged, and then I sat next to Blue and stroked his back. He sprawled on his side soaking in the attention, his tail wagging, thumping on the porch floor. I cradled his head in my hands and kissed his face. "Welcome home, Blue Boy," I whispered in his ear. His whole body wiggled. He got up and gave me sloppy kisses on my cheeks. My heart ballooned with joy having him home where he belonged. I thought of the other dogs still at Sweet's and wished they could all be rescued. I questioned if the knowledge gleaned from animal research was worth the ethical cost.

"I hope you're home for good," Grams said.

"I wish. It would be suspicious if I didn't go back. As soon as I can quit gracefully, I will. How's Blue doing?"

"He seems okay. I miss his howling. I try not to laugh at his raspy little howl. Poor guy. He's eating good. Other than losing his bark and being thin, he doesn't seem to have any ill affects from whatever he went through. But then dogs are forgiving creatures," she said. "He still follows Cody, and he plays with Shadow like they're old friends."

I called the dogs and put them in the fenced-in portion of the yard before Grams and I went inside. I would never again leave them loose in the yard without supervision. Thanks to Jarsma, I even had a hard time relaxing when they were in the fenced yard.

"Are you hungry?" Grams asked.

"Not really, but I haven't eaten much so I should be hungry." Her question made me think of Daniel's delicious dinner, which made me wonder what he was up to. I didn't relish seeing him again on either a personal or professional level. I was surprised he hadn't called after he abruptly ended our date. I worried that he may be suspicious of me. I hoped he was just overwhelmed with the break-in, but how overwhelmed could he be? Only two dogs missing. The breach of security could easily be remedied so it wouldn't happen again.

I sat at the kitchen table while Grams busied herself putting together a quick lunch. We spent the next hour eating and drinking lemonade while getting caught up with each other's lives. Grams made it very clear she didn't appreciate the quiet when Cooper and I were gone.

"I don't like living alone. Not because I'm old or scared. I like human companionship, someone to talk to, someone to cook for, someone to eat with."

"I'm with you. I don't like a quiet house either, especially when I don't even have a dog to talk to."

Grams laughed and admitted she talked to the dogs.

"Have you seen this?" she asked, handing me a newspaper clipping from Friday's paper. The headline read, *Local Man Arrested for Murder*.

I read the article. Sam Grensward had been charged with the murder of Gary Jarsma. "I thought the two of them were friends."

"More like business partners. And like most partners, it sounds like they had a falling out."

The article stated Grensward confessed but insisted Jarsma's death was accidental. He panicked and decided to get rid of the body by dumping it off the bridge into the river. He didn't admit any wrongdoing in running the shelter but did say there might have been some misunderstandings. He wouldn't elaborate on advice from his attorney.

"I'd say they both got what they deserved," I said.

"I'm glad he's gone. Anyone will be better than him."

Later I went to the barn and whistled for the horses. Dappy responded to my high-pitched call and led the other two horses in the race to the barn. I gave them each treats and led Dappy into the barn and saddled him. I called the dogs. Cody raced to my side with Blue and Shadow right behind him. The scene made me smile, then laugh. But the ride wasn't the refuge it used to be––Cooper was missing. I never dreamed I'd be trading Blue for Cooper. It was shortsighted to think returning to the farm would ease my guilt or loneliness.

I called Cindi at the shelter. She was surprised and pleased to hear from me. I asked if we could get together. She was too busy with an influx of dogs to talk and suggested we meet for dinner at Scotty's in Ludington.

I helped Grams weed the garden and later mowed the lawn, a job Cooper used to do. I welcomed the work. I loved being outside, and it was good to be tired at the end of the day.

I met Cindi at 6:00 at Scotty's. Already she seemed like an old friend, and we greeted with a hug. I glossed over the latest happenings in my life and told her Grams had shown me the article about Grensward.

"I was shocked to hear it, but it makes sense," she said. "With Patrick Carlson asking questions and threatening a lawsuit against the county, I'm sure the situation was tense. Somebody was going to be blamed for Patrick's dog disappearing from the shelter and both Jarsma and Grensward were equally guilty and greedy."

"They're both out of the shelter, that's what's so great," I said. "How are things going there?"

"You won't believe this, but the county commissioners voted in favor of making me the new shelter director. Lindsay Cook, the interim director, didn't return to work after the police asked her questions about Grensward. She left her keys and a letter of resignation on the front counter. I called the county controller, and he came and picked up the letter. The animal control officers are starting to uncover how many animals have been illegally taken from the shelter, and Lindsay must have been involved."

"I'm stunned. I liked her and thought she was as dedicated to the animals as you."

"It surprised me, too, but rumor has it Jarsma paid her cash to look the other way. Money talks."

"But, congratulations on the job. The commissioners couldn't have made a better choice. So what changes are you going to make?"

Cindi glowed as she talked of her plans. She was the perfect person for the job. "It's going to take time, but I think we're on the right track. There's more than $3,500 in the forfeited spay/neuter deposit fund, and the commissioners voted in favor of us using it to spay and neuter animals before they're adopted. Right now we require a refundable deposit and a contract that says the new owners have to get the animal fixed to get the deposit back. But many people don't do it and forfeit the money, and the county doesn't have the manpower to enforce the contract. Soon the animals will be fixed before they go to their new homes."

"That's great. Something that should have been done years ago."

"We're negotiating with veterinarians in the county to do reduced-cost spay/neuter surgeries to make it affordable. The adoption fee will include the cost of the surgery. We're also going to offer a free spay surgery for female dogs and cats for county residents who bring in litters of puppies and kittens. It's crazy to have the same people bring in litter after litter."

"That's a great idea."

"And now that the shelter isn't giving animals to research, more people are volunteering. We've increased the hours we're open and are considering being open seven days a week. Why be closed on the days most people are off work? We're also working to put more animals on Petfinder."

Cindi had a long list of improvements and changes she wanted to make. "My goal is to make it a no-kill shelter, where we find every adoptable cat and dog a new home. And I'm looking for a trainer who will help with the dogs that have behavioral issues."

"Pretty lofty goals."

"Lofty, but doable with the right people––people who are committed to the idea. That's why I'd like you to come work with me. I think we'd make a great team."

"You're offering me a job?"

"Full-time if you want it."

"I'll have to think about it ... and I couldn't start right away."

She laughed. "That sounds like a yes."

"It does, but not a definite yes. I need to think on it. My dad has been telling me I should get a job, and I am starting to feel like I need to do something."

Cindi asked what I had been up to the last few days. Although I felt I could trust her, I couldn't tell her the truth. The fewer people who knew the whole truth the less chance of it leaking to the wrong people. I told her I had been visiting my friend Sara in Grand Haven. Not a total lie. We talked for more than two hours with most of the conversation revolving around the shelter. It was exciting to know positive changes were happening.

When I got home I sat at the kitchen table and called Sara to see what news she had of Cooper.

"What timing. I was just about to call you," she said.

"Sorry, I couldn't wait. I'm going a little nuts wondering."

"First of all, he's doing fine. His leg is healing, and there's no sign of infection. They know he's wanted in California, and he's still a suspect in the break-in at Sweet's. In the next few days he'll be transferred somewhere, but I don't know where yet."

"Do you get to see him?"

"I shouldn't. He's not my patient and it might look odd if I show too much interest in him. But on the other hand, everyone knows I feel sorry for patients who don't have family or friends. So I feel safe seeing him once a shift."

"You saw him today."

"I did. He said to tell you not to worry. He's doing okay. His parents are supposed to be here tomorrow. He sends his love. Oh, and he asked about Blue."

"I can't believe he asked about Blue. Tell him Blue couldn't be better. It's like he never left. I'm glad his parents are coming."

"Me too."

"Tell him I miss him, and that I'm back at the farm because they closed Sweet's until Wednesday. Tell him it isn't the same here without him and that I love him, and I'll be waiting for him. No matter how long it takes."

Later that evening Taylor called. He was relieved to hear Cooper was okay, but disappointed the authorities discovered he was wanted and a suspect regarding Sweet's. He promised to keep in touch.

I helped Grams with the evening chores, giving grain and fresh water to the horses and feeding the barn cats. The mosquitoes were too thick to sit outside, so we sat in the house and talked until bedtime. I let the dogs out one last time and climbed the stairs to my room. I felt like the Pied Piper with Cody, Blue and Shadow following me to my room.

I wasn't anywhere near ready for sleep. I popped open my laptop and searched the Kalamazoo area television news sites for updates on Sweet's. One report said they had a person of interest in custody. I assumed it was Cooper and hoped it wasn't Erica. They didn't say anything more about missing animals, but they did say records were missing that would set research back by months. Must be the computer Taylor took.

I changed into my pajamas and tried to do some reading, but concentration eluded me. Instead I turned out the light, and sat near one of the open windows and stared into the night. Refreshing cool air drifted into the room. The random flicker of fireflies dotted the darkness––a private show put on by nature. Rustling noises of nocturnal critters doing whatever they do when the sun goes down broke the quiet.

Once again I found myself contemplating the changes in my life over the last several months. It was unsettling how fast things could change and what twists and turns fate played with my life. I saw the truth in the old saying: The only constant in life is change. I didn't like change, but I was learning to adapt.

Staring into the night was like seeing into a crystal ball. What I needed to do was suddenly clear––at least for the next few days. In my life, long-term goals were a joke.

I would go back to the apartment tomorrow evening. I would go to work Wednesday and find a reason to quit as soon as possible. Maybe Dr. Madden's advances could be my excuse. I'd take the job at the shelter and wait until Cooper returned. It didn't matter how long. I would wait. I'd keep busy and enjoy the time with Grams. I had a plan.

It felt good to crawl into my own bed, my own pillows and sheets. The best part was the dogs; they didn't even wait till I was asleep to jump onto the bed. They cuddled so close I could feel their body heat. I didn't feel quite as alone. It was almost as if Blue had never left.

But sleep didn't come easy. Nor did it stay. For some reason I woke at 2:10 and was instantly alert. I listened for unusual sounds, but the only thing I heard was the heavy breathing of sleeping dogs. I felt safe knowing whatever woke me didn't wake them. But there I was thinking again, forever thinking. And all I could think of was Cooper. My heart ached. I missed him with every breath. Finally I got up and went to his room. The dogs woke and followed. Cooper's belongings were still there. A shirt draped over the back of a chair. His riding boots behind the door. Books were stacked on the desk along with a notebook. I opened it. It appeared to be a journal. I refused to invade his privacy, closed the notebook and put it in the top drawer. I climbed into Cooper's bed, buried my face in his pillow and pulled the covers up around my neck. His scent was strong and it filled me with peace. I felt his warmth. Enveloped in the memories of his love, I slept.

Chapter 25

The dogs woke me with their restlessness. Their nails clicked on the hardwood floor as they paced about the room. Once in awhile they wrestled like bored little boys. It took me a moment to realize I was in Cooper's room. It was 8:30––I couldn't believe I had slept so late; no wonder the dogs were antsy. I took them downstairs, let them out into the fenced yard and waited for them to do their business. A note from Grams said she had gone into Ludington to a garden club breakfast. On her way home she'd get groceries. I was on my own for a few hours. I showered, made toast and sat on the porch swing drinking coffee. It was another beautiful summer morning. Birds were singing and I already took the warmth and green of summer for granted. While relaxing on the swing, I had the idea of writing Cooper a letter. I would take it to Sara and she could smuggle it into him. Maybe they would think his parents took it to him. It didn't matter. Grand Haven was a minor detour on the way to Kalamazoo.

I spent the next two hours composing a generic letter, making sure there were no clues to my identity or to any of the events of the past few days and weeks. I wrote about my Blue car and how it ran great after getting it back from the shop. How I hated to be without a car and it was good to have it back. I wrote about gardening and how my family, especially my grandmother, was enjoying the summer. I mentioned getting a new job and how I would be working with Cindi. I also told him how my boyfriend was being deployed. I didn't know where, but I was worried and would miss him. It was unclear how long he would be gone, but

I'd keep busy until he returned. I thanked him for his friendship and all he had done for me in the past. I asked if he remembered the picnic at the lake and what a good time we had. I wished him luck and told him the family would keep him in our prayers. I signed it Maggie. Maggie was his favorite barn cat. I imagined Cooper reading between the lines and laughing at my attempt to write in code.

When Grams got home, I asked if she would read the letter to make sure there were no clues that would give away my identity. She laughed as she read it.

"Good hints," she said. "I think he'll catch on. I don't see anything that'll give you away. Even signing it Maggie is off-base."

"I'm going to take it to Sara on my way to Kalamazoo so she can deliver it."

"I'm glad you let me read it. I guess I didn't realize things were getting so serious between the two of you."

"I denied it at first, but I couldn't help myself. He's special and so patient and understanding, I couldn't help myself."

"I'm happy for you. I sensed he was special the first time I met him. It's just too bad he's in so much trouble."

"I'll wait. Cindi offered me a job at the shelter, and it'll keep me busy. I can wait."

Grams was pleased that I'd be working at the shelter. She mentioned she might volunteer, and I knew Cindi would be pleased with her help and insight.

By 3:00 I was cruising down US 31 toward Grand Haven. A few hours of hanging out with Grams had been relaxing. I wasn't looking forward to tomorrow, but I was looking forward to returning to the farm as soon as possible. I left Sara a message that I would be stopping by for a brief visit. I hoped she would come straight home from work. If not, my plan was foiled, and I would have to leave the letter somewhere outside her house. But my worry-induced attempt at a Plan B was a waste of time. Sara called me back immediately; she was already home. She had a split shift and would be going back to the hospital that evening.

"Perfect," I said. I told her about the letter. She said she could get it to Cooper that night. Nights were slow, and she'd already planned on visiting him during her break.

Sara was a steady force in my life, and seeing her always had a calming affect on my attitude. She greeted me with a heart-felt hug and tea and homemade cookies . She didn't have any more news of Cooper but knew he was still at the hospital. She would sneak up to see him on her break and promised to call me when she got home.

"No matter how late. If I go to bed I'll have the phone on the night stand."

We walked down to Lake Michigan. Even though it was cool for June, people were out sunning themselves, but only young kids were brave enough, or maybe excited enough, to go into the cold lake water. The campground at the state park was full of trailers and tents. A festive atmosphere filled the park with people sitting around chatting and snacking.

"To be so carefree," I said.

"No matter the problems, when it's vacation they're left behind," Sara said. "It's always uplifting to walk in the park. The attitude is contagious, at least for the time you're here."

The walk was invigorating and burned off some of my anxiety. With Sara's encouragement, I felt better about going back to work in the morning and finding a reason to quit.

"You just don't want to make them suspicious. The break-in occurs soon after you start and then you quit shortly afterwards. Wouldn't look good."

"I know, but I want out."

"Play it by ear, but keep your cool."

I was in Kalamazoo by 7:00 and at the apartment by 7:20. Erica waited for me. She hadn't heard a thing from anyone since we left Sunday and only knew what she watched on the news. She was relieved Cooper was okay but dismayed he was under guard and being investigated.

"I don't think they can tie him to Sweet's. The bullet they removed from his leg disappeared. What else is there? His story is he got into a fight. Someone pulled a gun and he got in the way of the bullet. He passed out and next thing he knew, he was being dropped off at the hospital. He keeps asking if they found his motorcycle yet."

"Will they want to talk to whomever he was with?"

"Probably, but he was with people he had just met. He's been traveling by himself. With any luck, they'll just send him back to California for questioning in the fire at the horse slaughterhouse."

I asked if the police had been back to talk to her a second time and she said no. She felt comfortable with their reaction to her answers during the first visit. "I'm not worried. I refuse to think about the negative possibilities."

"I think we're good. I just have to be cool at work and figure out a way to quit." Erica gave me the same warning Sara did, not to give them a reason to be suspicious of me. We stayed up till midnight talking. Even then I was still wide awake––what did I expect after sleeping in so late?

Sara called. She had been able to get the letter to Cooper, and he looked well. She said she'd call when she had more news.

I knew I wouldn't sleep well, so I took two Tylenol PMs. I knew they would knock me out. I needed a restful night of sleep and the pills would do it. I worried that I might become an over-the-counter drug addict. But the need for sleep overpowered my concern.

Dread and a sense of impending doom rode with me to Sweet's the next morning. So much had happened since I had last worked. It seemed as if I had been gone for weeks. In reality, it had been four days. Stewart greeted me with a big smile and wave. It lessened my fear. But then I spotted Dr. Madden's car in its parking spot, and my stomach knotted. I focused on my breathing to steady myself.

Jackie sat at her desk.

"Good morning," I said.

She looked up, smiled and echoed my greeting. It felt normal.

"Can I ask what's been going on?" I asked.

"If you've been watching the news, you know as much as I do. I just got here ten minutes ago and haven't talked to anyone yet."

"I have been watching the news," I said.

"We'll have to wait and see what Dr. Madden has to say."

"I saw his car in the lot." It sounded lame, but I was at a loss for words. "Anything in particular you want me to do this morning? Or should I continue what I was doing Friday?"

Jackie shrugged her shoulders. "It all needs doing."

"Is everything okay? Are you okay?"

"Honestly, I don't know. I've tried to find out what's going on, but I get nothing. I don't understand. So I'm waiting."

"I'm sorry."

"There's nothing to be sorry for. You haven't done anything wrong."

With that I went to my desk. Jackie had no idea what her words meant to me. *I hadn't done anything wrong.* But I felt bad Jackie was out of the loop. She seemed like an insider to me. I got the impression she knew Dr. Madden intimately, and he didn't keep secrets from her.

I put my mind on autopilot and started transcribing tapes. At 10:00 Dr. Madden came in and asked if I would come to his office. I tried to stay on autopilot. I didn't say anything. I took off my headset, sat it on the desk and followed him out of the room. I felt like I was being summonsed to the principal's office. Like I had murdered someone and was being led to a firing squad. Jackie was already seated in his office waiting for us. Dr. Madden asked me to take a seat. He then sat down behind his desk. His gaze shifted between Jackie and me as he spoke. It was all business.

"As you must already know, there was a break-in Saturday evening. The security guard shot someone, but whoever it was escaped. We thought we had a suspect, but it's not panning out. Some valuable research data was taken. The Board of Directors met yesterday and decided to put everything on hold until they can get an understanding of what happened. This means we'll finish what work we have started and put everything else on hold."

"What about your project?" I asked.

"It's being terminated."

"Terminated? Why?"

"I can't go into details."

"I'm sorry. I know what it meant to you."

"Thank you. What this means to you, Alison, is you're out of a job. You'll get two weeks severance pay. Jackie, you'll stay on a few days to help get everything wrapped up. I'm not sure if or when you'll be called back after that. We'll work out an agreeable severance package."

"I don't understand," Jackie said. "On the news it sounded like a minor break-in, a couple dogs missing. I don't see how that can result in the place closing."

"I'm sorry I can't disclose more information. For now it's the best I can do."

In disbelief, Jackie and I stayed seated for a few moments. Dr. Madden stood, clapped his hands and told us we could leave. I looked at him and there was no hint of anything personal having gone on between us. I got up and left. Jackie followed. We talked for a few minutes in the hallway. Then I gathered my stuff and said goodbye to her. She gave me a hug and said she was sorry.

"I don't understand what's going on," she said again. I felt sorry for her.

I half expected Dr. Madden to appear before I got to the door, but he didn't. I was relieved; yet disappointed. It was all too odd. But as soon as I got to my car, I felt an enormous sense of freedom. It was over. I stopped and chatted with Stewart for a few minutes. I told him I enjoyed getting to know him and regretted I lost my job. He was surprised by the news.

"Everyone is tight lipped. I don't have any idea what's happening," he said. "I'm sorry to see you go. You're one of the few people who acknowledged me when you drove through. I'll miss you."

I went back to the apartment, gathered my stuff and left a note for Erica. I invited her to visit at the farm whenever she felt things had cooled enough. I hoped she would keep in touch. I couldn't get out of there fast enough. By noon I was heading home. By the time I got to Grand Rapids, I decided to take the scenic route home––via Grand Haven.

Sara wasn't home. I left a note on my car that I went for a walk and would be back by 3:00. The blue sky and cool air invigorated me, so I made my way to Morning Star Cafe. After lunch I took the long way back to Sara's, window-shopping along Main Street and strolling the boardwalk along the Grand River. I even stopped at the pet boutique, Must Love Dogs, and bought gourmet biscuits for the dogs. I bought an ice cream cone and sat on a bench to watch boats in the channel. Sailboats motored out to the Big Lake along with yachts and fishing boats. I loved the earthy smell of the river. Tourists strolled the river walk and a few joggers and bicyclists wove their way between the slow walkers. I left the boardwalk before it entered the state park and merged into the pier, the home of Grand Haven's landmark lighthouse. From there I followed sidewalks back to Sara's.

It was on the last leg of the trip back that I began to entertain the idea of visiting Cooper in the hospital. Did I dare? I recalled what Dr. Madden said about the suspect not panning out. If he wasn't a suspect in the Sweet's break-in, maybe I could pretend to be a friend from California. After all his parents had been notified and were in town to see him. They could have told other people, and close friends might have wanted to see him. I got excited at the prospect of seeing Cooper. I couldn't wait to get Sara's thought on the idea.

Sara was home by the time I got there. "He was excited to get the letter. He was expecting his parents so I didn't stay."

Before I asked her what she thought of me visiting Cooper, she gave me the bad news. Cooper had been taken away sometime during the morning. She went to see him at lunchtime and his room was empty. Rumor had it he was being taken to California. Tears trickled down my face. I couldn't help but cry. How ironic that at the same time I was being set free, he was taken into custody.

"It's almost more than I can take," I said.

"No, it's not. You've handled worse. Much worse. Focus on Cooper's love and the fact that he's okay physically. He could have been killed."

"You're right." She made me feel guilty for getting Cooper involved in my problems.

"In the big picture, it's just a minor complication," she said.

I really didn't want to hear what she had to say. No doubt she was right, but I needed understanding, a shoulder to cry on. I wasn't ready for the hard-core reality of the situation. Part of me had hoped and thought Cooper would be released and come back to the farm. I was in my own personal fantasy world. My way of avoiding the truth was to deny it.

I thanked Sara profusely for all she had done for me: for being a friend I could always count on, for taking the puppies, for helping Cooper, and for sticking with me through all my ups and downs––especially the downs. "You're right. It'll work out and I do know how fortunate I am that Cooper didn't get hurt any worse than he did."

I cried most of the way home. Luckily traffic was almost non-existent. I felt the same abandonment and loneliness after Thomas died and my marriage fell apart. I was numb.

Chapter 26

A soothing rain is falling outside my open bedroom windows. A wisp of cool air drifts into the room and is delightfully refreshing. It's been a month since Cooper was hauled off to California. I heard from Taylor, who visited him in jail, and Grams received two letters from her longtime friend Lucia–Cooper's grandmother.

From all accounts Cooper is coping with the situation. But what choice does he have? He has a lawyer, and they're considering a plea deal. They worried that a jury would see him as a domestic terrorist, and he'd be sentenced to years in prison. I send him messages through Taylor. But what can I say? I'm sorry. I miss you. I love you. I'm doing okay. The weather is great.

I started work with Cindi at the shelter two weeks ago. It's emotionally draining. I didn't realize there were so many ignorant and uncaring people in the world. They bring in litters of puppies and kittens and think we will find them homes. Don't they realize the majority of their neighbors are also dropping off litters? Who is supposed to adopt all these animals?

Cindi did recruit a vet to do spay surgeries for the females who produce the incoming litters. The majority of the owners are thankful for the free surgery. In the long run it will make a difference. In the meantime we resort to euthanasia. I hate it. But for the moment there is no alternative.

The shelter is full. Foster homes are full. We've extended the hours we're open to make it easier for people to adopt. We have photographs and biographies of animals on Petfinder. We're working with animal rescue groups, which help with dogs, but there are just too many cats and kittens. Cats are proficient breeders. Kittens as young as six months or younger can have babies. They can have several litters in a year, and it's common for a litter to contain six kittens. All of them are sweet, lovable fluff balls who deserve a home of their own.

I'm bringing my work home...literally. We have three new barn cats who I couldn't stomach being killed. Thankfully, Grams agrees with me. What's another barn cat as long as it's sterilized?

I got a snail-mail letter from Erica. She hasn't been contacted again regarding Sweet's. She's comfortable with the situation and is ecstatic that Sweet's may permanently be closed.

Taylor gave the laptop to a national animal rights group that has been fighting against animal research. Preliminary findings revealed Sweet's was falsifying research results. It looks like Dr. Madden was remiss or maybe arrogant enough to keep the real results on his personal computer along with the results the company released or published. It was his personal laptop that Taylor stole. I often wonder if he mistakenly left it in the lab because of his excitement of our date. Wishful thinking. I never heard from him again.

Blue has taken to following me around. Probably because of the extra kisses and hugs. I still can't believe he's back home.

So my plan stands. Stay with Grams, work with Cindi and for however long it takes, wait for Cooper.

The best news is I got a letter from Cooper. Written in his own handwriting. What a treasure it is. He smuggled it to his sweet grandmother to mail to me. I won't reveal what he said. But I will say I read it every day, and will do so until he returns to me.

Epilogue

Dog 281 was inspired by my sister's black Labrador retriever, Fraser, who disappeared from Montcalm County in mid-Michigan in 2000. She did everything she could think of to find him:

She hired a pet detective.

She put up hundreds of posters with the word REWARD in bright red letters.

She distributed postcards with Fraser's photograph and description.

She frequently checked the county shelter as well as shelters in surrounding counties.

She ran a "Lost Dog" ad in the local daily newspaper for a year.

Despite her efforts, Fraser never came home. It was if the world was flat, and he fell off the edge.

Fraser was a 6-year-old couch potato who loved being taken for walks. Fraser disappeared when my sister and her husband were on vacation and his routine was interrupted. He had been left in the house with the doors unlocked. When my niece came home from school the door was open and the only thing missing was Fraser. It was in January, during a stretch of colder than normal temperatures.

Fraser was wearing a collar—a brand new one that Santa had just brought him. But Santa hadn't switched his tags from the old collar to the new one.

Montcalm County was (and still is) home to a USDA Class B animal dealer. In Judith Reitman's eye-opening book *Stolen for Profit––How the Medical Establishment is Funding a National Pet-Theft Conspiracy,* (Pharos Books, 1992), Reitman details how family pets can end up in medical research.

There are currently eight USDA Class B animal dealers who sell cats and dogs for research in the United States. Three of them are in Michigan.

Did Fraser paw the door open that cold day in January? Possibly, it was an old wooden door that didn't latch unless pulled tightly to ensure it was closed.

Did he take himself for a walk, get lost in the nearby woods or swamps, and die from exposure?

Did someone find him so that he became a couch potato in their home?

Or did someone enter the home and steal him?

Did Fraser somehow end up in the hands of a Class B animal dealer?

We may never know.

As I was putting the finishing touches on this manuscript, the Physicians Committee for Responsible Medicine published information about experiments at Wayne State University in Detroit, Michigan. The University continues to use dogs from animal shelters for heart research. The following information is from PCRM's web site, www.pcrm.org.

Dec. 16, 2011, Physicians Committee for Responsible Medicine

Dog Experiments at Wayne State Violate Michigan's Animal Cruelty Law, Doctors Say

WASHINGTON—Painful forced-exercise heart experiments on dogs at Wayne State University violate Michigan's animal cruelty law, says a legal complaint filed by a doctors group on Dec. 14 with the Wayne County prosecuting attorney. The Physicians Committee for Responsible Medicine (PCRM) wants Wayne State prosecuted for felony animal cruelty for forcing dogs to endure lengthy treadmill tests after multiple major surgeries.

Wayne State's experiments have resulted in unrelieved suffering and death for hundreds of dogs, including a husky named Jessie, a hound-Labrador mix named Charlie, a Dalmatian mix named Queenie, and many other former companion animals obtained from state animal shelters.

"Felony animal cruelty charges should be brought against Wayne State, and the use of dogs in painful heart experiments should be halted immediately," says John J. Pippin, M.D., F.A.C.C., a cardiologist and director of academic affairs for PCRM. "Michigan's animal cruelty law was enacted to protect dogs and other animals from forced exercise and unrelieved pain such as that experienced by Charlie, Jessie, and Queenie."

According to medical records obtained through Michigan's Freedom of Information Act, Charlie experienced two major surgeries to place medical devices in her body and had weeping wounds where catheters protruded. In violation of Michigan's ban against cruelly working animals, Charlie was forced to run treadmill exercises even when she had a high fever and vomited almost daily. Jessie's suffering was not as prolonged as Charlie's, since she died suddenly in February of this year soon after her first surgery. PCRM has obtained a photo of a third dog, Queenie, who died in Wayne State's laboratory in 2010.

The doctors' nonprofit states in its legal complaint, "Wayne State University's use of dogs in cardiovascular forced exercise experiments does not represent the 'humane' research protected by Michigan law, and we request that Wayne State University be charged with felony animal cruelty under MCL §750.50(2)(b) for cruelly working hundreds of dogs by forcing them to endure lengthy treadmill tests after multiple major surgeries."

Founded in 1985, the Physicians Committee for Responsible Medicine is a nonprofit health organization that promotes preventive medicine, conducts clinical research, and encourages higher standards for ethics and effectiveness in research.

Wayne State University's Inhumane Dog Experiments: Queenie's Story

PCRM obtained shelter and veterinary records through the Michigan Freedom of Information Act for Queenie, a Dalmatian mix who was used in one of the experiments conducted by Donal O'Leary, Ph.D. These records show that Queenie suffered immensely at the hands of O'Leary and his staff at Wayne State University in Detroit.

Queenie was found stray in early 2009 by residents of Gratiot County, Mich., who kept her for weeks before surrendering her to the Gratiot County Animal Shelter on June 15, 2009. After 10 days at the shelter, she was transferred to R&R Research, a Class B "random source" animal dealer.

Queenie was sold to Wayne State University, and veterinary staff noted that she was "curious, gentle, [and] friendly" when she arrived on Sept. 16, 2009. Lab personnel renamed her "Lafayette," and she was assigned to the experiment "Integrative Cardiovascular Control During Exercise in Hypertension." She began treadmill training on Sept. 23, when she was noted to be "distressed."

Queenie remained "spooky" during her presurgery treadmill training, even jumping off the treadmill when one of the experimenters entered the room. She had to be given a bath on Oct. 15 because she had "fecal material all down [her] left side." Her training continued until Dec. 1, when she had a left thoracotomy—a major surgery in which her chest was opened to implant devices in her heart.

After surgery, Queenie had to wear a jacket, t-shirt, and cervical collar so she would not pull at her stitches or at the foreign objects now in her body. Her face and paws were swollen, she was "whining [and] vocalizing a bit," and she vomited immediately after being placed in her cage. By Dec. 8, she was back on the treadmill.

As Queenie healed from her first surgery, she experienced irritation, scabbing, leaking fluids, and other ill effects. She seemed "agitated," "intent on cleaning feces from [her] rear," and was "whining for attention." On Dec. 15, she underwent another procedure—this time, experimenters placed catheters in Queenie's neck and behind her abdomen.

Queenie's recovery was more difficult after the second experiment. The next morning, Queenie was found lying on her floor and "reluctant to get up out of [her] cage," vocalizing when laboratory technicians tried to assist her out of the cage. Queenie did not want to move, and lab technicians placed a muzzle on her to stop her from making noise and attempting to nip.

Queenie's incisions constantly seeped large amounts of fluids. After relentless licking, sores appeared on her paws and right hip. She was forced to wear an even larger Elizabethan collar to stop her from further aggravating the sores.

Queenie was forced to run on the treadmill again. Initially, the experimental devices were not turned on so she could serve as her own experimental control. When the devices were later turned on, constant problems with the devices' electronic signals occurred, which prevented the experimenters from collecting data. Still, according to her veterinary records, Queenie was forced to run on the treadmill, and experimenters gathered data when they could, dodging bites from this once-friendly dog and frequently stopping the experiment to clean up feces.

By March 2010, Queenie was hypertensive. In April, she was noted by one lab technician to be "acting very timid – like she can't get [up]...shakes while getting up (back legs)... won't get up for me." That same day, she underwent treadmill experiments again. Two days later, Queenie's leg became caught in the treadmill and she stumbled. For the next two weeks, Queenie was seen "tip-toeing" and limping, but she was still forced to run.

Queenie was used until June 2010, when experimenters accidentally cracked one of the devices implanted in her while "packing up probes" after a treadmill training session. They attempted to fix the device, but it broke again, retracting into Queenie's body. On June 29, 2010, more than one year after she arrived at the Gratiot County Animal Shelter and more than nine months after she arrived at O'Leary's laboratory, Queenie was killed.

Queenie was just one of the hundreds of dogs used in O'Leary's experiments at Wayne State University. Please take action to end these experiments before even one more dog has to suffer:

Wayne State University:
Inhumane Dog Experiment Overview

For 20 years, Donal S. O'Leary, Ph.D., has been performing inhumane dog experiments to study heart failure and related diseases at Wayne State University in Detroit.

After learning more about these experiments, Mel Richardson, D.V.M., a veterinarian with more than 40 years of experience with animals, stated, "In my experience, no matter which pain-relieving agent used, dogs undergoing these procedures would be in constant pain."

Here is a brief overview of what will happen to a dog assigned to O'Leary's experiment "Integrative Cardiovascular Control During Exercise in Hypertension":

Week 1: Treadmill training begins.

Weeks 2-3: The dog undergoes a left thoracotomy, and medical devices are placed on his arteries. Cables entering through his ribs and underneath his arm are fed through his body toward the heart and exit the body between his shoulders. This surgery is followed by seven to 14 days of recovery.

Week 4: Cuts are made in the dog's neck and leg to place

catheters in arteries and veins. The catheters are fed through the body and exit slightly behind the catheters from the previous experiment. A large incision is made to place more devices on the dog's arteries. This surgery is followed by seven days of recovery.

Weeks 5-13: Control experiments are performed, and the dog must run on the treadmill once or twice per day for 35 to 45 sessions.

Weeks 14-26: Hypertension is induced by reduction of blood flow to the kidneys.

Weeks 27-30: The dog endures treadmill sessions again, now with hypertension.

Months 5-8: The dog is killed after all data have been collected.

Hundreds of dogs have been subjected to this pain over the past two decades, and it is time for these experiments to end. The story of Queenie, a Dalmatian used in these experiments, is particularly heartbreaking.

Class B Dealers: Animals Sold for Experiments

When families have to give up their animals for adoption, they hope that their former companions will go to a loving home—not to inhumane medical experiments. Despite statements from the National Academies of Science and the National Institutes of Health declaring Class B dealers unnecessary and recommending that they be phased out, Wayne State University still purchases dogs from these "random source" dealers who buy animals from shelters, auctions, and individuals to sell at a large profit.

The majority of the dogs used in the experiments of Donal O'Leary, Ph.D., are from R&R Research, a Michigan Class B dealer with a history of Animal Welfare Act violations. R&R Research is currently under investigation by the U.S. Department of Agriculture (USDA), and has been cited eight times for obtaining animals illegally since 2007. Senior USDA officials have requested that R&R Research's license be revoked, but the company remains in business today.

Michigan residents have taken the issue of Class B dealers to their county and state legislators with varying success. In

2009, Montcalm County District 3 Commissioner Ron Retzloff expressed concern over R&R Research before a vote on Class B dealers, saying, "I don't feel it's right to continue to do business with a place that has violations...Basically, it's saying we condone the violations because we continue to do business with [R&R]." The commissioners later voted to end pound seizure in Montcalm County.

Unfortunately, Class B dealers can still purchase dogs from Gratiot County and Mecosta County shelters in Michigan. Local activists have worked tirelessly to foster and adopt all of the shelter animals to prevent any more from ending up in experiments, but a few inevitably end up in experiments. When the Gratiot County Animal Shelter is empty, R&R turns to another local Class B dealer, D&M Resources, for Mecosta County shelter dogs.

Michigan state legislators have failed to reintroduce a bill that would ban pound seizure and put Class B dealers like R&R out of business, and R&R's contract with Gratiot County is not set to expire for years. PCRM is working to put this unscrupulous company out of business another way—by ending the experiments that use R&R dogs. Please take action to stop the inhumane heart failure experiments at Wayne State University and take away a large source of R&R's business.

For more information on animals used in research and USDA Class A and B animal dealers visit the following sites:

American Anti-Vivisection Society: www.aavs.org

Humane Society of the United States: www.humanesociety.org

Last Chance for Animals: www.lcanimal.org

Physicians Committee for Responsible Medicine: www.pcrm.org

Rescue + Freedom Project (formerly Beagle Freedom Project) www.rescuefreedomproject.org